The Dangerous Duke of Dinnisfree

A Whisper of Scandal Novel
Book Five

by
Julie Johnstone

Dedication

For Samantha Grace and Ava Stone, who have always been there for me with friendship, advice, and excellent brainstorming sessions. This book would have stalled at the beginning if not for the two of you. Anyone who will listen to me ramble my way through the infancy stage of an idea for a book is a true friend.

And for my husband, who gallantly took up the role of Mommy and Daddy several times so that I could finish this book. I love you! I could not write a more perfect hero.

Kisses ~ Julie

Author's Note

Dear Readers,

During research on the Regency Era, I became fascinated with the trial of Queen Caroline, who is best known as Caroline of Brunswick. Her husband, King George IV of the United Kingdom, had been determined to gain a divorce from her so he'd had the Pains and Penalty Bill introduced into Parliament to prove that Caroline was adulterous and, therefore, not fit to be his queen. Of course, it was well known that there was no love lost between them, as the king had never been a faithful husband and his attempt was ultimately unsuccessful.

As often happens with me, this bit of information sparked a host of ideas in my mind, and thus, the plot of *The Dangerous Duke of Dinnisfree* was born. This book is a work of fiction with real people in it, but it is largely based on situations from my own imagination. There were indeed letters that came out during the divorce proceedings that painted the king in a very negative light, but how these letters were discovered I can only speculate, which is exactly what I've done here. I hope you enjoy the story!

All the best,
Julie

One

The Year of Our Lord 1820
London, England

*A*rabella's shoes tapped against the tile floor of the Stanhope Home for the Mentally Impaired. Every window she passed as she walked down the corridor was wide open, and she wrinkled her nose at the stench that blew in from the river. Her mother often complained of the terrible smell, but Mrs. Henderson, the warden, had said the windows must remain ajar because becoming overheated made some insane people's conditions worse. Arabella didn't know for certain if this was true or not. How could she? She was a seamstress, not a physician or the wife of one like Mrs. Henderson.

Arabella had to rely on the woman's word—quite an upsetting thing for someone who'd learned a long time ago to rely only on herself. It made her nerves tingle, but circumstances left her no choice, much in the same way fate had left Papa no choice but to rely on *her*. Once his lower body had become paralyzed and he was confined to a wheelchair, he'd been forced to trust her to provide everything—food, clothing, even the caretaker who watched him when Arabella went to work.

Just as her mother had trusted Arabella to pay the monthly bill for this place, with its white walls and the whimpers of sadness that rang through the halls. Otherwise, Mother would be sent away to Bethlem Mental Hospital, a horrid place for the deranged, where more than moans resounded in the corridors. Arabella had visited Bethlem— or Bedlam, as many had taken to calling it—when she didn't think she would be able to scrape enough money together for the Stanhope Home. The hospital was damp, dark, and smelled of feces, and she'd seen dozens of patients chained naked who appeared to be starving with their skeletal frames. Upon leaving, she had vowed to sell her body before sentencing her mother to that misery. Thankfully, it hadn't come to that.

She quickened her pace, hastened by the memories of Bedlam. Cries of horror filled the silence there, and fear colored the eyes of all who peered out from the tiny windows of their cells. Arabella's throat constricted and her nails curled into her palms, breaking the soft flesh of her skin. She winced and forced herself to relax her tight fists. It wasn't right to treat people so poorly simply because they had no money.

Her family was perilously close to destitute, and ever since visiting Bedlam, her nights had been haunted by dreams of her mother being imprisoned there. Arabella clenched her jaw and focused on the hunched back of the guard, Stewart, who walked in front of her. His shoulder blades protruded against the faded-blue material of his uniform, and his repellent odor wafted back to her with each step they took. Her nose wrinkled in disgust.

He turned the corner, and with the sunlight shining through the window, she got a better look at the angry, red scratch on his cheek that she'd noticed when he'd let her into the home. It reminded her of the terrible scratch her old cat, Matilda, had given one of the neighborhood boys when he'd tried to hurt her. Arabella narrowed her eyes, a terrible suspicion rising. Had Stewart been harming one of the women here? He was always sending inviting, disgusting looks that she ignored, but if you were a patient here, trapped in a room, unable to leave... A sour taste filled her mouth.

Suddenly, Stewart paused at the door to Mrs. Henderson's office and turned to Arabella with a leer on his face. He swallowed and his Adam's apple bobbed. "If Mrs. Henderson gives you trouble about that blanket for your mother, pass it to me and I'll get it to her. I don't mind doing you the favor." His gaze trailed away from her face and down her body before returning upward.

Arabella stiffened. "No, thank you. I'm sure Mrs. Henderson will be agreeable to allowing my mother a blanket from home." She didn't know if the warden would be congenial or not, but she was not about to take a favor from this man. His dull, lust-filled eyes told her what he'd want in return. It was the same thing the creditor, Mr. Branburry, had expected in exchange for not taking all their possessions when Papa could no longer pay the bills. Arabella had simply told the man what time to arrive at their house to empty it. She still felt a tug of satisfaction when she recalled his gawking face. She'd explained to him in careful, controlled tones that she'd rather have nothing to wear, read, or sit on than allow him to touch her.

Stewart leaned toward her; her nostrils flared at the heavy scent of urine that wafted from him. "One day," he snarled under his breath, "you'll realize how much you need a man." He swiveled around and knocked on Mrs. Henderson's door.

Arabella clutched the frayed, wool blanket that had been her only one. *Need a man?* She almost let the sharp laugh in her throat free. She'd had a suitor, Mr. Benjamin Fowler. Thinking of him didn't even make her heart skip a beat anymore. She'd realized that she had not really been in love, but rather, infatuated with the idea of love. She'd thought his blue eyes kind and his heart pure and would have probably married him. But he'd proven just how deceitful appearances could be. He'd told her in very polite words that he could never marry a woman who likely had insanity tainting her blood, no less a traitor for a brother. She didn't bother to tell him that she was adopted. His willingness to leave her had shown he was not worth her breath. Nor did she trouble to remind him that there was no actual proof that her brother Daniel had been attempting to flee his regiment when he'd been shot and killed. The evidence Daniel had sent before dying showed a different story. She had letters from him, telling of things his commander had lied about. And his commander had been courting the same woman as her brother... She had no doubt he'd been jealous of Daniel, but no one would listen. The false words of a shifty-eyed captain would never convince her, even if it had convinced the rest of the world.

A giant lump formed in Arabella's throat and she swallowed it back. Now was not the time to become misty-eyed over all that had befallen her family. She suspected most men would have done just as Benjamin had, but she didn't care to find out. She slaved all day to simply put food to the table, house herself and her father, and ensure her mother continued to receive proper care. The last thing she desired was the trouble of a man.

"Mrs. Henderson says you can go in."

Arabella snapped her attention to Stewart, who was already striding past her with long, gangly steps. Her gaze fastened on that dark slash on his cheek. *Could* that be the mark of fingernails from a woman who had clawed at Stewart's face in self-defense? Her stomach pitched downward as she thrust her shoulders back and took determined steps through the door and into the warden's office. She would make sure that Stewart had no contact with her mother anymore.

Mrs. Henderson, dressed in a severe black gown, sat behind a large, gleaming mahogany desk. She raised a creamy hand to her coif of brown-and-silver hair. "Miss Carthright, I'm glad to see you here today. I was about to pin you a note."

Arabella's chest tightened. "I know my payment is overdue."

Mrs. Henderson nodded. "Two months. I could overlook one month, but two..." The woman clucked her tongue.

Arabella slipped her mother's wedding ring off her finger. If Mrs. Henderson demanded security until she received the money Arabella would soon have, this ring was all she had to offer. There was no other institution like this in London, and she refused to see her mother go to Bedlam. "I will be able to pay by tonight," Arabella promised, pressing the wedding ring between her thumb and forefinger. This time her words were true. The gowns Lady Conyngham had commissioned were finally complete after hours of tedious toil, and the lady had promised her ten pounds if all four garments were ready within two weeks. She planned to deliver them to Lady Conyngham after leaving here and collect payment. Of course, she had to pay ten percent to Madame Chauvin as the proprietor of the dress shop and the one who had given her the job. But Lady Conyngham had said that if she was pleased, she would give Arabella a bonus on top of the agreed-upon pay.

Mrs. Henderson tapped her nails against the wood, the *clack, clack, clack* filling the silence and making Arabella's nerves sing. The warden let out an irritated sigh. "Miss Carthright, this is not Bedlam, where they take people who can pay nothing. This is a *private* home owned by a generous lord who took up the cause of the deranged after his own beloved wife perished at Bedlam. Yes, he *does* dip into his own pockets to keep this home afloat, but his generosity does not include your mother being here for free." Mrs. Henderson's painted mouth twisted into a sympathetic smile. "I wish we could be more accommodating, but running this place is costly."

"I understand," Arabella quickly inserted.

"It does not seem you do," Mrs. Henderson replied in a sharp tone that made Arabella's temper notch up.

She ground her teeth. It would not do to argue the point.

Mrs. Henderson picked up her quill pen, glanced down at the document before her, and began writing. A sinking sensation filled Arabella's entire body. She leaned forward but could not make out the words. "What are you doing?"

The warden paused and fixed her dark eyes on Arabella. "I'm writing to the hospital to let them know that your mother will be delivered there tomorrow morning."

"No, please!" Arabella snatched the paper off Mrs. Henderson's desk and thrust the ring in front of the woman's nose. The warden's eyes widened a fraction as she stiffened in her chair. The leather squeaked with her movement. "Don't make this harder than it has to be."

"It doesn't have to be hard at all," Arabella replied, moving the ring back and forth in the air. The small, well-cut diamond caught the light and cast a glow in the shadows. "Take this ring as collateral. I vow I'll bring the money tonight." Though coming tonight would mean paying her father's caretaker an additional wage to sit for longer hours today. Arabella would do it, and make up the deficit of funds by skipping dinner for the next two weeks.

With pinched lips, Mrs. Henderson slowly outstretched her hand.

Arabella deposited her mother's wedding ring in the warden's open palm, and as she did, a hard knot of despair lodged in her belly. This was the only possession of her mother's that Arabella had left. The ring symbolized a happier time, and giving it away like this—She swallowed hard. Well, handing it over was like handing over all the happy memories she had left, too.

Dash it all! Tears burned in her throat, but she'd die before relenting to the silly fear that was trying to consume her. She was not giving the ring—or her hope—away forever. She licked her dry lips. "When I bring you the money, you can give me back the ring."

Mrs. Henderson held the ring close to her face. Her droopy eyelids pulled upward, forming three folds of skin over her eyes. She bit the ring and nodded with a grunt of satisfaction. "I will take this ring as payment for the two months you owe. The first is on Monday. That gives you three days to secure two more pounds for the upcoming month. Be here then with the money or your mother will be gone by day's end."

Arabella stared at her mother's ring. She could not lose it. "What if I bring you the six pounds we owe tonight? Will you return the ring to me in exchange?"

Mrs. Henderson gave her a flinty stare. "I have a previous engagement tonight. I cannot wait around for you," she snapped. "And if you want this ring back so badly, it will cost you seven pounds. You may pay me Monday morning and not before. I've no idea when I'll return to the office this weekend, and I'm not planning my time around *you*. Are we clear?"

Oh, they were clear, all right. Mrs. Henderson was going to pocket some money for the favor of letting Arabella pay late, but there was nothing she could do about it. "Yes," she forced, nearly choking on the word.

Mrs. Henderson smiled and deposited the ring in her desk drawer with a *clink*. Arabella's chest tightened. At least the ring was not gone for good, unlike her mother's mind. She took a deep breath. Her responsibilities to her mother and father were her top priority, and she'd not fail them, just as they'd never failed her.

"I brought a blanket for my mother," she stated in a

firm voice. "She complains of always being cold. Will you see that she gets it?"

Mrs. Henderson nodded. "Certainly," she said in a falsely accommodating voice. The warden motioned to her desk. "Leave it here, and I'll give it to the guard to take to her."

Apprehension ran down Arabella's spine like quicksilver and curled in the pit of her belly. "I'd rather Stewart not be around my mother anymore. Is there another guard perhaps that could…" Her words trailed off at the flash of anger that crackled in Mrs. Henderson's eyes. Arabella blinked, sure she saw incorrectly, but no, Mrs. Henderson suddenly appeared livid, her lips pressed white and gaze burning.

"What is your grievance with Stewart?" The question slashed through the air with the snap of a whip.

Arabella stiffened. For her mother's sake, she could not back down. "He's made lurid suggestions to me, and I would prefer another guard if you don't mind."

"Lurid suggestions to you?" Mrs. Henderson's voice rang with disbelief, even as she swept her gaze over Arabella.

Heat flushed Arabella's neck at the woman's blatant appraisal of her person. The warden's face paled as her eyes met Arabella's. "Please take my apology."

A sigh of relief escaped Arabella. "You needn't apologize for your guard."

Mrs. Henderson nodded. "I'm afraid I must. Stewart is my son."

Her son? The distant manner in which Stewart's mother treated him almost inspired Arabella's pity until she recalled his leer. That same tingling apprehension that swept down her spine moments ago now danced up her skin, making the hairs on the back of her neck prickle. Despite Mrs. Henderson's seemingly unmotherly attitude toward Stewart,

Arabella suspected by her pinched lips that the warden was none too pleased to have her son criticized, be it true or not.

"I'm sorry. I did not know."

"That's quite all right," Mrs. Henderson said in a tone of forced cheerfulness. "Of course, Stewart should not be making lurid suggestions to you. Though"—the warden's gaze dropped to Arabella's chest where her old gown pulled too tight across her assets—"you should take care to dress more modestly."

"I'll keep that in mind," Arabella said through clenched teeth.

Mrs. Henderson smiled. "I'll switch Mr. Black to your mother's room, but it hardly seems necessary. Your mother does not have the youthful beauty that you do."

Arabella heartily doubted the warden's pig of a son cared, but since she had no proof, she forced her own smile to her face. "I thank you for your understanding."

"Of course," the warden replied, smirking slightly. "The other guard's salary is a bit higher, and with one more patient for him to handle, I'm afraid I'll have to charge you five more shillings a month. But you seem the sort of daughter who would do anything for her mother, am I correct?"

Arabella had the very unladylike and very sudden vision of lunging across the desk and smacking the woman's smirking face. Instead, she jerked her head in agreement. Two pounds and five shillings a month was a fortune! She'd have to secure more work somehow. Her head pounded with a sudden rushing of blood in her ears.

"Excellent," Mrs. Henderson crowed while waving a hand toward the door. "You may go. I'll see you Monday morning with payment. Don't forget the increase."

"I won't forget," Arabella managed to reply, though she was seething inside.

She turned on her heel and showed herself out. She

didn't waste a moment lingering in the halls but headed straight for the exit since it wasn't a visiting day. She'd come back tomorrow to see her mother, and by then, she'd have the money for this month and hopefully she would have Lady Conyngham as a future client to aid with some of her family's financial burdens. And if Lady Conyngham was very pleased, perhaps she would recommend Arabella to her friends.

Not an hour later, Arabella sat on a plush, navy-blue velvet settee in the most decadent drawing room she had ever seen. She was glad that the stuffy butler had demanded she wait here instead of following him up to Lady Conyngham's bedchambers. Arabella had been momentarily incensed that the butler appeared not to believe she was expected *and* had been instructed to proceed to the bedchamber to fit Lady Conyngham. But as she wiggled her bottom against the soft cushions and slid off her right slipper to curl her toes into the lush Aubusson rug of tan, wine, and indigo, a sigh of delight escaped her and her irritation melted away.

She'd never been in such a grand room. What a treat not to have a hard lump protruding from the settee, and the carpet... She ran the tip of her toe back and forth over the lush weave. They'd had rugs before most of their possessions had been taken away, though nothing near as fine as what was currently under her feet. Closing her eyes, she imagined this carpet was in her home, taking the place of the cold, bare floor. She only allowed the wishful thinking for one moment before she snapped her eyes open and stuck her foot back into her shoe. She trained her gaze on the boxes that contained the gowns she'd sewn. Arabella didn't like the envy that was filling her heart. She had food and a roof over her head, and that was a great deal more than many poor souls in London had. *No more pining over rugs and settees.*

She stood and bent to pick up her seamstress bag and the boxes so she would be ready when the butler came to fetch her. As she straightened, the drawing room door opened, and the butler entered. He stopped just inside the room and motioned to her. "Come. Lady Conyngham will see you in her bedchamber."

Arabella barely refrained from saying, *I told you so.* She wanted to, to be sure, but the butler's splotchy, red face told her either he was winded from the walk or he'd perhaps been chastised by Lady Conyngham. Regardless, Arabella was not so uncharitable as to gloat. Unless he pushed her with more snobby looks. She was only human, after all.

He turned slowly on his heel without so much as a backward glance or a word and led her at a snail's pace down the hall and up the majestic winding staircase with its breathtaking scrolled iron railing. No doubt the man was tired from the trek up and down the stairs, so she followed in silence with her boxes, content to gaze at the beautiful stained glass windows that lined the staircase. There were four, and she'd never seen the likes of them.

When they arrived at the top of the stairs, the butler stopped in front of a bedchamber with dark double doors. The butler raised his hand, presumably to knock on the door, but it swung open and a man burst out, almost knocking the butler down.

The dark-haired man, thick locks disheveled and cravat dangling from his neck, bowed slightly to the butler while offering an apology, and then he fixed his burnished gaze on Arabella. He didn't seem a bit surprised to see her, which was odd until she considered that, of course, he must have heard the butler announce her arrival. A slow smile spread over his face, and then, before she knew what he was doing, he had taken her hand and raised it to his lips to place a kiss there.

"You are exquisite with your bright blue eyes and sable hair," he murmured. "And quite the seamstress, I hear."

"I've said no such thing," came a feminine, distinctly irritated voice from behind the man.

Arabella snatched her hand away and quickly curtsied to Lady Conyngham, who stood in the doorway in a shocking state of dishabille. Arabella did her best not to gape at the woman, but honestly, who with any sense pranced around in a sheer dressing robe for all to see what God had given her? A quick look at the butler told her that he was having the same thought. High color touched his cheeks, and he snapped his mouth shut and shot his gaze toward the floor. For a moment, the inability to decide what to do paralyzed her, but then she quickly spoke. "Good afternoon, Lord and Lady Conyngham. Thank you for—"

An eruption of laughter from both of them drowned out the rest of Arabella's hastily planned greeting. She frowned. What had she said wrong?

Still chuckling, Lady Conyngham stepped toward her and eyed her with a sharp, rather unfriendly narrowed gaze. She dismissed the butler with a flick of her hand. "Go, Mr. Gregory."

The butler moved quicker than Arabella would have thought possible of him. Lady Conyngham, who was a good five inches taller than Arabella, stared down at her, her light eyes darkening and narrowing further. "This man is not my husband." She fluttered her fingers at the gentleman still standing by the door.

Arabella's gaze went back to the gentleman before she could stop herself. Not only was his cravat untied but his shirt had been tugged loose at his neck. She stared at the multitude of lip prints perfectly made on his neck and upper chest, revealed by his open shirt. Slowly, she pulled her gaze back to Lady Conyngham and desperately tried not to look at the woman's mouth, but it was as if her whole face had suddenly been consumed by enormous, ruby-stained lips.

Arabella licked her own lips and winced when she realized what she was doing. "I'm sorry. I assumed since he was coming out of your bedchamber—" She bit down on the inside of her cheek to stop herself from prattling any more nonsense that would worsen the already rapidly disintegrating situation.

"Never assume anything, Miss Carthright. It shows how foolish and ignorant you are."

"Elizabeth," the gentleman chided. "Don't be so testy. Or jealous. You know my heart is yours."

Yet, Lady Conyngham's heart *should* be with her husband only. Or at the very least, her bedchamber reserved solely for the lord of the house. What a sticky mess.

Arabella pondered how not to get embroiled further in the lady's private affairs, nor continue to rile her possessiveness over this man. Excusing herself seemed the best recourse. "I'll wait in the bedchamber for you, my lady."

"How very wise of you," Lady Conyngham snapped, even as her lover, who was standing behind her, winked at Arabella, as if to say he would tame any ruffled feathers. Arabella certainly hoped he could, though she had serious doubts. The lady did not seem in the mood to be appeased.

Arabella prayed she was wrong. Within minutes of Arabella's entering the opulent, royal-purple bedchamber and setting the gowns out, Lady Conyngham breezed into the room, her mouth swollen and red with fresh kisses. She stopped in front of the settee where Arabella had carefully laid out the four gowns she had created. Lady Conyngham plucked up the first one, a deep-burgundy cloth, and fisted it in her hands. "This is not the color I ordered," she said, tossing the frock to the ground.

Arabella's heart plunged downward with the garment. The blasted gown was the exact color that had been ordered. She took a deep breath and hoped she sounded soothing and not angry. "Lady Conyngham, I assure you this is the same burgundy you said would nicely suit to scandalize the *ton*."

Lady Conyngham's eyes widened a fraction, so Arabella knew the woman recalled saying the words. Yet, her mouth twisted into a vicious grimace. "I would never have said such an intimate thing to you. You are incorrect, and I won't take this gown."

Arabella swallowed the curses she wanted to fling at the woman. The lost revenue would cost her dearly, but letting her pride get the best of her and saying what she really felt would undoubtedly cost her more. Fierce anger burned in her throat, but she managed to say, "Of course, my lady." She motioned to the ice-blue gown Lady Conyngham had exclaimed would match her eyes perfectly, undoubtedly the cool color suited her heart, as well. "What of this one? Won't you try it on? I'm sure you will love it."

"Never be sure of anything. Especially not men who vow they love you. Men are liars." She stalked over to her dressing table and snatched up a gold box. A multitude of stones embedded the closed lid. They glittered in the sunlight streaming in through the windows. "They try to cover their lies and false hearts with pretty baubles," Lady Conyngham growled. "Trinkets are not love. Real love is what I desire! I don't want these trinkets. I want utter devotion!" She'd fairly screamed the words as she reared her arm back and threw the box. It hit the wall with a loud *clank* and slid down to the floor, landing with a clattering noise that made Arabella grit her teeth.

When the room fell to silence again, she tried to think of something to say to calm the tempest that was Lady Conyngham. Before she could utter a word, the woman bent down and swept all the gowns off the settee and onto the floor. "Get out. And take the gowns with you. I no longer want any of them."

A cold sweat instantly dampened Arabella's brow as her stomach squeezed and started to turn violently. This simply could not be happening. Lady Conyngham had to take the gowns. "I'll come back tomorrow, my lady, when you are feeling better."

"You sound exactly like my pathetic husband! I won't want these gowns tomorrow or ever. I could never wear them now. I've been betrayed." She glanced wildly around the room while turning in frantic circles, then stalked to the gold box she'd thrown and kicked it. "Duped! Left to sit, wait, and hope in vain! As if I would simply do so because *he* rules! I won't wait like a child." She kicked the jewelry box again.

Arabella stared in awe. That box, if sold, could likely pay for her mother's care for the year. Wild laughter filled the air, causing her to flinch. She dragged her gaze back to Lady Conyngham, who was glaring at her.

"Do you hear me?" the lady demanded.

As if the woman needed to ask, but Arabella forced a nod. The woman must have been angered by her lover. Perhaps their dalliance was now ended. Whatever the circumstances, it did not change the fact that Lady Conyngham *had* ordered the gowns. She simply had to take them or pay for them at the very least. Each one had been made exactly as the lady had demanded.

"Lady Conyngham, regardless of what has happened with your *friend*, you *did* order the gowns."

The lady drew her eyebrows into a high arch. "I will *not* keep them nor pay for them, and *you* are giving me a megrim."

Arabella's hands went clammy and her vision swam. She blinked rapidly. The woman had no care for anyone but herself. There would be no reasoning with her.

Lady Conyngham cocked her head. "I'm going to speak

with my portrait painter now, and I do not want you here when I return. Understand?"

Arabella understood the woman was a hateful witch who was needlessly jealous. She also comprehended that to say so could worsen her already terrible problem. "I'll be gone," Arabella said in the calmest voice she could muster.

"Excellent." Lady Conyngham turned to leave but paused near the door and swiveled back around. "I'm afraid I'll have to tell Madame Chauvin what a terrible disappointment your creations were." She smiled a cruel, twisted smile. "I don't think you have a promising career as a seamstress. I'd try the brothel if I were you. You dress as though you crave attention."

Arabella was so angry she was left momentarily speechless. Lady Conyngham took full advantage of the moment and promptly quit the room. Blast the woman to the devil!

Outside the door, Arabella heard a deep male voice speaking in a soothing tone, and then Lady Conyngham screamed, "Mr. Gregory, get rid of that damned atrocious jewelry box! I never want to see it again!" The angry tap of slippers on the stairs filled the air, after which all fell silent.

Arabella shook where she stood as her blood roared in her ears and pounded through her veins. She squeezed her eyes shut and sucked in gasps of air to calm herself. After a minute, the roaring subsided, though as she raised her hands to her gown, she noted they still trembled. She tugged at her gown, trying to loosen the way the material clung to her breasts, but it was useless. The frock was too small, had been for quite some time, but there was no money to purchase material to make a new one.

A brothel, indeed. Arabella's principles were just fine, too-snug gown or not. Lady Conyngham was the one who had misplaced her morals, with her sheer, frothy white robes and her lover.

She made a disgusted sound and wearily bent to pick up

the clothing that had been thrown to the floor. Losing this money was bad, but deep within, she feared the worst was yet to come. Madame Chauvin liked her, but not so much that she'd jeopardize losing Lady Conyngham as a client by keeping Arabella as an employee.

Bile rose in her throat, and she struggled against the urge to curl into a ball and pretend all this had not just happened. In three days the money to pay for her mother's continued care was due, not to mention that she needed to pay her father's caretaker and buy food.

She shoved the gowns into their boxes. Even if Madame Chauvin paid her the meager salary she was owed, which Arabella was uncertain would happen, it would not make a drop in the giant bucket required by Monday. Arabella swallowed her mounting fright. She needed money, and she needed it quickly. Standing here like a fool was not getting her closer to solving her problem.

She started toward the door but stopped when her toe hit the gold jewelry box. She glanced down and her heart began to hammer. She could take it. Lady Conyngham didn't want it anyway.

Arabella squeezed her eyes shut and opened them again, perspiration covering her brow. Tremors engulfed her entire body, along with clamminess, yet she crouched down, her knees popping as she did so. She breathed heavily as she set her packages on the floor and reached out to touch the box. She ran her index finger over a large emerald and snatched her hand away, feeling as if she'd been burned or, better yet, branded a thief. Taking the box was wrong.

"Take it," a deep, amused voice said behind her.

Her heart gave a hefty jerk as she twisted around and faced the gentleman who had started all her trouble.

He offered a mock bow, his hair flopping over his eyes. As he came up, he flicked his hair back, walked over to her, and held out his hand. She took it but left the box, which he immediately bent down to scoop up and then thrust at her. "Don't be a foolish nitwit. She no longer wants it. She ordered it thrown out." He eyed her for a moment. "I heard what she said to you. I hear everything." His silky smooth voice surrounded her.

Arabella glanced at the box and back to him. "Don't you want it?" He'd given it to Lady Conyngham, after all. It seemed as though he'd desire to have such an expensive thing back in his possession.

For a moment, his stare turned incredulous, but then laughter filled his eyes. "No, I don't want it. That box fills my mouth with distaste. *You* can have it and sell it for whatever you can get for it. In fact, I'll help you."

"You don't even know me."

"Ah, but I do," he replied. "You are a desperate woman in need, correct?"

She nodded.

"I've been desperate before. One can always recognize a fellow troubled soul."

She nibbled on her lip. "How can you help me?"

"I know a man who can sell the box for you. He's incredibly discreet, and he'll know how to find suitable buyers for you. Understand?"

Arabella nodded, as a hopeful flutter filled her belly. "Could you arrange a meeting for me this afternoon?"

He smiled but shook his head. "No, Mr. Winston is not in Town currently, so you must bide your time."

Her legs suddenly felt as if they could no longer hold her up. Hope had been teasingly offered, only to be cruelly dashed away. She needed money now. Not next week. Perhaps she could find another buyer herself.

As though the gentleman had read her thoughts, he shook his head. "Don't even consider it." The words were a command and a fierce one. "You may sell only to Mr. Winston. That is my requirement for giving you this box.

You cannot disappoint me."

What the devil did he mean "disappoint him"? She started to ask but then clamped her jaw shut. It was no matter if he said odd things, if he could help her. "I need money now," she admitted, shoving aside shame in favor of survival.

A strange glint filled his eyes, almost a knowing one. "I can offer you another way if you trust me. Do you? Do you trust me?"

Wariness enveloped her. What choice did she have? "Tell me."

"You are exquisite. And young. Are you untouched?"

She flinched away from his words, and what they suggested. Yet, did she have a choice any longer? She curled her toes downward against the desire to flee. "I'm an innocent, yes."

"I knew you would be!"

She furrowed her brow. He didn't know her, therefore could not know such a thing, but she supposed his suggestion that she looked like an innocent was far better than Lady Conyngham's declaration that Arabella looked like she should be in a brothel. Even if at this point the cruel words did foretell her future.

"Go on," she whispered hoarsely.

"You could make a fortune selling yourself. I know a woman who could arrange a showing for you."

The way he watched her made her feel as if he was trying to judge something. Maybe he wanted to be sure she had the nerve to do such a thing?

She forced her cold lips to form words. "A showing?"

His posture relaxed suddenly and an almost imperceptible smile came to his face for the briefest moment before it disappeared. He nodded, his gaze darting to the door. He produced a cream-colored calling card and handed it to her. "Call on me here. Tomorrow."

Arabella took the card, looked at it, and froze. She knew this address: number six, Golden Square. It was the townhome directly across from Madame Sullyard's hotel, which was not really a hotel but a rather infamous brothel.

"I'll set up the appointment," he said, interrupting her recollections. "And I'll have someone near during the meeting and after to ensure all goes as planned. Don't worry. I am going to look out for you." His gaze moved away for a moment, then settled on her once again. "Bring the box when you come to see me tomorrow."

"But you said Mr. Winston was not in Town."

"Bring the box," he repeated.

"That's silly. Why don't you just take it, and you can help me sell it when Mr. Winston returns?"

He looked momentarily angry but then shook his head. "Better for you to carry it away from here than for me to do so. Elizabeth and I have, um, shall we say, unfinished business, and just because she no longer wants the box I gave her does not mean she wants me to have it."

She supposed that made sense, yet she felt as if he was holding something back. "Why are you helping me? Really."

His eyes held an almost secretive look, yet his smile was gentle. "Truthfully, I've no choice."

What an odd thing to say. Of course he had a choice.

They stood in silence staring at each other until he spoke once more. "You... you remind me of my sister. She would have been your age. One and twenty, are you?"

Arabella nodded. There must be a profit involved for him if he helped her, yet she had precious few other choices. In fact, unless a miracle occurred, she had none. She glanced quickly down at the card again and looked at his name: J.I. DEVINE.

"What does J.I. stand for?" To trust a man, one needed to know his full name. Her father had always said that names told a great deal about a man, and thanks to her father, she knew the origin of most names.

"Judas Iscariot, but don't you dare ever tell a soul."

Her mouth dropped open.

"You're gawking," he chided.

She snapped her jaw shut. "Who the devil wouldn't when told the person they just met is named after the apostle who betrayed Jesus for thirty pieces of silver?"

Judas—heaven above!—shrugged.

She narrowed her eyes. "You are not serious, *are you?*" It was a hopeful statement as much as a question.

"Completely. You know, I'm offended." He scowled down at her.

"You're offended?" she heard herself ask in disbelief.

"Yes, indeed. You are the very first stranger I have ever told my real name to, and you are acting as if I'm the very apostle who did the dirty deed."

Heat warmed her cheeks. "I'm sorry. Truly, I am, but why would your parents name you Judas Iscariot?"

His gaze bore into her. "Because I was born of betrayal, I suppose. In fact, my mother has never even met me, but I've seen her portrait. I have her eyes. And my father's lips."

She stared at his eyes. They were the color of a chestnut and had an interesting shape. They rounded near the nose and slanted on the outer part. And his lips were thin on top but shaped like a bow on the bottom.

"Are you always this honest?" she asked incredulously.

"No," he retorted with a chuckle. "I feel peculiar today."

She had no idea what to think of this man. "Were you not raised by your father?"

He shook his head. "I was raised by a witch." He frowned. "My sister was, too, but her witch flew away. Mine still lurks around."

Sadness flickered across his gaze and dissipated as quickly as it appeared. The man was odd indeed and spoke in strange riddles, but she was too desperate to care.

"Now, Miss Carthright, you may call me Jude, never Judas. I'm sure you can understand why."

She nodded. "Jude is not a name, though."

"I know," he said, his voice suddenly intense. "Which makes it very fitting for me."

She cocked her brows. "Meaning?"

"I am not who I seem. Do you see?"

She wasn't entirely confident she did. "As in you are no Judas?"

He inclined his head. "Something like that. Now, I told you my secret because I believe we shall be friends."

She really didn't have any friends. Work and caring for her parents didn't permit the luxury. She prayed she didn't regret this, especially given his name. Her father would tell her to run in the opposite direction, yet the man could not help with what his father had branded him.

"Friends only," she said sternly.

He chuckled. "Yes. I told you that you remind me of my sister. I shudder to think of you as anything but a comrade."

"Excellent," she murmured and tugged on the box, which he relinquished easily.

"Come find me at the address on that card tomorrow at precisely four in the afternoon. Now, run along, Miss Carthright. The tigress will return shortly, and she'll eat you alive if you're still here."

Arabella didn't like the way he thought of her as helpless to defend herself, but after depositing the jewelry box in her seamstress bag and gathering her things, she quickly obliged. When she reached the front entrance, the butler gave her a suspicious look, and she inadvertently clutched the bag to her that contained the box. He opened his mouth, as if to say something, but another gentleman stumbled into the foyer at that moment, also heading for the exit, and the butler pressed his lips together and showed them out.

The man held an easel in his hands and had a bag that appeared to be full of supplies slung over his shoulder. As the door closed behind them, he turned to her and bowed. "I am Mr. Fitzherald, formerly Lady Conyngham's portrait painter as of a few short minutes ago," he fairly snarled.

By his angry tone, Arabella would say that Mr. Fitzherald had gotten a dose of Lady Conyngham's temper today, the same as Arabella had received. "I'm Miss Carthright. Formerly the seamstress. It's a pleasure to meet you."

He smiled as they descended the steps and swept his arm toward the curricle that the stable master was leading toward them. "Would you care for a ride to your home?"

She eyed the curricle wistfully. It got awfully tedious walking everywhere, but riding in a curricle with a man—a stranger at that—was not the done thing, even if she was on the verge of selling herself. She shook her head. "I prefer to walk, thank you."

"But it's not safe!" he exclaimed. "A woman as lovely as you walking alone…"

"Oh, I've managed to stay safe all my life," she replied. When he looked as if he would protest again, she quickly added a firm, "But I thank you. Good-bye." She moved to stride ahead of him but stopped when he called her name. "Yes?" she said, facing him once more.

"I insist you let me follow you to ensure you get there safely. I do not feel right letting you walk alone."

She shrugged. "If you'd like." She did not have the time or inclination to argue with this man.

She went straight home to check on her father and drop off the jewelry box. The idea of carrying such an expensive case out on the streets made her feel tense. And what if Madame Chauvin saw the box? Arabella didn't want anyone to know she'd taken it, even though Jude had given her permission. She felt a bit like a thief. As she neared her home, she turned to wave good-bye to Mr. Fitzherald and offer him her thanks for his unnecessary but kind gesture.

She entered her house and called, "I'm home!" while maneuvering through the tiny door with the garment boxes and her seamstress bag. She deposited the packages on the floor by the entrance and paused a moment to stare at the little dark square of wood that contrasted so greatly with the lighter wood that surrounded it. The entrance table previously sat over that square, which was why the wood had not been bleached by the sun that filtered in through the small windows on either side of the door. The table was gone, and soon her innocence would be, too, she thought sourly.

"Are you done for the day, daughter?" came her father's low, crackly voice from the kitchen at the back of the townhome.

"Just stopping in before I go to Madame Chauvin's," she replied as she hurried down the hall and into the kitchen. She offered Alice, her father's caretaker, a smile. Alice grinned back, her blue eyes twinkling and her soft, wrinkly skin turning a slight rosy color. Arabella set the bag containing the jewelry box on the counter and then bent down to kiss her father on the cheek. He smelled clean like soap today, not like the strong-smelling mixture of horseradish juice, mustard, turpentine, and goose grease that so often lingered on him.

Arabella stood and saw the still-full bottle of the rheumatism lotion on the counter, which explained why her father smelled good. Alice must have made it but not had time to rub it on him yet. Alice reached for the bottle, but Arabella got there first.

"Go rest, Alice. You look a bit peaked."

Alice fanned herself, making a few strands of her silver hair move with each burst of air. "It's hot in here today."

"It's hot outside, as well," Arabella said. "I'll rub the

concoction on, but then I have to go to Madame Chauvin's. I won't return late," Arabella promised.

Alice nodded. "I'll sit for just a minute."

"Sit for twenty. Then I have to depart."

Alice patted Arabella on the shoulder as she kneeled in front of her father and began rolling up his pant legs to put the pain-easing ointment on him. He had a dollop of noodle stuck on his chin. She smiled up at him as she took the napkin Alice held out and cleaned his chin. "You missed a spot."

He chuckled. "I always do. Tell me of Lady Conyngham's."

Arabella made a show of opening the lotion and pouring it into her hands. Really, she didn't want her father to see her face because she knew he'd see through her lies. He was very observant, and he didn't need to worry.

"It went splendidly." Was her voice high? Brittle? It sounded false to her own ears.

"Splendidly," he echoed as she began to rub the white lotion onto his misshapen legs. Lack of use had done this to her poor father.

"Mm-hmm," she responded, not wanting to compound one lie with another. The less she said, the better.

He reached down and caught her hands, his big one enveloping hers. His grip was still strong from years of blacksmithing and wielding heavy tools at Buckingham Palace. She knew how much he missed the job he'd lost after he'd had his stroke. He rarely spoke of his time there, but when any of his close friends came to visit and mentioned the king or queen, her papa always tensed. It made her think he harbored anger over being dismissed, but really, what could they have done? He could not do the work that was required of the lead blacksmith.

His brow furrowed. "Are you certain it went splendidly? You're usually bursting to tell me all the details of your day and what you accomplished."

She bit her lip. Well, all she'd managed to do today was lose an important client, take something that didn't belong to her, and agree to sell her body. She most definitely would not be telling her father any of that. He'd have another stroke if he knew what she planning, and this one would possibly be the thing that killed him.

She forced a smile to her face, her cheeks aching, and she looked up. "I'm sorry, Papa. I'm preoccupied with having to see Madame Chauvin. In truth, Lady Conyngham didn't react exactly as I had expected, but things still turned out well."

Lies, lies, lies.

Her nose twitched with her deceitfulness. She quickly put the cap back on the bottle and stood. "I better be going. As I said, I'll be home early."

She gave him a kiss on the cheek and then moved to the counter to get her bag so she could hide the box in her room. As she picked it up, she lost her grip and the bag fell to the floor with a clank. From where she stood, she could see the box inside the bag. Her heart jerked that her father might have seen it, too. She scooped the bag up, but as she did, he spoke.

"What's that in your bag?"

"It's for Madame Chauvin from Lady Conyngham," she instantly replied, hating to lie *again* but feeling she must protect him. She didn't wait for him to speak. She scrambled out of the kitchen and to her room where she hid the bag in the only piece of furniture she had left—her wardrobe. Then she dashed out the door, calling her goodbyes.

The distance between her home and Madame Chauvin's dress shop was not great, but it seemed to take forever as her guilt and worry made her progress slow. Her mind turned. What would she say to Madame Chauvin about what had happened, and how was she going to persuade the seamstress to keep her as an employee?

As soon as she walked into the shop, Madame Chauvin gave her a pitying look, and Arabella's heart sank. Lady Conyngham must have already sent word. How bad of a picture had the woman painted? She opened her mouth to explain, but Madame Chauvin shook her head and held a note—it had to be *the* note—toward Arabella. "This was delivered to me only moments ago by Lady Conyngham's footman."

Arabella set down the packages she had been holding and took the note with her trembling fingers. She stared at it. What nastiness had Lady Conyngham written? She bit her lip. "Will you let me tell you my side?"

The compassionate look on Madame Chauvin's face became even more pronounced. "Of course, my dear, but it will not make a difference. I cannot keep you as an employee. To do so will cost me Lady Conyngham's business, and that of all her friends. Unfortunately, the lady has a great many influential acquaintances. As much as I want you to stay, and as sure as I am that you truly don't deserve this, it would destroy my business. I have my children to think of. The loss of income from the dresses you made for the lady will set me back significantly as it is."

Arabella's heart squeezed as she pictured Madame Chauvin's three children hungry. The seamstress offered Arabella the money that was owed her for the previous week's work, but Arabella shook her head. "I cannot take it."

Madame Chauvin's mouth dropped open. "Come. You need it just as much as I do."

It was true, but she did have a way to make the money she needed, even though her skin crawled when she thought about selling her body. But sell it she would, rather than cause three children to go hungry or her mother to be sent to Bedlam. "I'll be all right."

Madame Chauvin hugged Arabella to her and when she withdrew, she grasped her by the shoulders and stared into her eyes. "You may tell me your side now if you wish, but there is no need. I know Lady Conyngham is vain, and no doubt you somehow pricked her vanity."

Arabella nodded. "'Twas something like that. She had a man there, not her husband, and I think she became jealous of his greeting me."

Madame Chauvin clucked her tongue. "That woman plays a dangerous game."

"Do you mean because her husband might discover she's unfaithful?" Arabella asked.

A momentary look of discomfort crossed Madame Chauvin's face. "No. I mean because it's whispered that she's the king's mistress and seeks to make *him* jealous."

Shock took Arabella's breath for a moment. "Well"—her memories of today tumbled over one another—"it was certainly not the king I met today, nor was it her husband."

Madame Chauvin nodded. "As I said, the lady plays a dangerous game, and whoever is bedding her is either a fool or has a treacherous agenda himself."

Unease fluttered in Arabella's stomach. Did Jude have some sort of agenda? Was she a fool to trust him? Wanting to be alone with her thoughts, she bade Madame Chauvin a hasty farewell and set out toward her home and very uncertain future. Though the June day was still rather warm, it could have been the dead of winter for the chill that had taken hold of her.

Two

London, England
The Sainted Order Hellfire Club
The Next Day

*J*ustin's father had always said that what defined a man was not how much power he possessed but how he wielded his authority. By the age of eight, Justin had recognized that his father was a cold, hard man who exercised great power with stony calculation. Yet, he was an honorable man due respect. The same could not be said of the king. He exerted his power like a fool and was, thus, known as one.

With much grunting and maneuvering of his enormous purple-silk-clad stomach, Prinny, King George IV, settled back in his velvet chair, clutching a snifter with his beefy fingers. Despite the breeze that constantly ran through the Sainted Order's private underground room, beads of sweat rolled over the lumps of flesh that concealed Prinny's cheekbones. As he raised his glass to his fat, cracked lips, they dropped—one, two, three—to join the dark splotches of brandy that sloshed over the snifter onto the king's lavish shirt.

The young page, Thomas, scurried from the corner with a napkin in hand. He started to blot at Prinny's shirt, but Prinny swatted his hand away. "I'll have your hand cut off next time you touch me without asking my permission first," Prinny snarled.

Thomas scuttled backward as his dark eyes grew big. He clutched his hand to his chest as his lower lip trembled. *Damned Prinny and his penchant for demoralizing anyone he perceives as weaker.* "His actions are my fault," Justin interrupted before the boy cried and got himself in further trouble.

"How?" Prinny demanded.

Justin eyeballed the boy with a look he knew conveyed that Thomas better display utter agreement with whatever Justin was about to say. "I instructed him before coming in here to take initiative and not speak unless spoken to first."

Thomas's eyes popped even wider, but he quickly nodded, obviously more than willing to go along with any lie that would save him. In truth, Justin had never said a word to the boy, but it would be their secret. Prinny snorted and flicked a dismissive hand. "Go then and remember from this day to ask before you touch me."

The boy nodded and dashed out of the room without a backward glance. Prinny's mouth pulled into a pleased smile that made Justin want to shake him.

Prinny may be King of the United Kingdom of Great Britain, Ireland, and Hanover, but he was a drunken, obese disgrace who wielded his power with the care of an impetuous, stubborn child. Given he was on his third drink in five minutes, it was safe to assume becoming the official ruler had not sparked an epiphany to change his ways.

The thoughts were factual yet traitorous, especially for a man who served as one of six personal spies for Prinny. Unease rippled through Justin, causing him to shift positions. With the thoughts rampant in his head, he wanted distance from the king to sort them out, but there was no distance to be had. Prinny had summoned him last night in the darkest hour, and though no man ruled Justin, not even the king, he had come. He had long ago vowed to put Prinny above all else, and Justin never broke a vow.

Justin reclined in the high-back leather chair, gaining himself a little bit of space. When people were too close he often felt suffocated. The chair squeaked as he allowed the full weight of his body to settle. A bone-weary tiredness threatened to consume him as his muscles relaxed. Thirty was too damned young to feel this exhausted. But the waters of the canal from Paris to England had been rough, and the horse journey here even harsher with the rain turning the ground to muck.

Prinny set his glass down and leaned forward, closing the distance Justin had gained. He barely resisted the urge to shove his chair back. Instead, he looked at the king, whose eyes were growing more sunken each time Justin saw him.

That gaze, seeming almost lost among the folds of flesh, fastened on him. "I've created a bit of a problem for myself," Prinny said in a slurred whisper, though they were the only two men in the shadowy, candlelit room. Two guards stood on alert outside the door, as was customary, but Justin didn't need them or anyone to help him protect Prinny. All he required were his hands, and in the rare circumstance he needed more aid, he was never without his dagger or his pistol, not even when he slept.

He drew in a long, silent breath. Prinny was always creating unnecessary problems for himself. "What's occurred, Your Majesty?" It had to be messy for the king to have called him away from his current assignment in Paris, ferreting out traitors to the Crown.

Prinny nodded, the layers of skin between his chin and chest folding over one another. "It involves my mistress, Lady Conyngham."

Justin clenched his teeth, striving not to show his disgust on his face. He didn't believe in marriage for several reasons. He'd witnessed firsthand through his parents' marriage what being wed to a cold, hard man could do to a woman. And despite the fact that he'd once hated the very traits in his father that his mother had fled the marriage and him because of, Justin had understood for quite some years that he possessed the same exact qualities his deceased father had. He would not make a good husband. However, he did believe that if one was fool enough to wed, one should remain faithful and honor one's vows. He'd seen firsthand the havoc failing to do so could wreak. Prinny's infidelities left a sour taste in Justin's mouth and Lady Conyngham—married, as well—was a greedy, deceptive termagant.

Weary, Justin scrubbed a hand over his face, the two-day beard growth prickling his fingers as they slid downward against the hairs. "Why don't you simply tell me what's occurred."

Prinny nodded. "Elizabeth is quite angry with me."

Justin's right eye began to twitch. He hoped to hell Prinny hadn't called him back from an important assignment to settle a dispute with the king's current mistress. It wouldn't be the first time, but Justin had sworn to himself after the king's previous mess with his former mistress that it would damn well be the last. "What seems to be the trouble?" he asked, snagging the decanter off the table.

"She refused to admit me to her bed," the king grumbled.

"As I'm sure you don't want me to try to persuade Lady Conyngham to open her bedchamber doors for you, what exactly is it that you want from me?" Justin hoped his tone was laced with just enough admonishment that if the king *had* intended to request his aid, Prinny would rethink the appeal.

He didn't particularly care to defy the king outright, but in this instance he would. As he waited for Prinny to answer, he poured two fingers of liquor in the empty glass in front of him and then took a sip of his brandy. The liquor slid down his throat and loosened the tension.

Prinny twisted the thick ruby-encrusted gold ring on his pinky several times before speaking. "I need you to retrieve some letters for me."

Justin set his glass down with a *thunk*. Surely the king was not such a fool as to write a love letter to his married mistress at a time when he was seeking a divorce. Prinny knew damn well that Queen Caroline had spies about trying to secure proof that he was unfaithful, just as he was accusing *her* of being. The damnable bill that Prinny had gotten introduced to Parliament to take away Caroline's rights as Queen Consort and grant him a divorce on the grounds that she was adulterous would be the king's undoing, exactly as Justin had predicted. And why not? This was the king at his most hypocritical. Yet, it was Justin's job to protect the king. "Expand," he managed in a civil tone, despite his disgust.

Prinny cleared his throat. "Some weeks ago I told Elizabeth I couldn't be seen in public with her until the divorce hearing was finalized against Caroline. I didn't want to restrict where I saw her, but I had to do so." Prinny's voice slipped into the all-too-familiar whiny tone of a king on the verge of a child's tantrum.

"Liverpool insisted you not see her in public?" Justin asked, already knowing the answer was yes, but with Prinny, sometimes a subtle reminder that even kings had to listen to others' advice could help avoid a fit.

"I hate the man sometimes," Prinny snarled. "If he keeps acting like he can tell me what to do, I *will* have him removed."

Justin nodded, even though he knew it would not come to pass. He didn't agree with everything Lord Liverpool did, but the prime minister had more wisdom in his pinkie than Prinny had in his entire head. "I understand," he soothed. "Perhaps after the divorce hearing is behind you…" Justin made a mental note to tell Liverpool that a gesture of peace

toward Prinny was imperative to pacify the king's fragile feelings. "The letters?"

"Yes, yes." He flapped his hand in the air. "Elizabeth threatened to send the love letters I wrote her to the papers if I refused to show my devotion to her in public."

Lady Conyngham was clearly not thinking straight. She should know better than to try to intimidate the king, and she should damn well comprehend that if the letters were printed she would be ruined. "I told you, no more love letters," Justin clipped. The words came out short and terse despite his best effort to soften his tone. Securing the last batch of letters the king had written to his former mistress had consumed too much time better spent on more important matters.

Prinny pressed his lips together, an odd strangled noise coming from his throat. "I know." He shrugged. "She insisted."

Justin's head throbbed. The king was a weak and pathetic fool, but that did not change the fact that he *was* the king. The letters, if made public, would destroy Prinny's chance of securing a divorce because they'd prove the king's unfaithfulness, which was exactly what Queen Caroline was trying to do. Rumors of the king's philandering ways were very different than definitive proof. Justin had half a mind to let the letters be printed. That would certainly settle matters nicely for the queen, but what if they were more than simple letters of adoration?

"Are they merely love letters?" he asked.

Prinny shot his gaze to his glass. "I might have disparaged the commoners who'd called Elizabeth a harlot the last time we were in public together. And I might have said I was going to cut off Howick's balls for making that motion in Parliament to abandon the investigation against the queen."

Jesus Christ. Howick was an important member of the

Whig party. He, along with his comrades, had the power to turn the already-disgruntled commoners against the king and raise an army to try to topple him from the throne. Justin ripped his cravat off with one hand, his skin stinging from the harsh slide of the material against his throat. He didn't want the king to get his divorce, but he'd not go to war to prevent it. "I'll leave momentarily and retrieve the letters from Lady Conyngham."

"It's not that simple," Prinny replied, his voice vibrating with tension.

That strain reached across the space separating Justin from the fool he served, and it enveloped him. The hairs on the back of his neck prickled, and his muscles grew tight one by one until his entire body hummed with alertness. Nothing was simple to those who chose to make it complicated. Justin lived only in the present, and each of those moments was orderly by his making. Therefore, life was simple. He did not allow things or people to upset him, and as such, he controlled every situation and person, rather than letting occurrences and others control him.

"Explain the complication, please."

"I received an urgent message yesterday that she no longer has the letters."

"What do you mean?" he said in an even, measured tone.

Prinny flinched. "She hid the letters in a secret compartment in her jewelry box, and the box has been stolen."

Justin felt the slightest increase in his heartbeat, so he immediately began counting in Japanese. *Nine. Ten.* His pulse ticked up more. *Eleven. Twelve. Thirteen.* His head ached. Damnation, he was tired. *Fourteen. Fifteen. Sixteen.* Mayhap he needed to try French or Russian. There had been times he'd had to count through several languages to keep his calm. Unbidden, a memory of his father spanking him for using a crop too harshly on his horse filled Justin's head. *Weak men allow their emotions to rule them, Justin.*

He was not weak. He shoved his memory and his feelings back into the chest where they belonged. The lid slammed and the lock clicked in his head. His heartbeat slowed to match the king's loud, uneven breaths.

"It will be fine," Justin said in a calm, reassuring voice. And it would be. He'd make sure of it. That was his job, after all.

Prinny's shoulders sagged with relief, yet he started twisting his ring again. He pulled his gaze to Justin's face with the slow reluctance of one with more bad news to reveal. "There's more."

Of course there was. There was always more with Prinny. Justin's emotions rattled in the chest. Being overtired had caused him to slip moments ago, but he'd not falter again. "Tell me and I will handle it."

Prinny sighed while nodding. "There was an emerald-and-diamond necklace in the jewelry box, too. I'd hoped the necklace would lessen her anger and make her see that one day all would belong to her."

"Go on."

Prinny shifted in his seat, the chair groaning with his weight. "It was Caroline's necklace, the one I gave her as a wedding gift." Prinny motioned to his neck. "A heart of diamonds—"

"With a center of the largest emerald ever known to be cut," Justin finished. He was familiar with the necklace. Everyone was. There was only one place in England where a necklace like that—or for that matter, an expensive jewelry box—could possibly be sold discreetly, and that was the Garden District. "I'll get the necklace, the box, and the letters back."

Prinny's lip curled back to reveal yellowed teeth. "I want the thief, as well. I'll see whoever dared to steal from me hanged."

Justin's facial muscles threatened to pull his mouth into a frown. Prinny's vindictive nature was showing. "Perhaps we should learn who the thief is first. They may not have known they were stealing from you, and—"

"No." Prinny spat, spittle flying from his mouth. He swiped a hand across his face. "It matters not. The person stole from me, regardless. I will see the thief hang."

Justin simply inclined his head and stood.

Later.

He would save that fight for later.

Arabella had slept fitfully and her morning had been busy with chores around the house, so by the time the afternoon rolled around, she wanted to take a nap, not dress to see Jude.

But get dressed I must.

Luckily, Alice was coming to collect Papa to take him to his monthly vingt-et-un card game and supper meeting with his friends. Despite the fact that going anywhere was so difficult for him, Papa insisted on continuing this tradition, and she did understand. She would not want to be stuck in the house all the time if she were him.

After helping him through his toilette, Arabella trudged to her bedroom to shake the wrinkles out of her only decent dress, a white-and-green striped day gown. As she reached to take the clothing from the wardrobe, her hand brushed the bag the jewelry box was in, and it gave her a start. She stared at the bag, hard. She could have sworn she'd hidden it on the bottom shelf and not the middle shelf where it now sat.

Her breath caught in her chest as she looked between the two shelves. No, she gave her head a little shake. Her memory of where she'd put the box must be wrong. And no wonder with everything clamoring in her head.

Pushing aside the worry, she took the box out of the bag. The embedded jewels shimmered, even in the dull light of her room. The box was heavy and made largely of wood inlaid with gold. Rubies, diamonds, and emeralds lined the outer edge of the lid, and there was a small spot for a key. She tried to open the box, but it was locked. She raised it in the air and shook it, gasping when something clanked around inside. Her hands trembled as she lowered it. Heaven above, she hoped she had not inadvertently taken a piece of Lady Conyngham's jewelry! But surely, the lady would not have demanded the box be thrown out with jewelry still in it. Unless she forgot... Arabella's stomach did a queasy flip.

Maybe Jude would know how to open the lock. And if there was jewelry in it, he could get it out and take it back to Lady Conyngham without her realizing it had been gone. Arabella turned the box over and studied it from every angle. The craftsmanship was beautiful with stunning carvings that looked very much like flowers swirling around one another. The box appeared to only have one compartment, but she couldn't know for sure until it was opened. Not that it mattered. She'd not be keeping it. She dressed quickly, bade her father and Alice good-bye, as the caretaker had arrived while Arabella was preparing, and set out to see Jude.

It took her over an hour to walk from her home to Golden Square. She'd been a child the first time she'd ever been to London's art district. She'd accompanied her mother, who'd been a seamstress as well, to deliver a gown she'd sewn for an Italian actress, Eleanora Servi, who had lived at number four, Golden Square. The woman had been the mistress of a duke, who had kept a residence at number five. Arabella remembered being in awe of the beautiful square with its magnificent garden in the center of the lovely townhomes. Mother had whispered in her ear to close her mouth and told her that if she thought the square was exquisite now, she should have seen it when the aristocracy had still lived there. Of course, the *ton* had long ago moved on to more prestigious streets.

The square had long ago lost its luster, but there was something intriguing and freeing about the place. The rules of etiquette that dictated Society did not seem to apply here. People were less stuffy, less formal. Chaperones were nowhere to be seen, and ladies drove carriages themselves without so much as a groom. She'd never witnessed a single person bow or curtsy to anyone, and the women were just as raucous as the men. It was grand! She'd been here several times in the last two years to deliver dresses that she or Madame Chauvin had created. The dresses were not for actresses, though; they were for the demireps who worked for Madame Sullyard. Arabella pressed a hand to her still-queasy stomach as she entered the square. Soon she'd be one of those women of questionable reputation.

The sounds of pianos and harps floated through the air to accompany the underlying buzz of gruff men's voices singing songs. She passed by a statue and could see the townhomes in the distance. Most had their windows open, likely to hear the music or to allow the sounds from the instrument within the home to float into the square to join the chorus. Groups of men stood around, either singing or chatting and smoking pipes that filled the space with the heavy scent of tobacco.

Her palms started to sweat as she made her way toward Jude's house. She slid her gaze to Madame Sullyard's establishment and stared at a russet-headed man whose back was to her. He stood outside speaking to Madame Sullyard, which in itself was very odd. Arabella had never seen Madame Sullyard leave her establishment, and she'd heard a rumor that it was because the lady had a strange fear of the outside world.

Arabella had excellent vision, and she could see even from the distance that Madame Sullyard did not look happy at all. She had a fierce frown on her face, but she nodded at whatever the gentleman had said. Arabella hesitated behind the tree as she observed the man. His beautifully cut coat accentuated his broad shoulders. She would bet he was an aristocrat from the dark, bottle green material of the cloth. It was either superfine or kerseymere. Very expensive, either way. As she stood staring, the gentleman turned toward her as if he sensed her gaze on him. That was ridiculous. Yet, he raised his eyebrows and a faint smile pulled at his lips. Her breath whooshed from her lungs.

He was tall and powerfully built, like a solid, unmovable oak. His slightly spread stance emphasized the force of his thighs and the slimness of his hips encased in tan breeches. A shaft of sunlight crested over the covering at the front door to Madame Sullyard's and struck the man's head. His thick hair gleamed like burnished copper. The faint smile at his lips spread to a slow, wolfish one. Heaven above! She was gawking, and he *knew* it! She darted out from behind the tree, marched in the opposite direction to Jude's door, and knocked. How utterly embarrassing to be caught gaping.

Her hand froze in midair. That man behind her could very well be a client of hers in a few short hours. The idea was terrifying.

The door flew open, and a hand shot out and dragged her inside. Jude stood before her, his gaze intense. He reached behind her and slammed the door.

Arabella shuffled backward until her shoulder blades met wood. Behind Jude stood an older, rather distinguished silver-haired gentleman in a gray coat and gray pants.

He smiled. "Hello, Miss Carthright."

She frowned, looking between the man and Jude. "How

do you know my name?"

The man's eyebrows twitched upward, and he shot Jude a questioning look.

Jude inclined his head as if to say, *Go on.*

"Judas told me just moments ago. Did you bring the box?"

She felt her own eyebrows rise.

"It's all right," Jude said. "This is Mr. Winston, the rare commodities dealer of whom I spoke."

Mr. Winston looked surprised by Jude's statement. Perhaps he'd not known Jude told her of him.

Jude looked between them with an odd, almost satisfied grin. "Mr. Winston came back to Town earlier than he had planned."

Arabella could barely contain her excitement. This meant she could sell the box and not have to sell her body! She took the bag off her shoulder and pulled the jewelry box out as she glanced at Jude. "There's something in it, but I don't know what. If it's valuable—"

"I'll get it back to Elizabeth," Jude supplied.

Arabella nodded with relief and thrust the box toward Mr. Winston. "Do you think you can sell it?"

The man looked from her to the box, and then to Jude and back again until Jude nudged him. Mr. Winston blinked as if surprised. A bead of sweat had appeared on his forehead. "Er, I'm not sure. My tools are in the other room to open it. I'll go examine it there and let you know momentarily."

Jude held a handkerchief out to him. "Still feeling ill, are you?"

The man frowned. "What?"

Jude motioned to the man's head. "You're sweating."

"Oh." He snatched the handkerchief from Jude. "Yes, indeed. I still feel ill." The man blotted his forehead as he turned and disappeared out of the small entranceway.

When the sound of his footsteps had faded, Arabella exhaled the breath she'd not even realized she was holding until that moment.

Jude bowed to her slightly. "You look lovely today. So fresh and innocent and trustworthy."

She quirked her mouth at his strange wistful tone. "Thank you, Jude." More than that seemed odd to her, though, starting with how she'd been dragged into the house. "Why did you snatch me through the entrance? As if someone might see me."

"Oh, that. So sorry." He shrugged. "When you knocked, I glanced out the window to see who was here, and I saw Madame Sullyard outside. I owe her a bit of money, you see, and I didn't want to give her the opportunity to ask me for it at that moment." He shrugged again.

"Oh. I assumed Madame Sullyard would be arranging my becoming a-a…" Arabella couldn't force the word *impure* out.

"She is. Or she will be. Would have been." He grinned. "But Mr. Winston is here now as I planned."

"As you planned? But you thought he was not in Town."

"Yes, I meant as I planned on occurring eventually."

"Judas!" came a roar from down the hall.

Jude flinched, as did Arabella, and he pulled his brow into a deep frown. "Wait here." He rushed out and disappeared the same way Mr. Winston had.

Arabella's chest tightened. She glanced around the small entranceway. There was nowhere to sit, which was a bit peculiar, but even more disturbing was the utter lack of any sort of decoration. Either Jude did not have the money to decorate, or he didn't care to, or he deliberately hadn't done so because… Why would someone put nothing personal in his home?

Before she could address her concerns, the solid clap of

footsteps coming toward her filled the silence. In the time it took to inhale a shaky breath, Jude rounded the corner, jewelry box in hand and his face tight with strain. Close on his heels was Mr. Winston. There was a necklace dangling from his right hand. Each step made the necklace sway, the gems glittering in the light. Arabella barely held in her gasp when she saw the enormous heart of diamonds surrounding a dazzling, huge emerald.

Mr. Winston strode in front of Jude before coming to an abrupt halt inches from Arabella. Her body tensed immediately, but she stiffened her spine and raised her chin. "Is there something amiss?"

His features hardened before her very eyes. "Did you open this box, Miss Carthright?"

His curt tone stirred her anger. She was tired of people being rude to her. "The box was locked," she replied, matching his cold tone icicle for icicle.

"I already know that," he retorted, his voice growing terser. "That was not my question."

She would have dearly loved to spin on her heel and leave this boorish man standing here, but she could not afford to. "I am not a magician," she said. "No, I did not open the box. I did not have tools to do so as you did." She purposely eyed the necklace he held. "I'm not quite sure what has you upset."

His face flushed, and he glanced at Jude as if it were Jude himself who'd upset the man.

Jude put his hand on Mr. Winston's shoulder. "Arabella, please forgive Mr. Winston. He is a man who is very passionate about the items he sells, and this jewelry case would have brought a great return to both of you."

"Would have?" she asked in a whisper. Her voice had abandoned her in a flash, along with a hefty amount of her hope.

Jude's eyes turned sad. "Yes, I'm sorry, but the case is

damaged and it appears that someone tried to pry the lock open, so the jewelry box has lost all value."

Arabella's gut clenched as she shook her head. "But that's impossible. I looked at the jewelry box myself this morning, and it was perfect."

"To an untrained eye, Miss Carthright," Mr. Winston said, his tone much calmer now than moments before, but he regarded her with distrustful eyes. The man still thought she'd tried to pry the box open! He moved his hand, and the necklace once again caught her attention.

"Jude, you *will* get the necklace back to Lady Conyngham, correct? I mean, you didn't know it was in the box *did you?*" Suspicion was stirring in her gut, though she prayed she was wrong. Had Jude had her take the box to get the necklace? It appeared to be worth quite a bit.

He shook his head. "I had absolutely no notion it was there. I promise you, and I vow I will return it discreetly tomorrow when I see her. Do you believe me?" His gaze bore into her.

Did she believe him? She nibbled on her lip. Did she have a choice? She had to believe him. She needed his help now more than ever. Finally, she nodded and Jude smiled.

Without a word, Jude clapped Mr. Winston on the back. "Since we have no more business," Jude said to the man, "I'll show you my small garden, as I promised." He turned to Arabella. "I won't be but a moment. Follow us and you can wait in the study."

Arabella nodded and trailed in silence behind Jude and Mr. Winston. When they got to the study, Jude paused. "Here you are. I'll return shortly."

She moved into the room as he and Mr. Winston continued toward the garden. Arabella was glad to see a very comfortable-looking settee in the room. Her feet were aching from the walk here. She strode across the small space toward the settee but jerked to a halt when she realized the jewelry box was sitting on the desk. She could not resist looking at the box one more time. A few steps closed the distance between her and the desk. She carefully picked up the box, which was open to reveal a velvet-lined rectangular space. There was only one compartment to the entire box. Arabella scrutinized the lock. It looked perfectly fine to her, but it was true that she did not have a trained eye.

Voices raised in argument jerked her out of her study of the case, which she nearly dropped in fright. She quickly set it back on the desk and glanced toward the window behind the settee. Jude and Mr. Winston stood in the garden and were clearly arguing about something. Arabella frowned. She hoped that Jude was standing up for himself. Mr. Winston may be devoted to his profession, but that gave him no right to be nasty. She was tempted to move closer to the window to try to read their lips, but before she could make up her mind, Jude turned on his heel and strode away while Mr. Winston departed out of what appeared to be a back entrance.

Within seconds, Arabella heard Jude approaching. He entered the room with a sigh and motioned for her to sit down as he went to his desk and took a seat. "I'm sorry about that, Miss Carthright. Mr. Winston is rather high-strung."

"At this point, I daresay it is acceptable for you to call me Arabella," she replied. He was privy to her downfall, after all.

Jude nodded. "I'm truly honored. Now"—he folded his hands together on top of the desk as he regarded her—"it appears things, as is usual with life events, have taken an unplanned detour."

"Well," she said, attempting to joke and make herself less nervous, "I suppose my downfall was planned."

His eyes impaled her. "Not by me, Arabella. I vow to you that."

Well, he did have a hand and he had been the one to offer her the solution, but she kept the thoughts to herself. His sudden intensity made her uncomfortable.

"It seems you will need my services to set up an appointment with Madame Sullyard, after all."

Arabella nodded, though her head suddenly felt impossibly heavy. "I—" She swallowed, her throat incredibly dry. "Yes."

Without a word, he picked up a bell and rang it. A man appeared immediately, dressed in full gold-and-burgundy livery. He regarded Arabella with wary eyes, but bowed to her, his salt-and-pepper hair unmoving from its slick-back state. "You summoned me."

Was this the butler? In all her nervousness, she'd not even truly taken note that a servant had not answered Jude's door.

Jude retrieved a quill, scratched something on a piece of foolscap with it, and held it out for the man. "Take this to Mary."

The butler secured the note and left without a word. Arabella fidgeted in her seat, her palms and underarms dampening with perspiration. What was she doing? She was not at all sure she could go through with this. Doubt seized her, and she scrambled to her feet. "I don't think I can do it," she blurted.

Jude came swiftly around the desk to her. He put his arm around her shoulder and patted her. "My dear," he said, squeezing her shoulder, "we can all do anything if necessity calls for it. Especially if it is to help someone we love. Or to protect them. Or to bring them to us as they should be."

Arabella immediately thought of her father and mother and bit down on her lip to stifle her cry. They needed her to be strong. She had to do this.

Jude released her and faced her, shoving a fallen lock of his dark hair out of his eyes. "I take it by the look of despair on your face that you must do this—obtain money—to protect someone you love."

"Two people," she whispered shakily.

"Then gather up your courage," he said with a wink. "I know it courses through your blood."

The door to the study opened and the butler entered. "Miss Morgan is here."

Jude nodded. "Thank you, Saxton. Show her in."

Arabella frowned. Who was this Miss Morgan?

As Mr. Saxton turned, presumably to retrieve Miss Morgan, a beautiful woman with fiery-red hair gathered into a high creation at the crown of her head swept into the room. She brushed by the butler without acknowledging him. Miss Morgan, Arabella presumed, flicked her green gaze at Arabella, and her eyes narrowed into slits. "She's too pretty. I don't like it."

Arabella felt her eyebrows draw downward, confused. What was this woman talking about?

Jude strode toward the woman, grasped her, and drew her to him in a crushing embrace that made Arabella's mouth fall open. He kissed Miss Morgan full on the mouth, covering her lips with his, and the woman moaned. Arabella's face heated, but her stomach fluttered and tingled. She'd never seen such an embrace in her life. People simply did not do such things in front of others, yet Jude, clearly, was different, as was this woman.

When he pulled away, he looped his arm around a rather dazed Miss Morgan and smiled down at her. "There now. I told you she reminded me of my sister and not to be jealous. You know you have my heart and my loyalty."

Miss Morgan preened up at him. "Silver-tongued serpent," she hissed, batting her long eyelashes at him. "What you requested should be simple. He's still there."

"Who is still here?" Arabella asked.

Jude flicked his gaze to her but did not reply. Instead, he

refocused on Miss Morgan. "Excellent. Were you safe coming over here?"

The woman scowled. "Why would you ask such silly questions? I'm always safe. You know Madame Sullyard."

"I do know the witch better than anyone," Jude said in an ominous tone.

Miss Morgan nodded. "She's too busy to notice my departure, and anyway, she trusts me implicitly."

Jude kissed the woman on the nose. "As she should, my pet. You are her right-hand girl."

"Jude, will you not answer me?" Arabella fairly growled. "*Who* is still there?" Did Jude have someone in mind for her? And if so, how in heaven did he know the clientele at Madame Sullyard's? Was it because of his secret relationship with Miss Morgan?

As Jude simply stared at her without replying, Arabella considered him for a moment in his dark blue coat with gold buttons and his inexpressibles that fit him perfectly. She really knew nothing about this man, and yet she was allowing him to dictate to whom she would sell herself, and he was not answering her questions.

She plunked her hands on her hips. "I thank you, Jude, for your help, but I demand a say in who I bed." Her stomach plummeted as she said it. It was a struggle to even think it. Doing the deed was unimaginable.

Miss Morgan snorted. "She's feisty. And ignorant of the ways of the underworld."

Jude nodded but offered Arabella a smile. "The demi-reps do not get to choose their clients, Arabella. Just ask Mary." He smacked Miss Morgan on the bottom. The woman didn't even blush.

"'Tis true," Miss Morgan—Mary—replied. "Jude was my first client, and I didn't want to bed him at all. I'd heard of his ferocious appetite."

Arabella pressed her hands to her cheeks. She'd have

perhaps been less embarrassed to be standing here stark naked. She had never seen such openness in talk or intimacy.

Mary smirked. "But then I fell in love with him."

"She'll do anything for me," Jude said matter-of-factly and with a grin.

Arabella scowled. Including allowing him to bed others like Lady Conyngham, she supposed. But what did she know? Mary surely bedded others, didn't she? Maybe they liked it that way. Arabella gulped at the thought. She could never stand to share the man she loved or allow another to touch her when her heart belonged to someone else.

Mary suddenly tittered with laughter as she stared at Arabella. "You *are* a funny one. You wear your shock on your face. You are beautiful *and* innocent of the wicked ways of the world. She is perfect, Jude. You've outdone yourself. Madame Sullyard will be foaming at the mouth to have her as one of her girls."

Jude scowled but nodded. "The witch will be pleased."

Arabella had a suspicion that perhaps she was not the first desperate woman in need of money that Jude had led to Madame Sullyard's lair. But she couldn't be angry. It didn't matter how she came to be here. She had to be here to survive, so she was actually grateful to Jude.

"Something simple has become complicated, which I don't like," Jude grumbled.

"It always does," Mary murmured. "You shall sort it out, I'm sure."

Arabella shifted from foot to foot. Were they now speaking of her or something else entirely?

Jude gave Mary a peck on the cheek. "Go. Time is wasting away."

Mary nodded and moved toward Arabella. "Come," she chirped in a startlingly cheery tone. "When I'm done with you, no man will be able to resist the temptation you present."

"Only one man," Jude said in what sounded like a stern warning.

Arabella dug her heels in when Miss Morgan tried to tug her out of the room. She eyed Jude. "What man? Is this man you speak of intended for me?"

Jude nodded. "I assumed you would prefer to find a benefactor and become his sole mistress rather than host a different man every night."

Bile rose in Arabella's throat, but she jerked her head in a nod. "You're correct." Her voice cracked.

"Mary will help you as I have instructed her to do. Listen to her and you will catch the interest of the gentleman."

Mary nudged Arabella in the ribs. "Then he may just take you under him," she teased in a throaty voice that made Arabella heat from head to toe. Mary winked at her. "And I daresay I doubt you'd find a complaint, though I personally wouldn't know."

Arabella's heart beat a vicious, painful rhythm. "Who is this man?"

"The Duke of Dinnisfree," Mary responded, and with a swift pull, Arabella followed her out the door.

Three

Justin wearily kicked off his boots and sat on the enormous bed. He gazed around the ostentatious wine-colored room that Madame Sullyard liked to refer to as "the king's room," because, she furtively had whispered, it reminded her of the king's style. Justin would never admit it aloud, but he could see why. Everything was over the top, overdone, and almost vulgar. It used to offend him for Prinny, the ugly things people would say to Justin about the king. People who didn't know that he was the king's spy, which was the entire world except for the other five men who worked for Prinny.

Now the comments amused him, and because of that, he couldn't decide if he'd become smarter or coldly cynical. It didn't matter. He reclined against the mound of pillows, propped his legs on the bed, and shut his eyes, stealing one brief moment of peace—likely the only one he'd get tonight—before the next demirep he needed to question entered the room. He leaned his head left to right, but the tense muscles in his neck stayed knotted. Between Lady Conyngham's incessant ranting when he'd gone to see her this morning and a long day of ferreting out details that had proven useless in discovering where the woman's painter, Fitzherald, might have vanished to, the vein on the right side of Justin's temple throbbed.

If Lady Conyngham's butler had not said he'd seen Fitzherald putting the bejeweled box into his bag, Justin would not have been inclined to believe the lady's assertion that Fitzherald was the thief. She was vindictive and manipulative, and she had been quite obviously unhappy with the painting Fitzherald had done. Justin laughed recalling the portrait that Lady Conyngham had shown him. It made her look less than lovely, which was a fair but dangerous depiction. Fitzherald had painted the bump on the right side of her nose to perfection and mirrored the too-thin upper lip exquisitely. In painting her exactly as she appeared, the man had sealed his doom.

Justin had grown to admire Fitzherald over the course of the day. Cleary he was a bold man to have created an exact likeness of such an obviously vain woman and then to have stolen the jewelry box as the payment Lady Conyngham had denied him. Justin firmly believed the man richly deserved that payment. In fact, he decided, slowly opening his eyes, when he located Fitzherald and retrieved the jewelry box, letters, and the queen's necklace, he would personally pay the man and help him to truly disappear out of the king's reach. Justin didn't even have a twinge of hesitation about what he was planning. Sometimes the greatest service he offered Prinny was protecting him from himself, though the king would never think so. Justin had learned that valuable lesson from his father, who'd served Prinny's sire and watched the man lose his mind while foolishly insisting he was fit to continue ruling.

Justin readjusted the uncomfortable pillow under his head, and the overpowering scent of flowery perfume filled his nose. It smelled like the one his mother had often worn. His pulse ticked up, and he began his counting ritual. When he got to fifty in Japanese, he purposely thought of his mother. It was a test he liked to perform occasionally to see if he was still the master of his memories. Since his recollections related to her were mostly bad, she was the perfect instrument with which to see if he could still control how his worst reminiscences made him feel. She'd left Father for another man and, in doing so, had left Justin, as well. She had not loved him enough to stay and endure Father's coldness. The betrayal that had once felt as if his heart had been ripped out no longer even made his pulse increase. It beat a slow, steady rhythm. He smiled grimly to himself. Test complete, he returned to thoughts of today.

The trail to get here had been tediously winding. An earlier gentle threat to Fitzherald's uncooperative former landlord had uncovered the fact that Fitzherald had moved out in the dead of night last evening, leaving payment for the remainder of the rent and a note that he'd not be back.

Justin had then tracked down a string of people who knew the man—a confectioner, a suit maker, a shoe-shop clerk, and, finally, a seamstress named Madame Chauvin. Madame Chauvin had just so happened to make a *glorious*— her words, not his—yellow silk gown for Fitzherald, who was purchasing it for one of Madame Sullyard's demireps, Ruby Rose, clearly an alias. Justin made a derisive noise in his throat.

Fitzherald had taken the dress that morning to give to the woman with whom he'd confessed he was in love. All that had occurred while Justin had been stuck listening to Lady Conyngham complain. He clenched his teeth, but when he realized he was doing so, he forced himself to relax.

Fitzherald had vanished. Ruby had vanished early this afternoon, too, leaving Madame Sullyard a note that she'd fallen in love and was never returning. Madame Sullyard had been only too glad to allow him to question the other demireps to see if any of them knew where Ruby might have gone, and the madam had vowed, for a hefty sum, to keep what he was doing a secret. Not that she really knew what he was doing. She was made to believe he was searching for Ruby because the girl was his sister. The demireps, however, had been told he was here to procure a new, experienced mistress. He'd stressed *experienced*. There was no point talking to any of the new girls because they'd likely know less, but none of the girls he'd questioned so far had been able to tell him anything. Or maybe they'd simply been too wary to divulge one of their own secrets.

It was time to change tactics and employ seduction. He yawned. He was not at all in the mood to bed a woman; he was that damned tired. He just wanted a bed—an *empty*, comfortable one. He let out a weary sigh. Usually, he successfully circumvented the need to seduce, preferring to choose his bed partners out of desire and not duty. Besides that, he never let a calculated seduction progress beyond the necessary kisses and caresses to gain the information he needed, unless the woman was no innocent and desired the encounter as much as he did.

If he was going to play the rake, he needed to get his blood flowing. He rose off the bed, raised his hands over his head in a stretch, and slowly laced his fingers before bringing them behind his head and arching his back. It didn't help in the least. He could have been knocked over with a feather at this moment. Weariness had lodged itself in his bones. The warm room didn't help the sleepiness, either. He strode over to the window and attempted to open it, but the thing was stuck. Swearing, he began to work at the lock, letting the curses flow in a calculated pattern of English, French, Russian, English, French, Russian…

Arabella peered through the cracked door into the distasteful bedchamber and gawked at the man who stood with his back to her. He jammed his hand against the window lock while cursing in English, then in what she thought was

French, and as for the other language, she had not a clue. *This* foul-mouthed creature with the anger problem was the gentleman whose interest she was supposed to capture?

The doubt in her mind compounded tenfold. Her stomach dipped as she followed the line of his broad shoulders, to his trim waist, and continued downward over his spread, powerful legs. Her breath caught. She recognized those legs! This was the man she'd been caught staring at earlier when she'd come into Golden Square. The one who'd been talking animatedly to Madame Sullyard.

Oh heavens. She couldn't go through with it. She took an inadvertent step back, only to have Mary's firm hand come to her back.

"Be brave," she whispered, her hot breath hitting Arabella on the shoulder as she spoke. Over the last hour of Mary fixing her hair, dressing her in an alluring gown, painting her face, and teaching her a few things about seduction, Arabella had learned the woman had a blind devotion to Jude, who she'd claimed had saved her by making her his mistress. A relationship like theirs would never work for Arabella. Mary was clearly dedicated to Jude, but considering Jude's affair with Lady Conyngham, his commitment to Mary clearly did not run as deep. *That* was typical in Arabella's limited experience of men.

Arabella twisted to say something to Mary, but the woman pressed a finger to her lips and motioned for Arabella to face forward again. When she did, her body stiffened. The duke had his shirt halfway off to reveal the lower part of a very muscular back.

Curiosity overpowered her nerves, and she stared as he drew his shirt slowly upward. The air around her seemed suddenly electrified. His shirt came all the way off, his corded muscles rippling under the dancing lights of the candles. His thick arms lowered, and an odd flutter filled her belly. It was not nerves, but awe. He was beautiful. She frowned, squinting at the strange markings on both of his shoulders. Were they painted? They appeared to be words.

He raised his arms again, jamming his hand against the lock with a thud. Something clicked, and the window popped open with a loud screech.

"Bravo!" Mary said from behind her, announcing their presence. Arabella froze, unable to look away as the Duke of Dinnisfree swung around.

For a moment, he appeared utterly surprised, and then the look was gone, replaced by an open smile. "I didn't hear you knock," he said, striding toward them with easy, confident grace. The closer he came, the more painfully aware Arabella grew of his shirtless state and the well-developed muscles of his chest.

Her brain forgot to make her aware that she was staring again, though a fact that registered when his green gaze captured hers, and in a deep voice traced with amusement, he asked, "Do you like what you see?"

Mercifully, her good sense returned with a bang, and she jerked her eyes to his shoulders. "I've never seen anything like that," she murmured, nodding to the markings and praying he did not notice the blush heating her face. Behind her, the swish of Mary's skirts let her know that the woman was departing. Arabella had the urge to run after her, but a simple thought of her mother and father kept her in her spot.

The Duke of Dinnisfree watched Mary as she departed. Arabella used his distraction to sweep her gaze over his profile once more. His russet wavy locks were cut short, but not so short that a hint of curl did not form at his neck. It made her smile, but she pressed her lips together as he refocused on her. If he knew she'd been assessing him, he didn't indicate it in the slightest, or maybe he was just that used to being assessed. He exuded power and a knowledge of it that made her belly tighten.

"They're tattoos," he said, interrupting her thoughts. His voice was courteous but patronizing. He thought her simple, did he? She leaned close to his chest to read the words, but her senses began to spin when the heat he gave off caressed her, and his scent... She inhaled sharply.

"You smell like fresh-cut wood and warmth," she blurted, then bit down hard on her lip. She had to try to sound more seductive and not like a naïve dolt.

He leaned so near to her that his unshaved whiskers brushed her cheek, making her shiver as he swept her hair back and took a long, deep inhalation. He did not pull back as she expected, but pressed his lips close to her earlobe. A chill raced down her neck, and she immediately brought her hand up to rub it.

He pressed a fraction closer. "You smell like—" His words stopped immediately, and he pulled away and scrutinized her. His brows dipped together. "You smell like horseradish and turpentine, a rather unique fragrance choice."

She burst out laughing. "That's not my fragrance of choice." She held her hands up. "I must not have washed away all the rheumatism medicine. I promise I don't smell like that *everywhere.*"

His gaze slid slowly down to her décolletage, and a sinful smile spread his lips, but when he leaned in, he sniffed her hair, and the wild urge to giggle rose up in her throat. Mercifully, she choked it down. When he was done, he drew back once more, and the genuine interest sparkling in his eyes surprised her. That couldn't be. Men searching for new mistresses didn't care about the women's lives, did they?

He startled her again when he took her hand in his much larger one, while deftly shutting the door with his foot. A whoosh of air and a click of wood resounded in her ears. "Come," he commanded and led her toward the bed.

Her legs were trembling so much that she stumbled and would have fallen to her knees, but the duke was there before she could blink, sweeping her up into a standing position and placing her hand on his arm. He turned his head and glanced down at her. "That's the first time my presence has ever made a lady almost swoon," he teased.

"I was falling forward, not backward," she said, unaccountably irked to be thought of as a woman who swooned. "When one swoons, one goes backward."

"Really?" he drawled. "Are you a swooning expert?"

She scowled. "Certainly not. I've never swooned in my life, and if I were going to faint it would not be over a beautiful man. It would be over something important, such as the death of a loved one." She flinched at her words and the reminder they brought.

He studied her for a long moment, a deep assessing look. "You are the most unusual demirep I've ever met."

Could he see that she was unlearned in the ways of mistresses? She had to do better. This man was her best hope. She wet her lips slowly with her tongue as Mary had taught her not half an hour earlier, and a sense of satisfaction coursed through her as the duke's gaze followed her movements. She drew her own gaze up to his slowly.

"I personally think being different is so much more interesting than being ordinary." His appreciative smile emboldened her to continue. "I'd daresay you feel the exact same way."

"Very bold of you, my dear. Tell, me"—he took her by the shoulders, his touch at once thrilling and frightening, and turned her to face him—"what makes you think you know how I feel about anything?"

His husky tone reminded her of the way the wind sounded when a storm was brewing in the sky. It rolled over her and whispered of a barely contained power within him. She could not afford to be meek or allow herself to be confined by the rules of propriety that had governed her life up to this very moment. She raised her hand and traced a finger over the tattoo on his right shoulder. His body showed no reaction to her touch, except his eyes. They tracked her movement like a seasoned hound hunting a fox. She was proud of herself for not trembling.

"Any man who has the word *Honorem* carved on one shoulder and *Justice* on the other is no man who embraces the commonplace."

His face closed as if guarding a secret, and his hand came to hers and moved it away from his shoulder. "Who taught you to read Latin?"

She caught the inside of her cheek, unsure why he suddenly seemed tense. "My father. I live with him." She nearly smacked her forehead with her hand. Mary had very clearly told her no personal details of her life. She was to maintain an aura of mystery. "I mean, I *used* to live with him," she blurted, her face burning from the lie.

"Don't lie to me, Miss—"

"Carthright. Miss Arabella Carthright." She curtsied, and his eyes widened infinitesimally.

"A curtsying demirep whose name means *Answer to a prayer*," he supplied as if she didn't know what her name meant. "You grow more interesting by the second. Tell me who you *really* are." It was a forceful command and a confusing one. Did he think she was lying?

"I really am Miss Arabella Carthright. And I really do live with my father. He has rheumatism," she said as proof.

"I thought all the demireps lived here."

"I'm new."

"I'm sorry, my dear," he said in felicitous but hard tone, "but I told them I only wanted to interview the experienced demireps." He took her gently by the elbow and guided her toward the door.

He was getting rid of her! She was going to lose her

chance to save her parents! She planted her feet, but it was useless. His gentle grip grew tighter, and he moved her forward with the ease of one moving a chess piece on a board. They got all the way to the door, and in desperation, she blurted, "I'm experienced!"

He made a derisive noise from his throat. "I mean experienced in *this* establishment."

She nodded furiously. "I am. I've been here a year," she lied. "I know all the ins and outs of the business. All the secrets." Heaven above, the sea of lies was going to soon be too thick to wade through. She'd just have to seduce him and make him forget that he wanted an experienced girl. She prayed to God she didn't toss her lunch. Her body went clammy at the thought.

He paused with his hand hovering above the door handle. "Do you know Ruby?"

"Yes," she answered without hesitation. "We were very good friends, but she's gone. She fell in love," Arabella added gently. Mary had mentioned he had a particular affinity for how the Ruby woman performed in the bedchamber, and if asked about her, Arabella was to say she knew her well and that the woman had trained her in the art of being a demirep. So Arabella did, without so much as a stutter, but with a hefty amount of distaste for the lies. She despised lying, but she detested the thought of her mother in Bedlam or her father homeless much more.

Something that looked very much like doubt flickered in his eyes and filled Arabella with a sense of urgency. With her stomach swirling, she turned into his chest as much as possible, since he still had a firm grip on her arm. She ran a hand up his chest, his muscles twitching in response as she made her way to his neck. What the devil had Mary told her to do? Kiss his chest? She couldn't remember for certain. Instead, she twined her hand into his short hair and raked her fingernails ever so lightly against his skull. A low growl emanated from him. That was good, she thought.

"Do you like my touch?" she whispered.

"Too much." He released her elbow and set his hands on her hips, then slid them slowly over her waist and up her sides, his fingers brushing her breasts as he went. She stilled in shock at his intimate but gentle touch. His hands traced a teasing path over her chest, barely skimming her hard nipples, and came to stop at her shoulders. He trailed a finger over her collarbone and paused at the hollow space where her pulse beat. "*You* are stirring my blood." His voice had grown thick and heavy. Was this what a man filled with desire sounded like?

She swallowed. "Is that a bad thing?"

"No." His galvanizing look sent a tremor through her. He moved his hands to her lips and ran his fingertips—as light as a feather—over them. Her eyes closed of their own volition at the strange pull in her stomach that his touch elicited, but she opened them at the sound of his voice. "So Ruby fell in love?"

The duke—she really needed to learn his Christian name—was obsessed with this Ruby person. Arabella dismissed the realization and concentrated on what was about to occur. It seemed funny to give herself to a man without knowing his Christian name. Plus, it would tell her something about his character. She'd have to find a way to ask him once he quit demanding to know about Ruby. Arabella frowned. Maybe he'd truly cared for the woman and it wasn't just a carnal fascination.

"Did you care for her?" she asked.

"In a way," he said rather evasively. Yet if a man she cared for had run off with another, Arabella doubted she'd want to admit how she felt to a virtual stranger. "Do you know where she went?"

"No," she said truthfully. She would have missed that he was irritated, except he shifted away from her ever so slightly and his nostrils flared. "I could find her," she rushed out, hoping he'd not care once they were together.

"Splendid," he said in a measured tone. He patted her on her shoulder. "You'll do nicely."

She'd do *nicely?* Arabella frowned. "But you haven't even kissed me. You don't even know if we would, er, suit."

"It doesn't matter."

"How can it not matter?" she demanded, suddenly offended for all the demireps. Was this how they were usually treated?

He let out a sigh, not irritated, almost emotionless. "It does not matter because I'd like you to help me find Ruby. I will pay you handsomely for your services, but I must have your complete discretion."

Arabella clenched her teeth on her irritation. So he'd come here tonight looking for this Ruby, and now he wanted to hire Arabella to help him locate her? The nerve! It was insulting. She felt utterly ridiculous for being insulted, but there it was. Her pride was bruised. She didn't want to sell her body, but she didn't care in the least for the all too familiar feeling of not being wanted. She'd had her fill of that emotion caused first by her real parents and then by her intended.

"You don't even desire me?" she demanded, shocked at her question the moment it left her mouth.

He'd started to turn the door handle, but he went completely still and spun toward her. He studied her with a curious intensity, his gaze raking down her body and back up to her face. He stepped toward her, so close she swayed backward. His hand slid around her waist to crush her to his hard chest. He brushed away the lock of hair that had fallen over her right eye, and then he cupped her chin. "Do you want me to want you, Arabella?"

"Yes," she murmured, utterly dazed by the satisfied gleam that had sparked in his eyes and the oddly protected way his embrace made her feel.

Four

What was he doing? The question reverberated through his mind. He did not need to sleep with this woman. He had what he wanted. Except suddenly, inexplicably, he'd gone from dead tired to fully alert, and he *wanted* her. Blood surged though his veins as she stared up at him with her smoky-blue eyes rounded in a perfect yet false picture of innocence. His desire wasn't so unexplainable, he thought, grimly aware of how weak a woman could make a man. If a man let a woman, that was. He never would.

This beguiling raven-haired woman wanted to give herself to him. Why the devil should he say no? She was a demirep. And experienced by her own assertion. And she was clearly disgruntled that she thought he was pining after Ruby Rose, who he'd never even laid eyes on. The exquisite creature before him had probably never experienced rejection. Far be it from him to sully her record.

"You are in luck tonight, my lady," he whispered into her thick, rose water–scented hair.

She gulped. "I am?"

He smiled. She was surprised. He rather liked that she didn't seem to comprehend how beguiling she was. It was most unusual for a demirep not to grasp the power she had over men. "You are." He leaned back and brushed his lips to her soft ones. "I want you completely."

In fact, it had been ages since he'd felt a surge of lust like the one taking hold of him. The desire to plunge into her and forget himself pounded through him and washed away any trace of weariness. He claimed her mouth in a kiss meant to show her exactly how desirable she was, except her mouth didn't open. Or rather it did, but she quickly clamped it shut on a squeak and almost bit his tongue. He jerked backward and eyed her. "What the devil?"

"I'm sorry," she rushed out, a blush as red as the ripest apple staining her cheeks.

"If you've changed your mind..." He'd never forced his attentions on a woman, and he certainly was not about to now.

"No!" she cried out. "I want you to kiss me."

Only kiss her? He jerked a hand through his hair. He was getting very odd signs from this woman.

"It's just that I don't even know your Christian name."

He almost laughed, except she had a very serious expression on her face. Never had a woman asked him his Christian name during a mutual seduction. They normally asked him to undress more quickly.

"It's Justin."

She grinned, and his chest actually tightened at the loveliness of it. He found himself wanting to smile, but he fought against it.

"That's a perfect name," she said. "Did you know your name means *justice?*"

"I'm aware," he replied, careful to keep his words neutral. He may be about to give his body to this woman, but he was damn sure not about to share his secrets. Still, an imprisoned memory slipped free of its cage and his father's voice whispered in his head, sounding just as he had moments before he died: *Continue the mission to find your mother. Seek justice against the man that stole her from me. Honor me.*

Justin clenched his teeth, then inhaled sharply to regain

his detachment. It descended slowly, and he allowed the memories to skip across his mind. His father had never seen the truth. He'd driven Mother away due to his inability to let her or anyone close to him. Justin had recognized the reality, but still he'd tried to obey his father's command to find her and bring her home. When his father had first made the request right after Mother had left, Justin had the missions carved into his body, one on each shoulder, in a bid to combat the doubt that battered him. She'd left willingly after all. If she missed him or his father, she would have returned. He'd found her a year before Father, on his deathbed, had begged Justin to continue the search, but he'd never told his father. In the end, when Father had lain dying and crying and mumbling about his lost love, Justin feared that by deciding to not force his mother to return he'd had a hand in his father's declining health and eventual death.

"Yes, Justin, is a very honorable name," she continued, her melodic voice chasing the memories back into their prison.

He focused on Arabella once again. She nodded her head decisively. "You may kiss me now."

She was an odd, odd demirep, but he liked her. He cupped her face and claimed her lips, and this time, when it seemed she might not open her mouth for him, he slid his hands to her bottom and hoisted her firmly against him. Her eyes flew open, and her mouth parted. He took advantage of the moment to slip inside her mouth. He groaned with pleasure at the hot, sweetness of the woman. She tasted of honey and a bit of lemon.

He circled his tongue around hers, and at first, she seemed almost unsure how to proceed, but then she tentatively took up the age-old dance of seduction that surely she knew by heart. Their tongues mingled and retreated before meeting again.

He broke off the kiss and swooped an arm under her

legs to cradle her to his bare chest. Her delicate hand settled over his heart, her panting hot breath caressing his skin. She gazed up at him with heavy-lidded eyes that had darkened to almost indigo, and suddenly, the tender touch of her hand against his heart was almost more than he could stand. It was the gesture. So intimate. He didn't normally allow such things, but his hands were occupied.

It took three strides to reach the bed, and he laid her in the middle of the silken covers, her black hair fanning around her face and contrasting vividly with the wine-colored background. He could not remember a woman ever stealing his ability to breathe, except his mother when he'd learned of her deception, but this woman stole his breath like a lightning-fast thief who struck unexpectedly. It wasn't her beauty, though her face would make a painter weep with joy and her body... He hardened instantly as he traced his gaze over the outline of the slender legs he could see hidden under her thin, silk gown. Her skin was a never-ending canvas of creaminess, and her high, firm breasts made his fingers tingle to bring her pleasure.

What was so alluring about her was the innocence that lurked in the depths of blue staring back at him. But it was impossible. She was no innocent.

As if she knew his thoughts, she scuttled backward until she met the mounds of pillows he'd leaned against earlier.

"What are you doing?" she rasped.

Her voice wobbled, as if she was scared. Every instinct he had sharpened, and he scanned a mental list of every-thing she'd said and done since the moment he'd met her. Something was not as it seemed. The lust-filled side of his brain rejected the knowledge that it was her and urged him to undress her and enjoy her, but his good sense embraced what his gut knew to be true: she was no demirep. He'd bet his life on it, but how far would she take this little act and why was she playing the part?

"I'm quite sure you know what I'm doing," he said in a purposely low, silken voice. "Surely, you've seen a man undress before." He deliberately held her gaze as he undid his breeches and slid them off. If her eyes popped any wider, she'd be in danger of them coming right out of her head. He clenched his jaw. He detested deception, even if she was attempting to keep him as her protector, and he damn well knew how hypocritical he was being, given he was also lying to her.

"Of course I've seen a man undress before," she stated boldly while pressing her hands to her fiery cheeks and bringing her knees up before her chest in a defensive posture.

"So is this a game you like to play? The innocent demi-rep?"

"Yes!" she exclaimed, relief apparent in her voice. "That's it. I adore games."

"So do I," he said and grinned in a way he knew made him look wolfish. The color immediately drained from her face. "In fact, I'd like to play one now. You'll be the innocent debutante and I'll be the gentleman who steals your virtue. Doesn't that sound amusing?"

She jerked her head in a nod, her lips now as white as her skin. She looked so pitifully scared he almost considered offering her quarter and telling her he knew of her ruse, but he suspected she'd deny it. He had to make her admit her deceit, and he'd learned long ago from his father's harsh lessons that in order to rip the truth from someone determined to keep it hidden, you had to attack like a wolf given a piece of raw meat. You had to chew up your quarry and spit them out in shreds, if necessary.

He'd been shredded by his father, and his father had learned all Justin's secrets, save two. Justin was no fool. He knew those secrets were only still secrets because his father had never thought to ask about them, never considered the possibility that his son could harbor discontent against him and understanding for why his mother had fled in the dead of night, leaving a note of apology and regret.

"Oh yes," Arabella finally managed to choke out. "That sounds so funny I might die."

He had to give it to her. She was clinging to her sarcasm admirably. "Excellent." He allowed the word to rumble from his chest and was pleased to see it had the desired effect. She sucked her lower lip between her teeth while unconsciously twisting a strand of her long hair around her finger. It should only be a moment until her ruse was up. He'd wager by the time he slipped her gown up her thighs, she'd be singing like a bird.

He kneeled at the foot of the bed and motioned to her. "Lie back, close your eyes, and pretend you're sleeping." He'd actually played out this fantasy for a very insistent, very eager French spy last year, and the memories were helpful now, though at the time he'd been more annoyed than impassioned.

"What for?" she gasped.

"Because you're the innocent debutante, remember? I'm the rogue who has come into your room while you're sleeping to steal your innocence."

"I see," she said in a weak voice. "Wh-what shall I do while pretending to be asleep?"

"Oh, moan and wiggle a bit," he said, struggling to keep a straight face. "Once I have you naked you can pretend to protest." It would never get that far. Even if she was able to hold out that long, he'd not let it continue on to that point.

"Yes, of course," she murmured and slid down onto her back until her head was flat against the bed. Her long, dark eyelashes lowered, and her hands grasped the material on either side of her. He paused a moment, thinking she might confess, but she lay stock-still and silent.

Curse the stubborn women of the world.

He reached forward until his fingertips touched the edges of her gown. She jerked in response, an obvious sign she was not used to a man's touch, but no protestations came from her. When he slid her gown up, gooseflesh covered her slender legs and she curled her toes, and after a minute, she gave an appropriate, though comical, moan. She sounded like a dying cat, not an aroused mistress. He had to bite his cheek to keep from laughing. The higher he raised her gown, the more rapid her eyes moved under her lids, and the quicker his pulse became. He allowed it. *This* was not losing control. *This* was enjoying the game.

He paused at her waist with her gown bunched in his hands and laid the material there. Underneath she wore very French, very appropriately demirep-style unmentionables. "Ah, Arabella," he murmured, as he contemplated what to do next. Touch her thighs? Part them? How far did this have to proceed, damn it? As much as he hated to admit it, he was aroused.

"Er, yes, Justin?"

He frowned. He'd never allowed any woman—hell, no one since his father—to call him by his Christian name, but it might seem odd for him to correct her now. "No more talking," he said instead and set his hands to the inside of each of her thighs. She gasped as a tremor vibrated under his fingers, and his own body went painfully hard. For a moment, his mission slid away, and all he knew was the woman underneath him.

"Don't be afraid," he whispered as he parted her legs and traced the delicate skin on the inside, first with his fingers and then with his tongue. *Jesus Christ.* He knew it was wicked, but he could not stop himself. Her soft, heated skin spun him out of control for the barest of seconds. Blood pounded through his veins and made his body throb with need for her.

He gritted his teeth and brought himself back under

control, his ears humming. When he became aware of her
again, he realized she was moaning sensually and wiggling
her hips in his face. "Do you have anything you want to
confess?" he ground out, his lust making even his throat
ache.

"No," she squeaked. "No, I don't."

Stubborn, stubborn wench. She was not going to relent,
so neither could he. Carefully, he slid her unmentionables
down until they were off. When he looked at her again, her
legs appeared rigid. He ran his hands back up her smooth
thighs, parted them once more, and rubbed slowly and
purposely up over the dark hair that covered her sex. The
second he hit the spot that would bring her the most
pleasure her eyes flew wide and she blurted, "Oh my God."

What happened after that, he couldn't damn well say.
Something—a leg? No, *hell*, a knee—came into his peripher-
al vision. He threw his arm up and deflected the oncoming
knee, but he saw the other one in the air too late. It rammed
into his nose with a sickening crack that sent his vision
momentarily black and left him breathless and speechless. A
Viking from days of old could not have offered a more
lethal blow.

"Oh my goodness, oh my goodness," she cried out and
scrambled—at least he thought she was scrambling, as his
vision was now spotty—toward him. Her thin arm slid
around his shoulder and her hand came to press against his
cheek. "I'm so sorry! Are you hurt terribly?"

The pain in his nose sent vibrations into his bones and
up to his head, and it pulsed with an immediate and painful
woman-induced headache. He gave his head a quick shake.
A colossally bad idea. Blood flew out of his nose like a
crimson stream. He let out a crazy bark of laughter, yet
with his nose bleeding it sounded very odd. He was grimly
amused that such a slight woman had almost taken him
down. Women were most assuredly nothing but trouble, as

his father had said time and again after his mother had left.

"I am not all right. You've broken my nose."

"No!" she exclaimed.

He forced his head up and leaned it back while giving her a sidelong glance. Warm rivulets of blood ran down either side of his face. "I've broken my nose enough times to know that it has, indeed, once again occurred. Give me a cloth."

Tight-lipped, she scrambled off the bed, then reappeared with a rag that she held as she hovered over him. "What shall I do for you?"

"You've done quite enough," he ground out, aware his temper had slipped. "Simply give me the cloth," he intoned with forced calm.

"I want to help."

"Arabella," he snapped, his temper slipping again. "I have to set my nose. You cannot help."

She nodded, yet hovered even closer. "I can. I reset my brother's nose three times. If you'll just let me, I can reset yours. It's a simple matter, and I really think it's better when someone else does it."

"No. Thank. You. I do not take help." His bloody nose throbbed with every word.

She scowled at him. "You are really very obstinate."

"I could say the same of you," he barked, jerked the cloth from her hand, and held it under his chin as he snapped his nose back into place. A long hiss of breath escaped him, and after counting to five in four languages, he managed to unclench his teeth and focus on her. "*You* are no demirep," he clipped, ground his teeth and offered in an attempt at cordialness, "madam."

She looked affronted, which was absurdly amusing. There was a pattern to this night.

"I am—"

He grabbed her by the arms—though it cost him dearly,

as pain rebounded from his nose to his head in sickening waves—and flipped her over his legs. He set his forearm over her back as she squirmed wildly and protested loudly. His control had galloped away, and astonished as he was that she'd somehow made his control disappear, he decided to let go for one moment.

"Release me, you beast."

"I will give you ten seconds to tell me who you are, and then I am going to flay your bottom like a naughty child until you spill the truth," he drawled, almost in amusement.

She glanced at him over her shoulder, her eyes flashing with anger and her face red. "I am a demirep!"

He waved his hand threateningly in the air. "You're sure about that? Because I've never met a mistress who goes rigid at a man's touch. Who clamps her mouth shut when kissed. Who breaks a man's nose in fear of being pleasured."

Her mouth opened and closed in a silent gasp, and her eyes glistened. Oh hell. Was she going to cry? His anger and amusement disappeared in a flash, and he started to ease his hold when she said, "I lied."

"Go on," he answered, easing her up and setting her beside him. She held his gaze instead of looking down or away. That small, strong gesture impressed him.

"I *am* a demirep. Or perhaps it's better to say I *will be* one after I've been bedded."

Jesus Christ! He didn't bed innocent women. They wanted professions of love and entanglements. "Tell me your story," he said calmly, though his mind was racing.

She nodded. "You were to be my first, but I can see that I have failed miserably. You must hate me." She started to scramble off the bed, but he grabbed her by the wrist.

He was astonished that she would be concerned for how he felt at all. "I do not hate you. Tell me your story."

She took an enormous breath. "I need money for my father and me to survive and to keep my mother out of

Bedlam. This job"—she sliced her hand through the air—"is my only hope. I must have the money by Monday, and if I don't, my mother will be shipped to the hospital. I needed to become a demirep, and you were to be my first, and hopefully *only*, client." She cast her gaze down then and shook her head. "I'm so sorry. I'll get them to send in another woman."

It was a struggle not to gawk at her. If she was truthful, she was likely the most selfless woman he'd ever met. "Don't be stupid. I don't want another woman." She could help him, and he *would* help her. He could no more leave this woman to the fate of becoming a demirep than he could leave the king to the consequences of his own folly.

She jerked her gaze to his, a severe frown marring her face.

"I'm sorry," he inserted. "I should explain. I didn't come here looking for a new mistress."

She nodded. "You love Ruby."

"What?" He laughed. "God, no. I don't even know the woman. I need to find her because she ran off with a man that stole something from me that I must have back."

"Oh." She quirked her mouth for a moment. "What did he steal?"

"It's of no importance to you." He tried, God only knew why, to make his tone gentle so her feelings would be preserved, but her lips pressed into a thin line and her dark eyebrows dipped over her lovely eyes.

He ran a hand over his suddenly itchy stubble. He needed a shave and sleep, but first he had to deal with this. "Why can your father not support you?"

"He's an invalid," she fairly growled at him. "Paralyzed from the waist down."

So he'd either wounded or irritated her. It was hard to know the bloody difference with the fairer sex. "I'm sorry."

She inclined her head but did not speak. Why the hell

did he feel compelled to bother with this chit? He stared at her—too beautiful, too vulnerable but bold, desperate, slightly untruthful, and in need. And she knew, so she said, how to find Ruby. That was why he was bothering. That was all. The end. Period. He was on a mission, and she was a part of what would make it successful. He did not need to know much else, yet he found he was curious.

"Why would you seek to be a demirep instead of finding reputable employment?"

"It's of no importance to *you*," she said with a smirk.

Now he had to know. "I insist, if I'm to trust you, that you tell me."

"Whyever would I want your trust?" she demanded. "You certainly don't have mine."

"Touché, Arabella. But I have something you need."

Her brow furrowed. "What?"

She was smart. He'd give her a moment to figure it out. He had a moment to spare, and he was quite enjoying watching how she quirked her mouth this way and that as she thought.

"Money!" she exclaimed. "But I thought—" Her gaze flew to his nose, and that single reminder promptly made him think of it again. The pain was still there, a bit duller but constant as the northern wind. "I thought," she began again, "that after I broke your nose, you wouldn't, well, that you'd rather not *bed me.*"

The last two words were whispered so low that he should not have been able to hear them, but he had excellent hearing. "You thought what?" he asked, cocking his hand to his ear. "I'm sorry, but I couldn't hear the last two words you said." He didn't know why he was teasing her, except embarrassment played across her face in the most fascinating way. He'd never seen anything like it. A blush rose in her cheeks slowly and then spread to a bright flame.

"I said I did not think you would want to bed me! Did you hear that?"

"I think everyone within a block from this brothel heard you," he replied with a chuckle. Her willingness to display her emotions was so opposite of how he was, but he liked it. He knew where he stood with her. His mother had always been angry, but she had never articulated why until the day she left, but it had been too late then.

A strand of long hair that had been dangling in front of Arabella's face suddenly fluttered upward as she let out an angry breath. "What exactly is it that you require from me?" she demanded.

Her words, almost exactly the same as the ones he'd said to Prinny yesterday, surprised him. Clearly, the woman didn't like to waste her time any more than he did. A pleasant discovery, indeed.

"All I require of you is that you lead me to Ruby. If anyone here questions you, retain the ruse that you are my mistress, so no one will become suspicious. For this I will give you—How much do you need to keep your mother out of Bedlam and keep you and your father fed and in your home?"

"Thirty pounds," she whispered.

He nodded. He could see that she thought it a great sum that he'd never give her. In actuality, the amount was paltry to him. His father had never given him much affection in life, but he'd given him a vast fortune upon his death that had proven to be much more reliable than love. Justin had given money to many in need, who had been thrilled to receive it and never once asked for affection from him. Not that he cared. He didn't. Soft emotions were not for men like him. "I'll give you half tomorrow and the rest after we find Ruby."

Her eyes widened, and she opened her mouth to speak, but he held up a silencing hand. "One moment, please. In exchange for your keeping our true relationship a secret, I will give you five pounds a month for one year, but"—he had to raise his voice over her gasp—"if you reveal our true relationship, the money will cease. Do you understand?"

She nodded. "You only want information. Not *me*."

Her chest rose just then with her full breath, and a surge of lust took him. He damned well wanted her, but to muddy the waters by bedding an innocent would be the height of foolishness, and he was *not* a foolish man.

She eyed him. "That's a lot of money to part with for someone you barely know."

Her attempt to get more information was admirable and amusing. He simply stared. Who was this girl willing to give her innocence to save her parents? She thought it deplorable what she had to do. He could tell in the way her eyes clouded and her jaw tightened when she talked. But she was ready to sacrifice herself for family. Something deep within him stirred. He could save her, so he would. It was simple.

She frowned. "Whatever the man you're pursuing stole from you must be very important."

He chuckled at her continued attempts. "I'll not miss the money, Arabella. I have more than I'll ever need. And as for what was stolen from me, if you continue to ask me questions, I may rethink needing your help." He didn't doubt that he could eventually find Ruby and Fitzherald alone. What concerned him was that Fitzherald would discover the letters from the king before Justin got to him, and the man would sell them to one of the king's enemies.

"I cannot think of a single other question for you," she replied instantly, "other than where shall I meet you tomorrow?"

"You tell me. Where do you think Ruby may have gone?"

Five

*A*rabella could not show any doubt. She kept her gaze steady on Justin's green, penetrating eyes. "I'll tell you in the morning after you give me the first half of the money." And after she asked Mary, who hopefully knew or could find out, where Ruby was.

He regarded her with the eyes of a hooded hawk. Did the man ever show emotion? He stood, grabbed his shirt from the floor, and put it on while staring at her. "I suppose that's fair. I'll pick you up at your home, then."

"No!" she shouted. She didn't want her father becoming suspicious.

He gave an impatient shrug. "Then meet me at the corner near your house. Just tell me the street name."

"No. That won't do, either."

"Why the devil not?" he snapped and gave his head a shake. His face grew calm.

The man was insufferably rude, yet somehow generous. He was a conundrum. He was her savior. But only if she met his expectations, which she would do anything to do. However... She took a deep breath. "Now that I know I can secure the money I need without destroying my reputation, I'd rather keep it intact, thank you very much. Therefore, I cannot meet you at the corner and risk possibly being seen climbing into a carriage with a gentleman and *no* chaperone."

"Exactly why I said I would meet you at your house."

She shook her head. "That won't do. What would I tell my father?"

"Tell him I'm courting you," the duke thundered.

She glared at him. "Do not yell at me, *Your Grace.*"

"You have the oddest effect on me, madam. I never lose my temper."

She snorted, and she could see his jaw clench.

He released it slowly. "I am sorry," he said in a stiff tone. "Simply do as I said and tell your father I'm courting you."

She shook her head. "My father would never believe that you are courting me."

He shrugged into his breeches, yanking them up as his brow furrowed. "Because I'm a duke, I suppose."

"No, you pompous jackanapes." The words flew out of her mouth before she could stop them. She drew in a calming breath. "Oh dear. Now I'm the one in a temper. Forgive me."

He shot her a magnanimous smile. "Done. I *am* a jackanapes for jumping to such a conclusion. Pardon, but I unfortunately dwell mostly amongst a supercilious, avaricious lot of people, and I've apparently forgotten not everyone sees the world in two classes—the *ton* and the lessers. I certainly don't, but I'm used to most other people thinking that way. So tell me, if it's not a class issue why would your father not believe I'd court you? You are beautiful, after all."

He thought her *beautiful?* Her mouth pulled into a smile that she immediately covered with her hand. She feigned a cough. How disconcerting that she cared at all how he saw her. She tilted her chin up. "He'd not believe it because I have no interest in being courted."

"A woman who thinks she does not need a man. How very novel." His words dripped sarcasm.

Duke or no duke, her savior or not, this man needed to

be put in his place. "Have you always been like this?"

His brows dipped together. "What is the *this* you think I'm like?"

"Distant." She thought for a second on the exact right words before saying more. "Jaded. Disillusioned. Cold."

He swooped toward her so fast she flinched. His arm slid around her back and drew her into his heat. "I can assure you," he said, his embrace making her body tingle all over, "that I can be very warm. Shall I show you?"

Was he taunting her? His challenging expression certainly said so. She pressed a hand against his chest to get some distance, but it was like pressing against solid, immovable stone. "I don't mean your flesh, Your Grace."

He smiled, flashing beautifully white teeth. "Ah, my heart." He released her at once but gripped her hand as she began to stumble and steadied her. "I do believe I was born this way," he replied, but for the first time since she'd met him, he looked away. "As for the rest of what you said"—he shrugged his massive shoulders—"who isn't jaded and disillusioned?"

"I'm not," she protested.

He swung back around and pinned her to the spot with an intense stare. "You most certainly are or you'd want to be courted. Some man has made you disillusioned."

She opened her mouth to protest but clamped it shut when she realized he was right. How irritating. "I think I prefer we don't discuss personal things," she grumbled.

"An excellent suggestion," he replied. "We have all matters between us straightened out except for where I am to meet you tomorrow." He stared at her expectantly.

She fidgeted for a moment, trying to decide the best place. "I've got to see my mother and pay for her keep. You may meet me at the Stanhope Home for the Mentally Impaired. With my money, please. *Outside.*"

She half expected him to protest, but he inclined his

head in agreement. "I'll see you there."

She nodded, her breath hitching as he turned and walked toward the door. She prayed she could find out what she needed to keep the money he was offering.

He was halfway out of the room before he turned around. "Do you need a ride home?"

"No," she rushed out, surprised by his offer. "My father stays up late sometimes."

"And you wouldn't want him to see me bringing you home."

"That's right," she nodded, relieved he understood.

"You're not walking, are you?"

The way his eyes had narrowed made her wary. He may be a cold, disillusioned man, but he struck her as the sort of gentleman who'd never allow a lady to walk alone through the dark. It was at once comforting and alarming. But she did not want to chance her father seeing Justin. She'd told her father she was working late, which was one short block from their house. And Madame Chauvin always had her eldest son walk her home when she had to work late.

"No, no," she assured him, praying neither her tone nor her expression gave her away. "I'm not so foolish as that."

"I'll sleep soundly in that knowledge," he said in a tone of mock seriousness, yet she had the oddest sense that he partially meant it. "Good night."

He was gone before she could respond. She stared at the door for several moments, waiting for him to return for some unknown reason, but after a bit, she put herself back into a presentable state, slipped out the door, and headed to Mary's room on the second floor, which was where Mary had told her to come when she was finished with the duke. Candelabras lit the shadowy halls, and she would have felt very alone if she hadn't passed several closed doors where the sounds of couples talking, laughing, and apparently thoroughly enjoying each other drifted into the hall.

When she rounded the corner at the end of the hall, she almost ran straight into Mary. "I was just coming to find you," Arabella whispered, conscious of all the people in the rooms surrounding them.

Mary leaned close to Arabella and grasped her forearm. "How was he?" The keen look of interest in the woman's eyes disconcerted Arabella. The woman seemed to have an odd fascination with Justin's sensual prowess.

"He was gentle," she replied. All this lying was making her gut ache, necessary or not. Besides that, the fewer falsehoods she offered, the fewer she had to remember, and she had vowed to Justin that she would let everyone here believe she was now his mistress.

Mary's painted lips came together in a pronounced pout. "Is that it? Just gentle? How utterly disappointing."

"I'm sorry," Arabella replied, trying to sound dutifully meek and remorseful. Really, she wanted to snort. The woman had clearly been expecting a wildly gushing tale.

"Humph," Mary replied. Then she twirled the other way, her crimson skirts swirling. "Follow me," she demanded over her shoulder.

Arabella did, and within moments, they were making their way back to the path they had taken to the brothel earlier. They crept around Jude's house until Mary opened the creaky gate that led to his garden.

Arabella's mind raced as she walked. "Mary, will Madame Sullyard demand a portion of the money His Grace is going to give me?"

Mary swung around and gaped at her, the white of the woman's eyes seeming huge in the black night. "Do you mean to tell me he truly asked you to be his mistress?"

Arabella nodded, slightly affronted by the clear shock in the woman. "He did, but he also wants me to help him locate the woman named Ruby you said he might ask after.

If I help him find her, he'll give me a bonus." That was close enough to the truth that she'd remember the lie.

Mary clucked her tongue while shaking her head. "I don't believe it."

Arabella's heart stuttered. "It's true!"

"No." Mary patted her on the shoulder. "I believe you. What I don't believe, though I should know better by now, is how Jude is always right."

"What do you mean?" Arabella asked with a frown.

Mary waved her hand as she turned and started up the few steps to Jude's back door. "Nothing. Just that he has an uncanny instinct for what people will do. He knew, absolutely knew, that the Duke of Dinnisfree would be entranced by you, and that, my friend, is no small feat you've accomplished. The Duke of Dinnisfree doesn't play the fool for any woman, or so I've heard."

Arabella pressed her lips together as she followed Mary into the townhome. Justin had not been captivated by her charms. He'd not even been intrigued enough to require she also bed him as part of the bargain. She should be thrilled and relieved. And she *was*, but she also felt the tiniest bit lacking. Why didn't she have that special something that would make a man fall hopelessly, give his life for her if necessary?

She snorted. She'd read far too many romantic novels in the late hours of the night. Her head was full of unrealistic fluff. She was not the type of woman to inspire undying devotion. She was the type of woman to inspire a man to leave her when things became complicated. Men could not be counted on, except her dear papa, of course.

Mary led her into the study where they found Jude. He was reclining on the settee with his feet propped up, papers in one hand and a tumbler in the other. He slowly lowered the papers as they walked in, and he smiled.

"How are you?" Jude asked, peering at Arabella with

concerned eyes.

"She's no longer pure," Mary answered with a snicker before Arabella had a chance. Mary breezed past Arabella giving her a narrow warning look that Arabella interpreted to mean, *He's mine.*

Even if Arabella desired a man's attention, it would not be a man like Jude. He was too... too soft and pretty. She preferred a man like... like Justin, devil take him. There was something broken about him that the nurturing part of her ached to fix, and he had a ruggedness that appealed to her. A sudden recollection swept through her of the way his strong hands had grazed up her thighs, causing incredible heat to pool deep in her belly and embarrassingly lower. Did he know how he'd affected her? Likely he did given the way he'd swaggered when he'd walked out of the bed-chamber, like a gentleman who'd been told before exactly how his touch set a body to flames.

"You're blushing," Jude said, interrupting her thoughts.

She pressed her hands to her hot cheeks. "Er, yes."

"Did you find him pleasing?"

She cast her eyes down to her slippered feet and nodded. "I wanted to thank you, Jude, for helping me. His Grace has asked me to be his mistress."

"Perfect."

She looked up, vaguely disturbed by Jude's response. It was an odd choice of words, as if Justin taking her as his mistress somehow benefitted Jude. What a ludicrous thought. Jude was simply being nice and was glad for her. She fidgeted with her gown for a moment, aware Jude was watching her but struggling to find the words to ask for the favor she needed. She couldn't tell Jude of what Justin really wanted, but the idea of lying yet again left a sour taste in her mouth. She swallowed her distaste. "His Grace would like to also find the woman you mentioned—*Ruby.*"

She did not miss the quick look of satisfaction Jude gave

Mary, nor her wink back to him. The hairs on the back of Arabella's neck suddenly stood on end. Was the exchange between the lovers something more, something hidden between them?

Jude swung his legs off the settee and leaned forward to set his tumbler and papers on the table. "Did he mention why?"

Arabella caught the inside of her cheek for a moment, struggling to calm her nerves. "It seems he was in love with her long ago and tracked her here. He simply wants to ensure she's well."

"He told you *that?* Those exact words?"

Jude had leaned forward and rested his hands—one of which had a bandage stained with blood around it—on his knees, an intense look setting his face into hard lines. Arabella nodded, even as her heart thumped so loudly she was sure it gave away her nervousness. Sweat trickled down her sides, despite the sheerness of the gown Mary had insisted she don. She had to change before she left.

"Yes," she asserted. "Do you happen to know where I can find Ruby? I'm to get a bonus if I can help him, and I could dearly use the money."

Jude stood and strode to her with Mary hovering behind him. "Ruby has gone to work at Crockford's Club. I'm sure the duke knows the gambling hell. It's a favorite amongst his group."

"Thank you, Jude," Arabella said and impulsively hugged him. Jude stiffened for the slightest moment but then returned the embrace, pulled back, and gazed into her face.

"Be careful, little bird. The Duke of Dinnisfree is known to be a dangerous man."

"What do you mean?" Arabella asked.

Mary was suddenly between them. She grabbed Arabella and thrust her gown into her arms. "He means the man is dangerous to women's hearts. Guard yours judiciously."

Arabella took her gown. "My heart is not involved, believe me. This is a business deal only."

Jude nodded. "Very good. Now that we've settled that, you better go change. You can use my bedchamber. Mary will show you the way. When you're ready, I'll take you home."

"No," Arabella replied. "But thank you. I'd rather my father not see anything and possibly become suspicious."

Jude scowled at her. "You cannot walk the streets of London at night alone, and I doubt a man in ill health such as your father waits up for you. Does he?"

Arabella stilled as she studied Jude. "How do you know my father is in ill health? I never told you that."

Jude cleared his throat. "You did."

"No, I—" Arabella pressed her fingertips to her temples. She was very tired and her thoughts were not near as clear as they needed to be, but she could have sworn she'd been very vague about her parents. *Hadn't she?* She tried to recall the exact words of her conversation with Jude, but she could not. "Perhaps I did," she answered lamely. "But in any case, he *does* wait up for me." Nor was it even that late yet. Her father never went to bed before ten, especially after attending his monthly card games.

"Then I'll simply drop you at the corner near your house. That will eliminate any danger of his seeing me and asking questions." Jude turned to Mary. "Show Arabella to my bedchamber so she can change her gown."

Arabella followed Mary down a dark hall and up the creaky stairs. As Mary opened the door to a large room containing only a bed on a dais and one wardrobe, Arabella was once again struck with how impersonal and bare Jude kept his home. She glanced around the room, looking for any trinkets that would make this room *his* and not simply anyone's, but she saw nothing. Not a brush, a picture, a book—nothing. Nothing that would tell you a thing about the man, who he was, what impassioned him.

She paused inside the doorway, wanting to ask Mary if she knew, but her words needed to be chosen carefully. She doubted Mary would freely give answers. "Mary," she said to the woman's back as she lit some candles, "Tell me how you and Jude met. I know he was your first client. Did Madame Sullyard pick him for you?"

Mary swung around and raised a candle between them, the flame flickering and casting shadows across her face. She shook her head. "No. He rescued me from one of Madame's patrons. The man who was to be my first lover was giving me a beating for daring to have an opinion different than his own." She snorted. "Lucky for me, Jude intervened."

Arabella worried her lip. "Jude seems to be in the habit of rescuing people." She was torn. Part of her wanted to believe Jude truly was helping her out of the kindness of his heart, but there was another part of her that had the suspicion he was using her. Yet how and why she could not say.

Mary nodded as she flicked her gaze to the door. "You better change quickly. Jude doesn't like to be kept waiting, nor does he like me to talk about him." The words were pointed. Arabella nodded, but she was determined to learn a bit more about this man who had taken her under his wing. She just needed to do so in a roundabout way.

"What was it that you and the patron were disagreeing about when Jude came to your rescue?"

Mary's face darkened. "Oh, the rat," she grumbled. "He said that Princess Charlotte died in childbirth because the queen was being punished by God for her adultery."

Arabella sucked in a sharp breath. That was a hideous thing to say, and Arabella could not believe such behavior of the queen was true. Her father had always said how kind Queen Caroline was, and despite the king's obvious dislike for his own wife, Papa had mentioned on several occasions that the queen only had kind and supportive words for the king. Of course, Papa had also joked, *What else could the queen do?* She was a smart lady, after all.

A huge lump formed in her throat. Her father was the most wonderful man. She didn't think most men gave a thought to how the queen must have felt being married to a man who held so little regard for her.

Mary clucked her tongue, snapping Arabella out of her thoughts. "My own sister died in childbirth, and I can promise you it was not 'cause my mama was adulterous. It made me so mad I forgot to hold my tongue, and I told him maybe Princess Charlotte's death was to punish the fat, filthy, immoral king and not our good Queen Caroline."

Arabella's thoughts tumbled in her head. Jude was sleeping with Lady Conyngham, who was sleeping with the king, and Jude seemed to care for Mary but not so very much for Lady Conyngham. Was it just lust, then? She assumed Jude's sympathies lay with the queen, so did it not bother him to bed a woman who slept with a man he held in such low regard, even if he was the king? Who knew with men... Jude probably felt it some great accomplishment to bed a woman who the king also bedded.

Arabella shivered. No doubt that could cost Jude his life if he was ever discovered. "Jude took your side, I assume."

"Certainly," Mary crowed. "Jude worships the queen as do all good English folk. Say"—Mary eyed her—"don't tell me you're for the king?"

"Of course not!" Arabella exclaimed. From the little she had learned from her father's occasional comments and the bit she'd read and heard in Town, it seemed the king was, indeed, an immoral man. He thought to rid himself of the queen by any means necessary, including destroying her character. Yet, Arabella was not foolish enough to speak against the king or queen to anyone she did not truly know and trust, which was her father alone.

She chose her words with caution. "I'm for husbands and wives being true to each other."

Mary nodded. "Me too. That's why I love Jude. He is true to me, though we're not married *yet*."

Arabella swung away, afraid her face would reveal what she knew. She was disgusted with Jude for allowing Mary to think he was faithful. If he truly cared for Mary why not rescue her from the profession? "I better change. It's getting late."

She heard the shuffle of Mary's feet as the woman moved toward the door. "Come to the study when you're finished."

Once the door shut, Arabella let out a relieved breath. She was grateful to Jude for helping her, but she didn't like that she felt he was not who he seemed, nor did she like knowing he'd been untrue to Mary with a woman who was the king's mistress. Arabella would likely never see Jude again, since she now knew where to find Ruby, so there was no point fretting about any of it.

She dressed quickly and made her way to the study. She stopped just outside the closed door when she heard Jude's raised voice mention her. She bit down on her lip and pressed closer to the door to hear.

"Damn it, Mary, I told you to watch your words with her!"

"You barely know her and you act as if you care more for her welfare than mine!"

"Don't be absurd," he thundered. "I told you that she reminds me of my sister."

"Oh, Jude!" Mary cried out, and then her words became mumbled.

Arabella sucked in a long, slow breath to try to calm her racing heart. Was Jude so private that he wanted Mary to mind what she said, or was it something else entirely? She'd never get answers standing out here. She pushed her shoulders back, gathering her courage, and knocked on the door.

"Come in, Arabella," Jude called.

Just as she was opening the door, Jude's butler, Mr. Saxton, appeared out of the shadows and swept her aside to open the door for her. Arabella gaped at his back. Had the man been standing in the shadows watching her eavesdrop? Her skin prickled.

She rushed into Jude's study. "I'd like to go now, if it pleases you. My father will be worried if I'm late."

"We cannot have your father worried," Jude replied, and within minutes, they were headed to his carriage, which the butler, who apparently also had the job of readying Jude's horses, was awaiting them. Jude handed her up and then climbed aboard the carriage himself and took the reins. As he moved the horses toward the street, she was about to give him instructions to her home when he turned the carriage in exactly the right direction.

She tensed. It certainly could have been a lucky guess. She was being silly. Jude could not know where she lived. Except within minutes, she realized that he did. He knew precisely where she lived, and he made every turn without asking or hesitating.

She gripped her hands in her lap, listening to the revolutions of the carriage wheels against the street. Fear numbed her, but she forced herself to face him so she could see his reaction to what she was about to say. "I never told you where I lived."

Jude's humming immediately stopped. He flicked his gaze to her and then back to the road. "Of course you did."

"No." Her pulse raced so furiously she felt dizzy, weak, clammy yet cold. She scooted as far away from Jude as she could get, yet kept her gaze on him. "No," she said again. "I never told you where I lived, and I never told you my father was in ill health. Pull over." Her voice quivered ever so slightly.

Jude kept driving, though it did seem he was slowing the horses. "Arabella, don't be ridiculous."

"Pull over or I'll jump."

To her utter relief, he drew the reins back and maneuvered the horses to the side of the empty street. He turned toward her, his expression unreadable in the shadows cast from the trees.

She wanted to flee, but she could not. This man had set up her meeting with Justin and she could not escape the gnawing sense that it had been for a reason other than helping her. "You are using me," she accused. "You are using me for something to do with the Duke of Dinnisfree and I want to know what. If you refuse to tell me the truth, I simply won't see him."

"Of course you will," Jude said in a smug tone. "You need the money. What choice do you have at this point?"

She didn't have much of a choice, but she'd make one nonetheless. She stood abruptly, intent on leaving, but Jude caught her wrist and held tight. Her pulse sped up as she looked at him.

He rose above her. "I'm sorry. Please sit, and I'll tell you what you want to know."

She hovered there, caught by uncertainty. Could she trust Jude? Did she have a choice other than marching away from him and Justin and selling her body? Her head ached, but she sat and faced Jude. "Who are you? *Really*. And what is it you want from me?"

Jude scrubbed a hand over his face, then spoke. "I'm a Bow Street Runner, and I'm working undercover to take down a smuggling ring. I need your help, but I must be able to count on you."

She slumped back against the carriage seat, wary yet relieved. *If* Jude was telling her the truth, it explained his odd behavior and the empty townhome that he likely didn't really live in. "What does your assignment have to do with His Grace, and how or why do you need me? I cannot fathom how I could help you."

Jude nodded. "I understand. Neither could I when my boss, the man you met at the townhome earlier, suggested I find a woman to get close to Dinnisfree. You see, we suspect he's part of a smuggling ring, and we've tried to maneuver one of our men into his confidence so we may be certain, but he won't let anyone close. He trusts no one."

But Justin had trusted her.

Her temple throbbed in time with her heartbeat. He had told her he was looking for Ruby because he was searching for a man who had stolen something from him, but he'd never said what. She felt ill. Every way she turned, deception greeted her, but she could see no other real choice, despite her blustering that she would leave.

And go where? her mind taunted. *Do what?* "What can I do?" she finally managed to ask, her throat dry and her mind racing.

"You are to be a distraction. We cannot accuse a man such as the Duke of Dinnisfree of being a smuggler without proof. We need proof. *I* need proof. You must gain his confidence. Get him to tell you exactly what he's doing and why he's looking for Ruby. We believe her lover is part of the smuggling ring, but she won't tell us."

"So you have Ruby?"

Jude nodded. "Yes, yes, of course. We'll keep moving her, but make it seem as if she was just where you lead Dinnisfree."

Arabella rubbed her arms to ward off the chill that had taken hold of her. "Whyever do you think he would trust me? He doesn't even know me." And she didn't know what to believe.

"Because you are good. He will sense it as I do. And you

are innocent of wrongdoing. Innocence is beguiling to men such as Dinnisfree and myself, my dear."

"And what sort of men are the two of you?" she demanded, fighting against her fear.

"Men who lost their innocence so long ago they've forgotten the feeling but who long to remember it."

"You speak as if you know His Grace."

"I've watched him long enough that I feel as if I know him as well as I understand myself," Jude replied. "Just as I feel I know you."

She shivered at the way he was looking at her, as if he really did know her. She inhaled slowly. "And what of honor?"

He shook his head. "It was not honorable of me to lie to you, but I swear I will never put you in a situation that will endanger your life."

"Of course not," she snapped, slicing a hand through the air. "You'd only trick me into losing my innocence and becoming a man's mistress so you could use me."

A pained expression crossed his face. "Don't look at it that way, Arabella. I don't. Things will work out perfectly, you will see. You're mad now, but you will thank me later."

"Thank you?" She scoffed. "You want me to thank you? I cannot in good conscience take any money from His Grace now, since I won't truly be helping him find Ruby. Do you want me to thank you for making my situation worse than it was?"

Jude gaped at her. "You must take the money. It would seem suspicious if you didn't."

She gave a sharp intake of breath at the mess into which she had somehow gotten herself. Jude was right. She *had* to take the money, regardless of her guilt. She had no other choice if she was going to save her mother, her father, and herself. Remorse and doubt gnawed at her. Another thought struck. She didn't even know what they thought

Justin was bloody well smuggling. What if it was something horrific?

"What do you believe he's smuggling?"

"Alcohol. We also believe Ruby's lover stole some of the money from Dinnisfree."

"What's the man's name?"

"Mr. Thorn," Jude snapped, as if her question somehow annoyed him. His attitude irritated *her*. She had a right to know as much as possible.

Jude gave her a fixed stare. "You will need to keep your eyes out for papers that may indicate him. Listen to everything he says. If it seems he has a lead on what he is looking for, you must tell me at once."

She sighed but nodded her agreement. She didn't know who to believe, but if she was going to keep her mother out of Bedlam and her father fed and cared for, she was going to have to do this. "How shall I contact you each day?"

"Meet me at the Sans Pareil Theatre tomorrow at five in the afternoon. I'll come in the back, you go in the front. The actors and actresses practice every day at that time and many poor people wander in to watch, so it won't seem odd that you do so if Dinnisfree should be following you."

"All right," she agreed, feeling wearier than she ever had in her life. "I'll walk the rest of the way home," she said in a stern tone. She wanted away from Jude at the moment. When he did not immediately release her, she stared pointedly at her wrist until he finally let go. She turned and descended the carriage, not looking back. The horses neighed behind her and the carriage wheels clacked against the cobblestones; Jude must have been maneuvering the carriage to head back to the Garden District. She chanced a glance over her shoulder and saw the curricle disappearing around the corner in the opposite direction.

She hurried the rest of the way home, not liking being out in the dark alone, despite her earlier bravado. When her hand touched the short railing that lined the steps to her home, she relaxed until, to her right, a shuffling sound reached her. She stilled and whipped her gaze in the direction of the large tree that stood next to her house. If anyone was there, she couldn't make the stranger out, nor was she going to stand around peering into the dark to try to do so. She scrambled inside the house and frowned at the darkness.

Alice always left a candle lit for her, so clearly Alice and Papa had not yet returned home. Arabella groped her way toward the study to where her father kept the claret. She was not normally one to imbibe, but she needed to calm her nerves. When she reached the study door, she palmed the wall to get to the desk without tripping. Something crunched beneath her slippers. It felt hard against the soles of her shoes.

When she finally retrieved a candle and lit it, she glanced down and stilled. Glass from the lone window in the room covered the floor. Fear froze her, but when the clock chimed, she blinked and then glanced at it—ten o'clock. Thank heavens her father was late.

She scanned the room, but nothing seemed out of place. With her heart pounding, she drew close to the window and jerked as a scream lodged in her throat. Illuminated in the moonlight was the Duke of Dinnisfree, staring in her direction, a pistol aimed straight at her.

Six

*J*ustin let out a relieved breath that it was Arabella. He'd been following her since she'd come out of the townhome across from the brothel to ensure she made it home safely and to learn what he could about her life. When she'd gone into her house, he'd planned to leave, but then he'd noticed the broken window. He started to lower his pistol when she spoke.

"Are you going to shoot me?"

Women never made him speechless, *until now*. He took in her wide, frightened eyes and her pallid skin. Bloody hell. The woman was not joking. She thought his shooting her was a possibility. Whyever would she think such a thing?

His natural caution took over. "Have you done something that warrants my shooting you?"

For a split second, a guilty look crossed her face before her eyes narrowed. "Certainly not," she snapped. "And you're lucky I don't have a pistol because if I did, I might have shot *you*. Why are you standing outside my window with a pistol?"

"I—"

"Did you follow me?" she demanded, putting her hands on her hips and giving him an incredulous look.

The woman had an admirable amount of gumption. He lowered his weapon to his side. "Certainly I followed you. What sort of gentleman would I be to allow a woman to walk home alone in the dark?" He ignored the fact that she'd been driven home, and he hoped she'd let it pass.

A look of utter surprise replaced the incredulous look on her lovely face. "I told you I was not walking home."

He nodded as he strode toward the window and stopped right in front of her. "Yes, you did, and I could only be certain of that by following you. Who was the gentleman that brought you home?" He'd tried to get a good look at him, but having to keep his own carriage so far back, he'd failed.

"That was my cousin Jude," she replied.

"Cousin? If you have a cousin, why did he let you go to a brothel to sell your body?"

"Not that it's any of your business, but he does not have any money to give me."

"That's no excuse," he grumbled. He didn't like to think she'd been abandoned by her own family. He knew the feeling all too well. If her cousin wasn't going to bloody well look after her properly, the least Justin could do was make sure her window had been broken accidentally and not by an intruder. He hoisted his leg up and climbed through the window.

"What are you doing?" Arabella demanded with a gasp.

He landed with a crunch of glass in—he glanced swiftly around the room—the study. "What does it appear I'm doing?" he commanded, a trifle irritated, more so that she was upending his calmness again.

She was annoyed? The ungrateful wench! He'd spent the past half hour ensuring she was safe when he could have been sleeping. Where the hell had his control gone? He started to count in his mind when she spoke.

"It appears," she said, in an acerbic tone, "that you have come into my house without being invited, after *stalking* me."

"Stalking you?" This...this ingratitude was a perfect example of why befriending people was more trouble than it was worth. "Miss Carthright," he clipped, reverting in anger to formalities, "I do not stalk women. Women follow me." He didn't give a damn that he sounded pompous. It was the truth.

Her nostrils flared as her eyes narrowed. "Who lives here, Your Grace?"

"What?" he asked, brushing stray bits of glass from his hair he'd gotten when climbing through the window.

"You heard me," she pressed.

"You bloody well live here," he thundered, then clenched his fists at his temper.

She nodded. "And as I bloody well live here, as you so rudely put it, is it not correct to say that *you* followed *me?*"

"All right," he barked. "I followed you. Are you satisfied?"

The sweetest smile came to her face, lighting her blue eyes and making his chest tighten oddly and his anger slip away. Respect replaced it. She had stood up to him without blinking an eye.

"Not totally," she said in a lilting voice that matched the sweetness of her smile. "I'd like to know why you followed me *and* why you had a pistol pointed at me."

"I followed you, *Arabella*," he said, striding past her and into the hall to check the perimeter for intruders, "because I thought you were lying when you said you were not walking home," he said in a low voice. "I had the pistol aimed at the *dark*, not knowing who may appear, as I saw the broken window."

"You saw the broken window when you were lurking around my house," she stated from directly behind him, her voice low, as well.

He *was* prowling. Damn her bedazzling blue eyes. But he'd been doing so because if he was going to trust her even a fraction, he wanted to know exactly who she was. He drummed his fingers against his thigh, trying to decide what to say.

"I admit," he whispered, "that I wanted to learn more about you and make sure you were telling me the truth, as I'm relying on you to help me with a rather personal matter. It is very difficult for me to trust people." He didn't know why he'd added the last bit. What a stupid thing to say. Then again, it was always best to keep lies as close to the truth as possible.

"I accept your apology," she said.

He could feel his brow furrow. "I did not apologize."

"Oh, but you did." Her words were a breezy whisper. "I do believe doing so must be so foreign to you that you didn't even realize what you were doing. Nevertheless, I accept. However," she continued, still whispering, "next time you want to know more about me, simply ask. I am an open book."

He cocked an eyebrow. "Which kind? A mystery?"

She frowned. "A very short, boring tale actually, until perhaps meeting you. Things are becoming more complicated now."

"I have that effect on people who know me," he replied, thinking surprisingly of his mother.

Arabella's heart-shaped face was turned up to him, and her blue eyes, flecked interestingly with streaks of gold, stared at him with an openness that defied what he knew of people. He blinked, but no, she still looked utterly honest. It was false, of course. No one was as truthful as they seemed. Everyone was hiding something.

Including you.

He tensed at the bothersome voice in his head and turned to complete his check of Arabella's house, but when her hand came to his arm, he stilled and waited. Her delicate fingers curled ever so slightly against his skin. Her touch, so innocent in its nature, was unexpectedly arousing.

"What are we doing?" she whispered.

"*I* am checking your home to make sure there are no intruders." And he was doing a poor job of it. Talking too loudly. Being distracted. Getting ruffled by her.

She pressed close behind him as he went from room to room, but the house was empty and did not look as if anything had been disturbed. They returned to the study, and upon searching the room, he found a rock under the writing table.

He picked up the rock and set it on the desk. "Has this ever happened before?"

"No. But there a good number of children who live in this area and many are often unattended, so I'm not surprised."

Her words eased his tension somewhat, but not so much that he was going to leave her alone. "What time is your father expected home?"

She bit her lip and glanced at the clock. "Any moment, I hope. He's late. You should go."

"No." He was quite sure his tone left no room for argument, but she set her hands on her hips once more and glared at him.

"I insist you leave."

He strolled over to the sideboard and swept a hand toward the crystal decanters. "May I? It's been a long night."

"No, you may *not*," she snapped and marched over to him. "Really, you simply must depart."

"I'm afraid I cannot."

Her lips parted and she looked as if she was about to argue further, but he held up his hand. "My conscience won't allow me to leave you here alone with a broken window. I'm sure it was simply the children, as you have said, but if it wasn't…" He shrugged. "I don't abandon those who are counting on me."

Her eyes widened, and then she sighed. "It's very hard to argue when faced with such gallantry."

"Gallantry?" He'd never been accused of being gallant. Ruthless. Coldhearted. Emotionally void. Yes, to all of them. But gallant, no. And he didn't like her seeing him as such when he was lying to her and using her. "I'm not gallant."

"Hmm." She tilted her head as if studying him. "Maybe not usually—I cannot say since I have only known you a few short hours—but insisting on staying here to ensure my safety is definitely the action of a gentleman."

"I'm a gentleman in name only, Arabella. Never forget that."

She sucked in a sharp breath. "Is that how you woo women? By telling them you're not a gentleman so they believe you are?"

"I am not wooing you. I would never do so. I'm *warning* you."

"Am I so undesirable, then?" Her voice wobbled with her vulnerability and pulled on a heartstring he'd long thought split. What a shocking surprise that the thing still worked. Why here? Why now? Why the devil her?

Her cheeks pinked immediately, and she twisted her hands together.

The why of it all struck him in the gut and caused an infinitesimal crack in his self-control. It was here, now, and her because she reminded him of himself when he'd been younger, weaker, and foolishly longing for the impossibility of his parents' love. That same sort of desperate longing dwelled in the depths of her eyes and resounded in her voice. He wanted to take her pain from her for a moment and give her a reason to believe she was wrong about herself. He could do that. What harm could that bring?

Arabella caught the skin on the inside of her cheek between

her teeth. The strain of the day must have caused her to go mad. That was the only reasonable explanation for what she'd just asked Justin and how her body felt as if it would fracture into a thousand pieces if this man didn't kiss her right then. He could very well be a criminal. Her mind knew this, but her heart didn't seem to care. She hadn't even known she'd longed to feel wanted anymore until meeting him. It smarted, his continued rejection and blasé attitude about her person. There was no denying it.

She'd always told herself that her biological parents' abandonment of her had been due to their own weaknesses, and she'd reasoned that Benjamin's rejection and abandonment had been due to his own poor character, as well, but she knew, she knew it was *her*. She was not desirable. Here stood a man who, by all rights, could demand she bed him, yet he'd rather not.

Not only was she mad, but there must have been something inherently wrong with her looks, with her desirability. She should be relieved beyond measure that he had not demanded such a thing, yet she wasn't. Not entirely. It would have been nice to be the one to decline his advances, not wonder why they never came. In fact—

Her last thought scattered as Justin reached out and cupped her face in his large hands. Her breathing stalled as her heart raced forward. "What are you doing?" she whispered.

"Showing you what you should know." The husky words reverberated with the promise of something illicit and unforgettable. One hand left her face and slid to her back to press her firmly against the hard length of his body. She'd never been with a man. The most intimacy she had ever shared was with Justin at the brothel. Her stomach tightened at the memory, and her cheeks heated at her lack of shame. His desire-filled eyes held hers. *He wanted her.* It was shocking, empowering, and frightening all at once. Yet, *her* question had started this, so she remained silent and let her mind go.

And go it went. To the wonderful slide of his hand over the planes of her back. And to his fingers tangling in the hair at the nape of her neck, then curling around her head to tilt it back before he bent his head to kiss her.

This time, when his lips touched hers and his tongue traced the creases of her mouth, she opened to welcome him in. He lit a flame within her with each swirl of his tongue, and when his hands came to her breasts and his fingers brushed over her nipples as they strained against the material of her gown, the flame burst upward, nearly consuming her. She groaned as she circled her hands around his waist to keep him close.

His thumbs flicked gently against her hard nipples as his mouth left hers and blazed a burning path down her neck to the valley of her breasts. Suddenly, his hands were cupping her breasts, and a growl emanated from him as he gently tugged her bodice lower until her breasts almost spilled from her corset. She couldn't think beyond the maddening heat and pulsing need between her legs to be shocked at her behavior. She arched toward him, desperate for more of his touch.

A draft of cool air caressed her skin as he dipped his fingers beneath the material and freed her heavy, aching breast. He took her taut nipple in his mouth and suckled it, pure explosive pleasure ripping a moan from deep within her as she curled her nails into his back. Blood pounded to her heart, her lungs, her brain, and just as quickly as he'd given her the pleasure, he wrenched it away by pulling back with a groan.

He stood for a moment, staring at her, his green eyes burning bright with what almost looked like wonder. The world around her crashed in on her, and heat flooded her cheeks. He reached out with a hand that trembled slightly and gently pulled her dress back up. "Never think yourself undesirable. You are so very much so that I almost forget who I am. I almost lose all control."

"And who are you, really?" she asked with a surprising calm she did not feel. Was he about to reveal that he was a smuggler?

His eyes took on a faraway look before he focused on her once more. "I'm exactly the man my father raised me to be."

The aching pain in his raw voice sent a tremor through her. She hardly knew him, but she could tell from his words that he was suffering, whether he realized it or not. She didn't want to add to that hurt by betraying his trust, yet what could she do? She needed to know more. "Justin—"

A slamming door cut off her words and made her flinch. Her gaze flew to the door as pounding footsteps resounded down the hall. Justin shoved her behind him, whipped out his pistol, and widened his stance.

As he raised the weapon toward the door, Alice called out to her. Arabella nearly cried out her surprise and relief. "Put the pistol away," she hissed as the door to the study crashed open and Alice, silver hair akimbo and face pinched, bolted into the room. Her eyes widened to two enormous dark globes as she stared at Arabella and Justin.

"Alice, this is—"

"It doesn't matter," the woman interrupted, waving her hands frantically in the air. "Your father has had another brain attack."

"What?" Arabella tried to take in a deep breath, but she couldn't.

Not again. Not again.

The room spun a little, and she reached out blindly for something to steady her. Her hand brushed hard flesh, and she faltered for a moment but then grasped the arm Justin offered her. It was solid and comforting. "Is he—" She stopped but forced herself to swallow and ask the question. "Is he dead?"

Alice shook her head violently. "No. He's very weak, and his speech..." She patted her glistening eyes with a handkerchief. "I cannot understand what he's trying to say. No one can. His words are slurred. I came straight here to fetch you." She sniffed. "One of the servants told me he got in an argument with someone, and then he had the attack."

Arabella sagged in relief against Justin. Slurred speech didn't matter a bit when compared to death.

"I can take you to him," Justin supplied. "My carriage is fast, and I can collect my personal physician along the way. He's the best in his profession."

A surge of gratefulness took her breath for a moment. "Thank you," she finally managed.

Justin nodded, and within moments, he'd maneuvered all three of them out the door and into his carriage with the efficiency of one who'd faced peril before.

As the carriage flew through the dark night, no one talked, for which she was thankful. Her throat ached too much to form words. She had insisted on sitting on the driver's bench with Justin, and Alice had sat with them, as well. Even though Arabella was pressed snug between Alice and Justin, she started to shiver and could not stop. Without slowing the carriage, Justin maneuvered out of his coat and handed it to her.

She silently took it, and as his hand touched hers, he grasped her fingers and squeezed them. "It will be all right."

She nodded, grateful for his comfort and, she realized with a start, thankful he was here to help her.

After stopping to collect his physician, Arabella told Justin the final turns to get to Lord Howick's home, he tensed beside her. Or perhaps it was her imagination? Why in the world would he be uncomfortable in Mayfair? She would be surprised if he did not live here, as well.

"Lord Howick's house is the third on the left."

"Yes," Justin replied, his voice cold and exact.

She turned to look at him. She was not imagining things. His face was set in angry lines. "What is it? Do you know Lord Howick?"

Justin nodded. "I do. We're in Parliament together. He's a Whig."

By the hard edge in his voice, she knew what he was going to say next. "I presume you are a Tory," Arabella said.

"You presume correctly." He was staring at her oddly as he maneuvered the carriage in front of the house. A servant met them outside. Justin helped Arabella down and the physician handed Alice out of the carriage, where they'd sat for the remainder of the ride. Justin then gave quick instructions regarding his horses before they all ascended the steps to Lord Howick's home.

Justin caught her arm at the top step. "How long have you known Howick?"

His eyes could have been emeralds for how hard they'd become, and his voice held a baffling accusatory tone.

She twisted her arm out of his hold, mindful that she'd only retrieved it because he'd let her. "I don't truly know him. I've met him once or twice, but my father always comes here for their monthly card games and suppers."

Justin frowned. "Monthly card games?"

She nodded, looking toward the door. "Please, Justin, can we discuss this later?"

"Certainly," he said in a perfectly cordial, precise tone.

They followed the silently waiting butler inside, and within moments, Lord Howick himself rushed into the room. He came to a shuddering halt, and his face turned a startling white. His dark eyebrows rose slowly into two disbelieving arches. He stared at Justin without speaking.

Arabella watched almost in a trance as Justin strolled forward, stopped a mere inches from Lord Howick, and motioned behind him to his physician. "As my presence here seems to have rendered you speechless, I suggest you simply show us to Mr. Carthright."

"Tensley," Howick barked. A tall, thin man in full livery scrambled forward. "Show Miss Carthright and the physician to her father."

Arabella glanced between Justin and Lord Howick. She was almost afraid to leave them alone when they looked as if they could gladly pummel each other to death. She nervously licked her lips. "Please, Your Grace," she addressed Justin. "I'd feel so much better if you would accompany me." She didn't have much hope that he'd agree, but at least she had tried.

"So sorry, Howick," Justin said in a tone that was anything but apologetic. "I'd love to stay and chat about your motion, the one that we both know will fail, but Miss Carthright's needs come before anything else at the moment."

Justin proffered his arm to her, and she took it, her mind almost dizzy with worry and confusion. She knew he'd likely only agreed to come with her because he clearly had a dislike for Lord Howick, yet there had been one second when his eyes had met hers that he'd looked almost thankful. For what? That she got him away from Lord Howick? She couldn't think on it now, though, as worried as she was.

As they started up the stairs, Lord Howick called to their backs. "You're on the wrong side, Dinnisfree, and you know it. Don't support the king in Parliament just because your father raised you to be blindly allegiant to the Tory party. You are a smart man. Use your brain."

Justin paused, and Arabella could feel the muscles in his arms bunch. She stole a sideways glance at him. His clenched jaw and the blue vein pulsing at his temple said more than any words. He was livid. He said something under his breath in a language she'd never heard, and after a minute, the tension seemed to drain out of him. He nodded as if to himself and continued to lead her up the stairs with Dr. Bancroft behind them.

At the guest-chamber door, Justin turned to her and opened his mouth as if to question her, but then he clamped his jaw shut and shook his head. "Later," he said in a cold voice. "I need answers later."

Was he talking to her or telling her? Before she could decide, he opened the door and all thoughts of anything but her father fled.

She raced to his side and knelt beside the bed on which he was lying. "Papa?"

He fluttered his eyes open and tried to talk, but the words, slurred and incomprehensible, caused him to cough so terribly that the physician asked her to step aside so he could administer some laudanum to calm him.

Arabella moved out of the way, anxiously shifting from foot to foot as he examined her father, who eventually drifted into a fitful sleep. She could feel the reassuring heat of Justin behind her and hear his even breaths. When Dr. Bancroft was finished, he turned to her, and as he did, Justin moved closer. For a moment, she had the absurd thought he was trying to reassure her that she was not alone.

Dr. Bancroft took her hand and patted it. "I believe, my dear, that he will recover. Time, of course, will only tell for sure, but I recently treated a patient with much the same history who had a second stroke, lost his ability to speak properly for a while, but regained mastery of the language at a remarkable speed. You will need to be patient and loving. Can you do that?"

She nodded as she swiped at the tears that came to her eyes. "May I take him home? I think he'd be much more comfortable in his own bed."

The physician nodded. "I see no harm in that." His gaze

went to Justin. "Will you—"

"Of course I'll help," Justin replied before the man had even asked.

Arabella's pulse quickened. Even with the stress of her father's condition, Justin was unnerving her with his goodness. Whatever he may be, innocent man or guilty smuggler, she was now indebted to him, and informing on him was certainly not the way to repay the kindness he'd shown her. She'd have to warn him to be careful without giving away Jude's identity. She wasn't going to help Jude, but that didn't mean she was foolish enough to court trouble with the Bow Street Runners because she'd revealed the identity of one of their undercover agents.

Seven

With the assistance of one of Howick's footmen and Dr. Bancroft, Justin and the other two men managed to get Arabella's father into the carriage without incident. Justin offered his hand to help Arabella into the carriage. As she set her hand in his, a man came outside who Justin immediately recognized as the queen's lawyer, Lord Brougham. Justin stiffened. Brougham was a dangerous Whig who'd like nothing better than to destroy the king and destabilize the Tory party. Brougham was also a man with no scruples and he'd do whatever it took, no matter how nasty, to accomplish his goals. Why, if Lady Conyngham's letter were to fall into the hands of a man like Brougham...

Justin's gaze flew to the carriage where Arabella's father lay, then to Arabella, to whom Brougham was motioning. Her eyes widened in surprise, but was it an act? How did her father know Brougham and Howick, for that matter? And where did the seemingly innocent woman fit into the political battle for the throne and the more personal battle between the king and queen?

Did Howick and Brougham know of the letters? Were they looking for them, as well? The questions fired through Justin's mind along with certain inevitable truths. It was likely they had spies in Lady Conyngham's household and around the king, just as the king had his spies in Queen Caroline's supposed lover's home and around her.

A hard knot formed at the center of Justin's belly as his hands curled into fists by his side. A predictable way to distract a spy from a mission was to send them on a goose chase. And what better person to lead a male spy astray than a seemingly innocent, exquisitely beautiful female?

His mind rejected the notion as Arabella walked toward the king's enemies, but doubt gnawed at him. Had his identity been compromised? Was Arabella innocent or duplicitous? He needed answers immediately.

He trained his gaze on Brougham's mouth and began to read the man's lips, grateful for once that his father had beat this one particular lesson of survival into him until he'd mastered it.

My dear, did your father happen to mention some letters to you?

Justin clenched and unclenched his fist as he watched Arabella's lips for her answer.

Letters? She shook her head. *My father has not received any letters.*

An unaccountable sense of relief filled him that she didn't know about the letters. It appeared her father did, however, and certainly Brougham, which undoubtedly meant Howick did, as well. How the bloody hell had Arabella's father become involved with two of the most powerful men in the Tory party?

Brougham started to speak, so Justin shifted his gaze. *Miss Carthright, I must ask, how do you know the Duke of Dinnisfree?*

Arabella's face flushed red, but she jutted her chin up. *He's courting me. I'm sorry, I really must be going.*

Justin quickly looked away as she strode toward him, but when she neared, he turned to her, silently proffered his hand, and helped her into the carriage.

They rode back to her home in tense silence, punctuated by an occasional moan from her father. Justin rubbed his knuckles back and forth in the palm of his other hand, trying to decide how best to get the answers he needed about her father and search her home without her knowing.

After they arrived and situated Arabella's father in the makeshift bedchamber that had once been the library, Justin concluded the best way to learn what he needed was to stay right here and try to insert a question or two as the night wore on. Eventually, she would fall asleep and he'd search her home.

Arabella sank into a chair beside her father's bed. "Papa, I love you," she whispered to him.

Justin shifted in his chair against the wall, feeling like a complete intruder. Her voice shook as she spoke, and her hand trembled as she raised it to her father's head and brushed it gently over his hair.

"Papa, don't leave me," she begged. "There's so much you've yet to teach me."

"Such as?" Justin interrupted, hating to do so but needing answers.

She looked at him and stared for a long moment before blinking, as if surprised. "I didn't realize you were still here."

He nodded.

"You must be tired."

"I'm used to going without sleep," he said.

Her brows furrowed, and a wary look settled over her face. "Why is that?"

"Oh," he hedged, sensing it was she who was probing when it should be him, "many things I do keep me up late."

"You should quit doing those things and stay home." Her words were sharp and emphatic.

What the devil?

"Your advice is noted."

"I hope so," she said, the word *hope* punctuated. "I'm sure many people, *particular people*, are interested in your every move."

Warning signals went off in his head. He leaned toward her. "What makes you sure of that?"

"Well, you're a duke. And you're rather fascinating."

"Am I? To whom?" He was done playing games, though playing with her these last seven hours most definitely had been enjoyable. Too enjoyable. He didn't want to think they were on opposing sides.

"To me, of course." She quirked her mouth. "Perhaps to others. Others who may think, oh, I don't know, that your comings and goings are so very intriguing."

His blood surged through his veins. She knew something. She knew something, and she was trying to tell him without saying the words. "Why would my comings and goings be interesting to anyone?"

She scowled. "Because smuggling is illegal!"

"Smuggling?"

She nodded. "You needn't pretend with me. I'll die before ever telling your secret." She eyed him. "*It is* your secret, yes?"

Bloody hell. Someone had convinced her he was a smuggler. But why? To get her to report on his movements? To keep him off the correct trail?

He crossed his arms over his chest and returned her scowl. "You are gravely misinformed, Arabella. I'm no smuggler."

She actually sighed with relief, which caused him to have to repress a smile. "Thank goodness!"

"Who told you I was?"

"One of the girls at Madame Sullyard's."

He studied her. She did not blink. Did not flinch. Her breathing was normal. Her eyes steady. Her hands still and her face calm. She was either telling the truth or she was a damned impressive and rather dangerous liar. His mind refuted the notion that she was a liar, which gave him pause. He always thought people deceptive, but not her. He *wanted* to trust her.

Shock ricocheted through his body. He would let this woman in far enough to help him, and then he would cut her loose, despite the fact that he'd much prefer to take her in his arms and take her to his bed. Being involved with a man like him was not for a woman like her. "Whoever told you that either wove a fanciful tale or they themselves were misinformed." He'd been the subject of a great many rumors in his life, so why not at a rumor in a brothel, as well?

Her father moaned, and she whipped back around in her seat and spoke to him in soft, soothing words full of obvious love. Justin leaned back in his chair, crossed his arms over his chest, and stretched his legs out in front of him as he listened to her talk to her father, who didn't respond. She spoke of his favorite dishes, saying that she would make them when he awoke, and as she continued to talk, Justin's mind wandered to his own mother. It was hard to believe she'd been gone for twelve years.

He could still hear her sobbing voice in his head after he had located her in Italy. She had told him how much she loved him but that she could never return to Father, and as a result, to Justin. Despite the fact that he had understood why she had fled Father, her ability to leave him, as well, had been surprisingly painful. Of course it didn't ache anymore. He simply didn't let it.

Arabella's animated voice drifted to him and interrupted his musings. He sat up a bit and concentrated. Bloody stupid to sit here thinking on things that could never be changed when he might miss a clue about Arabella's father. He leaned forward as she spoke.

"And when you are better, Papa, you must tell me more stories of your time at the palace. You know how I love to hear your stories."

Justin's ears perked. "Did your father work at Buckingham Palace?"

Arabella turned toward him and yawned as she nodded. "He was a blacksmith there for many years. His work caught the eye of the queen," she said with obvious pride,

"and she made him head blacksmith. He was so happy.
Mama was so happy, too, but then everything changed."
She scooted toward him as if she didn't want her father to
overhear her. "Daniel, my brother, went off to fight
Napoleon and was killed. In the report that his cavalry
leader turned in after Daniel's death, the man said Daniel
was trying to abandon his regiment out of cowardliness."
She curled her hands into fists. "My brother was no coward.
Do you know what I think?" Her words were harsh, her
eyes narrowed.

She was fiercely beautiful when angry. Justin shook his
head. "What do you think?"

"I think Daniel's commander was jealous of him. They
had been courting the same woman before they left, and I
swear the man sent Daniel to his death, and then made it
look like my brother was trying to desert his post."

"What makes you think that?"

"Letters!" she said, surging to her feet. "Daniel wrote
me letters, and in them he told me stories of things his
commander had done to him. The man would lie about
things all the time. Rations went missing and he'd blame
Daniel, and even if Daniel was not in camp that night, his
commander's word was taken over his. I tried to tell
someone—Papa did, as well—but no one would listen to
us."

The angry tears that flooded her eyes made his heart
ache. Without thinking, he brushed back a few of the tears
that trailed down her cheeks. The feel of her warm skin
under his fingers sent a shot of desire though him, but not
just for her body. It was more. A desire to cradle her.
Protect her. Help her.

Her mouth parted, and her eyes widened. He trailed his
fingers down to her lips and traced the creases of them as
his blood began to pound within. He wanted to kiss her
again, but now was not the time or place. He slowly drew
back his hand, but something had shifted. He felt it as if he

could grasp it and hold it. He trusted her. Bloody stupid and dangerous.

"Do you still have the letters?"

She nodded.

"Bring them to me and let me read them."

She frowned. "Why?"

"Because, my dear, if the letters are as you say, I may be able to clear your brother's name. I guarantee you, people will listen to me."

She leaped to her feet and was out the door in a blur. She returned before he'd had time to do much more than stand and pace the room. She thrust the letters at him. "There are four. Start with this one. It is the first."

He settled in and read the letters from start to finish. With each letter, his anger grew. When he looked up, she was watching him intently.

"Do you believe me?" she asked.

He nodded. "Yes, and I know Lord Halbrook, your brother's commander. He's despicable. May I take these letters?"

"Yes, of course. But what can you do?"

"I can get your brother's honorable name restored and Lord Halbrook dismissed immediately."

"However can you do that?"

"My dear," he said in a self-assured tone that he hoped would keep her from asking more questions that he'd have to answer with lies, "I'm the Duke of Dinnisfree. There are many things I can do that other men cannot. I have very powerful allies, and they listen to me." He'd get word to Davenport, his only true friend and the only man he trusted—as much as he could allow himself to, at least. Davenport could relay his request to the Duke of York, who had the power to clear Arabella's brother's name.

"Thank you," she cried, throwing her arms around him and hugging him fiercely. He froze, unable to move because emotion clogged his throat and had done something funny to his limbs. Her gratitude, the affection she poured onto him, had the effect on his body of being shoved into freezing water. He was not used to such things.

He sat there for a moment, his arms hanging useless at his side, and then, slowly, he wrapped his arms around her slight body and hugged her back. He'd never given a woman a hug beyond his mother. It was nice. Enjoyable, but slightly uncomfortable, too. This sort of embrace was more emotional than physical, and he didn't do emotional.

He pulled back until he could see her face. "What happened after your brother was killed?"

Her lips pressed into a hard line. "They informed us of his death and of his dishonor. Papa had a stroke and was dismissed from service almost immediately."

Justin was surprised the queen had not taken pity and let the man continue on in her service for a bit, in name only, of course. She was usually more tenderhearted.

"The king himself sealed the letter of dismissal and notice of dishonor," Arabella said, her voice vibrating with anger.

Damned Prinny! Justin barely controlled his tongue. Of course! It made sense now. Arabella was probably perfectly right that Lord Halbrook had been jealous of her brother and wanted to eliminate his competition. And Lord Halbrook's father and Prinny were close friends. If the son had appealed to his father and his father had appealed to Prinny... Well, Prinny was not known for his sound judgment.

Howick's accusation flashed in Justin's memory. Was he supporting the king simply because his father had ruthlessly hammered it into him to do so? Doubt crept into his mind.

Arabella yawned again, and Justin noted the purple smudges under her eyes. She needed sleep, but he required a few more answers first. "I suppose your parents despise the king for dismissing your father and setting your brother into the records as dishonorable."

"If they do, they never said as much. Mother lost her mind very shortly after Daniel died and Papa had the stroke. I think it was simply too much for her to take. And Papa..." Arabella shrugged. "He's always kept his own council and rarely discusses politics, though I do know the queen sent him a note expressing her apologies and regret, saying her hands were tied."

Justin nodded his head. That alone would be enough to make a man loyal to the queen and not the king. "I imagine you're tired," he ventured. He needed to search this home, and the sooner she went to sleep and he could do so, the better.

It didn't take long for Arabella to doze off after he'd convinced her to close her eyes and rest her head. He promised her that he'd watch over her father and if anything should seem amiss, he'd wake her.

Later, as he crept from room to room while continually darting back to check on Arabella's father, Justin was cursing himself. This woman was doing something to him. He barely knew her, yet she managed to anger him and amuse him all at once. And then, in the next moment, she aroused his desire. Since meeting her, he had doubted himself and his allegiance—things he'd never questioned before. She was a disturbance to the order of his life.

With great effort, he pushed her out of his thoughts to concentrate on searching the house. He did so methodically until he'd combed every room and the sun was creeping up in the horizon. He was well aware that the sense of relief filling him because he'd not found the letters was wrong. He should want to find them immediately, no matter who had them, and set the matter to rest for the king. But that had not been his reaction, and it was a problem. An enormous one.

Eight

By the time Justin fell back into the chair near Arabella, he had passed the state of tiredness that had plagued him and moved into a stage of being hyperalert. Bright orange and red shafts of light streamed through the window and touched the top of Arabella's dark, silky head. Justin stared at her, slumped against the side of the chair she sat in. He'd tucked a blanket around her earlier, and though it covered her from head to foot, she still looked alluring. Her dark lashes lay against her pale cheeks. Her lips were parted ever so slightly, and every once in a while she'd moan and turn her head to the side only for it to fall back against the chair as before.

When the sun came fully up and filled the room with light, her eyes fluttered open and she gazed at him with a wondrous expression. "You're still here."

"Yes." He was acutely aware of how his pulse notched up by simply looking at her. "I told you I would stay and watch over your father while you slept."

"I know, but—" She bit her lip.

"But what?"

"I didn't think you'd truly stay."

He shouldn't have. He had a hundred things he needed to be doing, one of which was to see Davenport so he could get Arabella's brother's name cleared. He also needed to search out the king's letters, but in order to do that he had to track down Ruby. "Where were you planning on taking me today to find Ruby?"

"To Crockford's Club." Arabella glanced between her sleeping father and Justin. "I'll ask Alice to stay with my father so I can go with you."

"That's not necessary."

"It is," she said with quiet intensity. "I need to take the money you are going to pay me to the Stanhope Home, so I must go out no matter what."

"All right," he nodded, understanding. Both her parents needed her, and she was trying to be strong and be everywhere at once. An impossible feat. He had a solution. "I'll take the money to the Stanhope Home for you."

"No." She shook her head. "I need to check on my mother and speak with her. I want to ensure she's being treated well."

"Do you have concerns that she's not?"

"Yes. The warden's son, well, he…" Her words trailed off and her jaw tensed. "I have reason to want to ensure he's not around my mother."

"Leave that to me, Arabella," Justin said, standing. Anger unfurled in his gut and spread through his body like fire, hot and consuming. Hell, he had to regain his control.

Arabella stood and faced him. "I can handle it," she said defiantly.

He set his hands on her shoulders and looked her in the face. "I've no doubt you can, but the cold hard truth is *I* can put the fear of death into the man and you cannot. Let me help you."

She opened her mouth as if she might argue more, but she slowly nodded. "For my mother."

"Yes," he answered, understanding her reluctance. Arabella relied only on herself, exactly as he did. It had to be difficult to trust him, but he'd not let her down. Not in this. "I'll be back to collect you in two hours."

◄Cᵒᵉᵗᵗᵉᵒᵉᵗᵉᵒᵊᵃ►

"Tell me again who this chit is to you that you'd beg such a favor?" Davenport asked, leaning back in his desk chair.

Justin tugged an irritated hand through his hair. He'd just spent the last hour bringing Davenport up to date on his current assignment, which included how he'd met Arabella and how she was aiding him. Hell, Justin had even revealed how Arabella had broken his nose, and he never exposed personal things. He was impatient to leave and collect his little helper.

Impatience. Anger. Irritation. It was unlike him to feel any of it strongly, but now each emotion washed over him like a wave. Davenport's assessing look was indicative that the man was just getting started with his probing questions, only further irritating Justin.

"She's no one," Justin clipped.

"No one?" Davenport quirked an eyebrow. "You have decided to bring this woman into your trust—"

"I never said that," he growled, drumming his fingers on the armrest of the leather chair.

Davenport placed his palms on his desk and stared hard at Justin. "You told me moments ago that this woman knew where to find the painter's lover who stole Lady Conyngham's jewelry box, therefore inadvertently taking the king's letters, did you not?"

Justin inclined his head.

"So you have put your trust in this woman that she's not leading you *away* from the letters."

"She's not, damn it," Justin thundered, surprising himself with the vehemence of his response when he'd raised those same doubts in his private thoughts. "You don't know her. She…she has an honesty about her, and a kindness," he said, feeling like a supreme fool.

"As do you," Davenport said. "And I fear your inherent

compassion is now clouding your judgement."

Justin frowned at Davenport's words. "I am not compassionate, and I never let anything or anyone sway me."

"Oh, really?" Davenport said in a sarcastic tone. "I know about the Morgans. I know you supported the family until you could find work for Alex, and I know you continue to aid them."

Justin stilled, his mind flashing to the guard the king had dismissed in a fit last year because Alex Morgan had dared to tell the king he should not stroll about the gardens without an attendant. Morgan had been absolutely correct. The king was not well liked and to go about without protection was folly. But Prinny liked no man telling him what to do and had dismissed Morgan and forbid anyone to hire the man. Morgan's wife had come to Justin begging for help when they could not feed their children, so Justin had done what he could. It was as simple as that. He narrowed his eyes. "How do you know that?"

Davenport smiled slightly. "Mrs. Morgan is now a cook in my household and my wife is quite chummy with the servants. She befriended Mrs. Morgan, who mentioned after you were here one day that you were like an angel sent to her family. You can imagine how the statement sparked Audrey's curiosity."

Justin could well imagine. Davenport's wife was rather inquisitive and not the type to be dissuaded when she wanted to know something. "I did what any man would have done had a woman come and pleaded for help and revealed that her five children were in danger of starving."

Davenport shook his head. "No. Most men would not dare to help a man the king had shunned for fear of Prinny's anger, but you dared because your compassion would not let you do otherwise."

Justin forced a laugh to cover his mounting irritation. "One act of charity does not make me compassionate or kind."

"I would be more inclined to agree with you if it were merely only one act of kindness, but it's not. You took that page Langley under your wing when he could not learn the simplest of tasks and you taught him his job. I've seen you personally on six different occasions slip money into the pockets of street urchins when you think no one is looking."

Justin's nostrils flared. "What is your point?" he demanded, not liking that Davenport knew about and was bringing up things for which Justin could not explain his motives. He'd felt a gut instinct to do those things and nothing more.

Davenport steepled his fingers in front of his face for a moment and regarded Justin over the tips. Finally, he lowered them. "I'll do you the favor you ask for her brother. You know I will. I've no doubt what happened with her brother occurred exactly as you've been told. But do me a favor."

"What?" Justin demanded, not wanting this conversation to go on any longer. He didn't talk about personal issues because he had none. Or at least he hadn't until now. He'd managed to go through life with one goal: to serve king and country. That had been enough.

"Let me do a bit of digging into her family, her father. You certainly should, and you know it. He held the queen's favor, for Christ's sake, and plays cards and sups with two of the queen's staunchest supporters. Don't tell me there's no connection between the woman's father, Brougham, Howick, and the missing letters. If nothing else, they must be looking for them, just as you are, but to use them in the queen's favor."

"I've already thought of that," Justin said grimly. He was well aware there was likely something connecting Arabella's father, the other men, and the letters. What it might be, he couldn't damn well say, but he didn't think

Arabella had anything to do with it. "I'm going to investigate it further," he relented.

"How?"

Justin gritted his teeth. "For a retired spy you're damned annoying and persistent."

Davenport flashed Justin a grin. "You mean a great deal to me, Dinnisfree. That's the only time I'll ever tell you that, so don't beg me to repeat it when you're feeling down about yourself."

Justin snorted as Davenport chuckled. "I'm supremely glad to see a crack in your armor of coldness—"

"There's no crack," Justin interrupted.

"There is." He pointed at Justin's chest. "It's just there. Right now, it's only a tiny fissure, but I think it would be the best thing in the world for you if it became a yawning cavern. *If* the woman is worthy of your trust, of course."

"I don't give a damn about giving my trust to a woman, or anyone for that matter."

Davenport gave him a smug look. "So says the fox to the wolf. I was exactly as you before I met Audrey."

"I'm not like you. I'm not going to change because of a woman."

Davenport shook his head. "You're already changing, you blind fool."

Justin, knowing there was truth to what Davenport said, stubbornly stared at his friend and allowed the silence to stretch between them. Davenport shook his head. "The old you would not know the personal history of a woman and her family unless that history served to get you what you want, and unless you want this woman, I cannot see how the favor you are asking of me benefits you at all."

"It doesn't," Justin clipped. He did want her, as Davenport had stated. He desired her, nothing more. Except it was a bit more. He also wanted to help her.

"Mmm, exactly as I stated. What are you going to do to

ensure you're not being duped?"

"I'm going to keep my damned eyes and ears open. I need not do more than that. I'm a trained spy, for Christ's sake. And she's a...she's a—"

"Woman you clearly desire," Davenport finished. "Desire can muddle the lines of duty. Take it from me."

"I've known this woman for less than twenty-four hours," Justin ground out.

Davenport made a derisive sound in his throat. "I knew within the first hour of meeting Audrey that she was the one for me. She had an odd effect on me, as no one ever had."

Hellfire. That sounded all too familiar, but he'd never admit it. "I'd never retire from the king's service over a woman as you did."

"Is that what you think?" Davenport growled as he whipped to his feet.

Justin nodded. Davenport had been married before his current wife to a double-crossing French spy who was now dead, and though his friend had never said it, Justin had always assumed Davenport had left Prinny's service because of his dead wife and uncertainty over where his loyalties lay—with the king or his wife.

"I retired," Davenport grumbled as he paced back and forth behind his desk, "because I started to doubt my allegiance."

Justin nodded. "As I said, your wife became more important to you than your king."

"Yes," Davenport said, voice low. "But I also doubted the king and was unsure that I believed in him."

Justin stilled.

"It would be very true to say that once I met Audrey I knew I would choose her over any person on this Earth, including myself. She has every ounce of loyalty I possess in my body, and that left no room to be a spy. But it does not mean my allegiance does not lie with the king, as long as he still has good men to guide him."

Justin's own doubts tried to rattle their cages, making him shift in physical discomfort. Davenport knew him better than anyone... If there was anyone he could talk to about his own loyalties, it was him.

"Would you say I'm blindly loyal to the king because of my father?"

Davenport sighed as he perched on the arm of Justin's chair. "I'd say your guilt drives you. I'm not saying you should abandon your loyalty because of it. You know the flaws in Prinny's character, and I have every faith that you understand that loyalty to him can sometimes mean doing what's best for him even when he doesn't realize it."

Justin frowned. "Are you suggesting I let the letters fall into the hands of Brougham, or Howick, or whoever the Whig party has searching for them?"

"Howick," Davenport replied. "Brougham wants to destabilize the Tory party, and that's dangerous at this time. I'm suggesting that once you secure the letters, you speak privately with Howick. He could use one of those letters to stop this nonsense about the king divorcing the queen. I'd say the letter needs to be one that is particularly embarrassing but cannot threaten the throne."

"I hate to admit it, but I have a certain admiration for Howick," Justin said.

"Yes," Davenport drawled. "The man is cunning while being ethical and not blinded like Canning."

"Canning? What of him? Has he involved himself in this mess?" The President of the Board of Trade was a Tory, but Justin also knew the man was secretly in love with the queen. Caroline, in her understandable despair of being utterly rejected by Prinny after they'd married, had turned to Canning. Justin only knew because his father had told him. No one spoke of it. Not the king, not the queen, and certainly not Canning. Justin's father had also told him that Canning and Caroline had produced a child from their affair. She had taken pains to hide her pregnancy and gone so far as to flee to a secluded castle. The child had been immediately sent away, as if he'd never existed.

"He has. You'd likely not know because you were away in Paris until a few nights ago, but Canning has threatened to resign his office over the king's treatment of the queen. Wouldn't you say that's quite the public profession of the depths of the man's feelings for her?"

Justin and Davenport had never once discussed Canning and the queen. There had never been a reason, but now there was a very immediate one, though Justin suspected from Davenport's knowing look and words that his friend had already gleaned that the queen and Canning had been in love, and perhaps still were.

"I'd say that if Canning was bold enough to publicly threaten to quit office over the queen's treatment, he is a man who would go to great lengths to protect her."

"He's not bold enough on his own," Davenport said. "Don't forget that." He stood and stretched his arms wide. "I'm sure I don't have to warn you to be wary of Canning. He's a Tory, but his heart belongs to the queen; therefore, his loyalty lies with her."

Justin nodded. "No warning needed. If you have any spare time and you want to follow Canning and report to me on his comings and goings, I'd be grateful."

Davenport grinned. "I was hoping you'd ask me that."

Behind Justin, a door creaked. He turned in time to see Davenport's wife, Lady Audrey, breeze into the room. She paused between Davenport and Justin, regarded them both with narrowed green eyes and then set her hands on her hips as she turned the full force of her ire toward her husband. "You were hoping the duke would ask you what?"

"Darling," Davenport replied in a soothing tone as he

moved toward his wife and wrapped his arms around her, "when will you accept that I will tell you all later? You can quit eavesdropping at my door."

Audrey bit her lip and offered a shrug and a sheepish look. "I'm uncertain. Truly, I don't mean to listen, but I've an ever-present fear you'll become bored with domestic life and go back to your old profession."

Justin tensed, as he always did when reminded that Davenport had told his wife he'd been a spy for the king. Of course, his friend had not revealed anything about Justin or the other spies, but he'd explained he could not keep the secret of who he'd been from his wife because it cast too much doubt in her mind.

Davenport gave Audrey a peck on her cheek. "No man could ever be bored with you, darling. You're a constant surprise, and it takes all my cunning skills to keep track of your comings, goings, and plots."

"I don't plot," she said with a playful pout.

"You do," Davenport teased. "You most definitely do."

Justin watched the exchange and his gut tightened as he realized that he was envious of the openness and obvious trust between them. Davenport had told his wife all his secrets. Justin's secrets were locked inside him, and he'd never have anyone to share them with. But he'd chosen that.

"You've not answered my question, dearest," Audrey said. "What were you hoping the duke would ask you?"

"He was hoping," Justin answered to save Davenport from feeling as if he had to be evasive to his wife, "that I'd ask him to follow Lord Canning."

"Canning?" Lady Audrey frowned. "Why do you care what Lord Canning is doing?"

"I care because our political views are not lining up lately, and I'm concerned he's trying to thwart something I'm striving to achieve. Now, if you'll excuse me, I need to be going."

"Don't leave on my account," she said hurriedly.

"I'm not," he assured her as he moved toward the door. "I've promised someone I'd do them a favor."

Lady Audrey grinned at him. "A lady?"

"Why would you assume that?"

"Because of the look that came over your face just now. The one that says a man's heart is engaged."

Justin scowled. "I barely know the lady, and my heart is most certainly not engaged."

"If you say so," Lady Audrey replied in a placating tone, but as he was walking out the door, he heard her tell Davenport, "Dinnisfree's heart is most definitely engaged if he's doing the lady a favor."

Justin stalked to the front door with her words echoing in his head. He'd know if his own damnable heart was engaged. It wasn't. Yet, as he climbed into his carriage and set out toward Arabella's home, his body hummed with anticipation. *Damnation.* His mission was not on his mind as it should be. *She* was in his thoughts. Her smile. Her concern for him when she'd tried to warn him that smuggling was bad. And her complete devotion to her father. Not to mention her creamy thighs and the feel of her breasts in his hands and mouth.

He groaned in irritation that he could not block her from his thoughts as he normally could do with anything. And then he began to count.

Nine

Arabella stood in front of Mrs. Henderson's desk with Justin by her side. *By her side.* She still felt as if she should pinch herself. Since meeting Justin, he'd done everything he'd said he was going to do and more. Not only had he provided a means for saving herself and her parents but he'd cared enough to offer his personal physician for her father, and now he was helping her with her mother's situation.

Mrs. Henderson's mouth was still hanging open. It had been that way since she had learned who Justin was. Arabella cleared her throat, and Mrs. Henderson finally drew her gaze to Arabella. "This is for payment for this month and the next."

"The next, as well?" the woman exclaimed.

Arabella nodded, feeling a little shameful about how nice it felt to finally have the upper hand, but not so shameful that she didn't intend to use it to protect her mother. "That's what I said," she replied, making her tone forceful. "It also includes the extra fee to have a guard other than your son attend my mother. And speaking of my mother, I'll take her ring back now." Arabella held out her hand.

With a huff, Mrs. Henderson opened her desk drawer, produced the ring, and deposited it into Arabella's palm. Happiness filled her as she slipped her mother's ring back onto her finger. Standing by Justin, she felt bolstered. "I'd like your promise that you will keep your word about the guard."

The woman waved her hand negligently in the air while gazing down at the money in her hands. "I already told you I'd make sure of it."

Arabella gritted her teeth at the woman's petulant tone. She opened her mouth to restate her request when Justin stepped forward and slapped his palm on Mrs. Henderson's desk. The inkpot rattled and a book that had been sitting on the edge slid off and fell to the floor with a loud *thwack*. Arabella gawked as he leaned forward until his face was inches from Mrs. Henderson's.

"My dear lady, I'm afraid I have to take exception to how rudely you are speaking to Miss Carthright." His voice was cool, collected, and unbendable. "She made a simple request. You should have given your word immediately. If you had meant to keep your promise, this would not have been a problem, yet you and I both know you didn't intend to do anything of the sort."

"I—" Mrs. Henderson started, but Justin gave her a look that could have cut stone and she fell silent.

"No man whose honor is questionable should have the care of others in his hands," he said. "Are we clear?"

Mrs. Henderson's face turned red. "My son—"

"Should be dismissed from employment here," Justin interrupted in a stern tone.

Emboldened by Justin's confidence that he'd get what he wanted, Arabella said, "The men who work here should also be required to go through a very thorough interview of their character. And they should be observed without advanced warning on a regular basis." There. She'd blurted her greatest hope for her mother's care.

She glanced sideways at Justin to see if he was looking at her as if she was a fool. As their gazes locked, her breath caught in her throat. His eyes glistened with what appeared to be admiration.

Mrs. Henderson snorted. "Who are you to make demands of me?" she snapped at Arabella.

"I've every right to expect my mother not be subjected to abuse from your son," Arabella retorted.

Mrs. Henderson gave Arabella a wide, annoying smirk. "The only person who can make such demands on me is Lord Stanhope, as the owner of this home."

"I happen to know Lord Stanhope very well," Justin said in a bored tone. "He's stretched quite thin with all his holdings these days, Mrs. Henderson. In fact, he recently approached me about acquiring one of his outstanding loans from him, and now that I think about it, he mentioned the loan on this home in particular." He flicked his gaze around the room and finally settled it back on Mrs. Henderson. "I've decided just now to take him up on the offer." Justin smiled even as his eyes turned cold as the thick ice of the Thames in the dead of winter. "Either dismiss your son today, Mrs. Henderson, or the first thing I'll do is terminate you *and* your son."

Arabella tugged on Justin's sleeve and he turned to her. "Her husband is the physician here."

He smiled grimly. "And your husband will be let go, as well. Furthermore, I expect Miss Carthright's excellent idea to be in place in two weeks' time. You will screen all employees and observe them unannounced. Are we clear?"

"Extremely," she said in a shallow tone. "Shall I dismiss my son or would you like to?"

"I think I'd like that honor," Justin replied in a voice that matched his glacial look. "Where might I find him?"

"In the women's east wing, doing his rounds."

Justin nodded. "I'll go now while Miss Carthright has a nice visit with her mother."

Mrs. Henderson jerked her head in a nod. "I'll personally see Miss Carthright to her mother."

"No need," Justin clipped and held out his hand. "Give me the room keys."

"But, Your Grace!"

Arabella could do little more than stare in shock. Was Justin telling the truth? Was he really going to purchase this place?

"I've neither the time nor the patience to argue, Mrs. Henderson. Hand me the keys now, or I'll take them from you."

Arabella gasped at the same time Mrs. Henderson did. A dangerous gleam had come to Justin's eyes. Mrs. Henderson quickly gave him the keys, which he took in silence. He then proffered his elbow to Arabella.

The moment they were out of Mrs. Henderson's office and far enough down the hall to speak without danger of being overheard, Arabella stopped and turned to him. "How much of what you said in there is true?"

His eyes sparkled much like a child's in the midst of a fun game. "A bit. I do know Stanhope. And I fully intend to leave here and go see him. I happen to know he's in dire financial straits, so I'll simply persuade him to sell me the place."

She felt her lips part in shock. "You'd do that for me?"

"I—" He furrowed his brow. "I suppose that—" His words faltered, silence engulfing him, and for a man whose face had shown precious little of what he was thinking, she could clearly see confusion. He scrubbed a hand across his face. "I'll do it for all the women here. I do it because if my mother had to be in a place like this, I would want her to be safe and unafraid, of being abused or otherwise. No woman should have to live in fear of a man."

Arabella's heart thumped wildly at his pain-laced words. She reached out and gently cupped his cheek. He flinched but did not move away from her touch. "You sound as if you have personal experience."

He looked away from her. "I do."

For a moment, she was certain he would say no more, but finally, he spoke. "My mother feared my father. He abused her emotionally, which I can tell you is just as bad as physical torture."

She nodded. She believed him, and as his haunted gaze settled on her again, she suspected he'd experienced both. This knowledge that he too was vulnerable, that he too was human, made her trust him and like him all the more.

"One day," he continued in that same troubled tone, "she fled, and I aided her by not stopping her. I swore to my father I'd find her and bring her back, but I betrayed him."

The guilt in his voice brought tears to her eyes. He stared not at her but through her.

"Then she betrayed me." His voice had grown blasé once more, and he focused on Arabella. "I found her and asked her to come back with me. Of course, she said no."

He offered the last sentence as if stating a simple fact. But it wasn't simple at all, and she saw clearly now that Justin used indifference to protect himself. Arabella's stomach clenched. "Did she tell you that?"

"Yes." He said the word with an utter lack of emotion.

"Your father," Arabella whispered. "What is he like?"

"He was a cold, hard man, just like me."

Justin was not cold and hard, yet she saved her breath. He saw himself exactly that way. "You said he *was* a cold, hard man?"

"Yes. He's been gone some years now."

"And your mother? She's not come back since his death?"

Justin shook his head. "I sent word to her to let her know. She wrote back that she would not be returning because she couldn't face the memories." He shrugged as if it didn't matter, but his omissions were the gateway to a depth of hurt he clearly refused to acknowledge.

"Oh, Justin," she murmured, her heart squeezing inside her chest. He flinched as if her pity struck him like a physical blow. A mask descended across his face, leaving it void of the little emotion she had seen.

"Come," he said in an irritatingly neutral tone. "You need to see your mother, and I need to deal with the guard."

She followed him in silence down the hall. He strode with quick, determined steps, yet she noted his stance was rigid, as if he were struggling to hold something in. As they turned down the corridor that held her mother's cell, a scream pierced the silence. Arabella's heart lurched as she gathered her skirts and raced ahead.

"Arabella," Justin barked and caught her at the elbow.

She tried to jerk free, but his hold was firm. "That's my mother's voice," she hissed.

He let her go at once, and they raced down the corridor, not stopping until they burst into her mother's room. Arabella cried out as her mother cowered in a corner, her eyes wild, her hair a ratted mess, and her arms flung over her head. Red welts covered her skin, and as Arabella turned toward Stewart, who stood across from her mother, she saw the crop in his hand. A guttural scream came from her as she charged toward him.

Justin grabbed her around the waist and jerked her to a stop. "Attend to your mother," he commanded.

She nodded her head, and Justin released her. As she struggled to stop her mother's thrashing and cries, Justin spoke in a menacing tone that drew her gaze.

Justin advanced toward Stewart, and in a blur had the man on his knees and the crop he had been holding in front of his neck. Arabella blinked, unsure how Justin had even managed it. He stood behind Stewart who kneeled in front of him. The man clawed at his neck as his face turned an ever increasing and alarming shade of red.

"You like to dominate helpless women, do you?" Justin demanded as he jerked the crop upward. Stewart answered with gagging sounds.

"You're a degenerate," Justin said as if he was simply informing Stewart that the weather was warm. "I know the perfect dungeon for you where creatures who were once men dwell and wait for the next victim to be delivered to their lair."

The guard moaned, and her mother cackled wildly, causing the hair on Arabella's arms to stand on end.

"Take him there!" her mother crowed. "Beats us all the time, he does. Calls himself King of the Insane! Take him there! Take him there! Let the crows eat his eyes out and feast on his heart."

"Mama, Mama, shh," Arabella cooed, wrapping her arms tightly around her mother. Arabella's throat ached with anger and sorrow. Her mother had truly lost her mind, but that did not mean she deserved this.

Stewart whimpered, and Justin leaned over the man and pressed his mouth close to his ear. "They'll show you torture methods there that will make you scream until your throat bleeds and fill your sleeping hours with nightmares that make you never want to shut your eyes again. I think I'll take you there," Justin said, matter-of-fact.

"No, please," the guard choked out.

"Shut your mouth," Justin said in a steely tone. His gaze came to Arabella and her mother. "What do you want me to do?"

Arabella considered his question as she rocked her mother back and forth and ran a soothing hand through her matted hair. The man deserved that dungeon and so much more. And she didn't even want to consider how Justin knew of such a place, yet she didn't think she could stomach sending any human to their torture and death. "Is there another way to teach him a lesson?"

"Certainly," Justin replied. He inclined his head and then yanked Stewart to his feet and toward the door.

"Where are you going?" Arabella asked.

Justin paused at the door and turned to her. "To teach this scum a lesson, as you requested. There is no point in you and your mother having to watch."

"Oh yes, I quite agree," Arabella murmured, even as her mother chanted, "Watch, watch, watch."

Arabella had calmed her mother and put cold cloths on her arms by the time Justin returned. Arabella licked her lips nervously at the spattering of blood on his white shirt. "You didn't—What I'm trying to ask you is—"

Justin's gaze bore into hers. "Of course not," he answered, as if she had asked the question. "I showed him a few select punches to his rather bulbous nose, and one particularly entertaining pressure point." Justin pressed a thumb between her collarbone and flesh, and for one second, numbness spiraled down her right arm. "Here, of course." He released the pressure at once. "I explained to him that if I pressed hard enough I could cripple him for life. He agreed to leave immediately, and I made sure he understood that in a few hours, I will have my own guards on staff here. He won't be back. Never fear."

"Oh, Justin!" She scrambled off her mother's bed and threw her arms around him. "Thank you. For everything."

"You can stay," her mother sang behind her in a calm, almost childlike voice. Arabella whirled around to her mother and gawked. Her mother actually held her gaze, then turned to Justin and smiled. "I like him," she said in that same childlike voice. "Makes me feel safe, he does. George used to make me feel safe."

Arabella blinked in surprise. Her mother had not said her father's name, or even acknowledged that she remembered him, since the day he'd had his stroke. "Mama." She started toward her mother, but Justin touched her arm and shook his head. She hesitated and her mother spoke again. "George was strong and reliable, but then he sent my Daniel to war against my wishes." Suddenly, she turned to Arabella. "Did you know George?"

Arabella swallowed back tears. "Yes, Mama. George, er Papa, is still alive." She'd had no idea that her father had sent her brother to war against her mother's wishes. She'd assumed they'd both agreed it was for the best.

Her mother shook her head. "No, George is dead. He fell over at my feet." She pulled and tugged at her hair. Trembling, Arabella reached out and took her mother's hands in hers. "No, Mama. Papa is alive. He had a brain attack, but he survived it."

"No. No. I killed George. I screamed at him that I wished he'd died instead of my Daniel, and then he did." Tears streamed down her face, and she raised a violently shaking hand to wipe them away. "I need my medicine," she said and started to twitch and scratch her arms.

Justin advanced on her mother. "What sort of medicine do you need, Mrs. Carthright?" he asked in a soothing, gentle tone that contrasted vividly with the previous growl.

"My dark medicine. I get it twice a day. Never with visitors here." She stared straight at Arabella. "Never with you. You're not to know because you'll want some. Not enough for everyone. Just me. I need it. Calms me."

"What? What are you talking about?" Arabella demanded, grabbing her mother who immediately screeched.

"Let me go! Let me go! My skin hurts! It burns and itches. And my head." She smacked herself in the head several times. "I need my medicine. *Pleeease!* I'll take the beating to get my medicine!"

Horrified, Arabella released her mother. "I don't understand. What have they done?"

Justin strode to the lone table in the room and snatched up a small dark bottle. He held it to his nose and cursed.

"Opium. They've been feeding your mother opium to either control her outbursts or, more likely, to ensure she never gets better so they can keep taking your money. I'd wager that Stanhope does not receive all the money you pay. I'll find out, but either way, she's addicted. This is full, so it must be time for the next dose."

"Please," her mother cried pitifully. "I didn't get my dose last night because I was bad and wouldn't take my beating silently. Please. Please. I *need* it!"

When her mother lunged for the bottle, Arabella grabbed her. "No!" Maybe this was the reason her mother had never come back to her senses. "No. You cannot have any more. You must come back to us." Arabella choked back her tears. "Come back to me."

"Give me my medicine," her mother howled and jerked out of Arabella's arms. Justin held up the bottle in one hand while holding up his other hand in a staying action.

"Get yourself under control," he ordered in a commanding voice that filled the room and stopped her mother's motion immediately. "I will give you some of your medicine, but you must calm down."

"Justin!" Arabella cried out.

He motioned for Arabella to come to him. She did so immediately. He turned to her and whispered, "She will have to be taken off the medicine slowly. Otherwise the side effects could kill her. I'll fetch Dr. Bancroft to aid her."

Arabella nodded. "Could this be hindering her recovering her mind?"

"Most definitely," he said grimly. "Opium keeps the mind clouded. I cannot promise you she'll come back to her right state, but if they have been giving this to her the whole time she's been here, then…"

Arabella clenched her hands together. "Now I wish you'd taken that guard to the dungeon you mentioned rather than letting him go."

Justin nodded. "Don't worry. I know where to find him. He'll be getting a visit to the dungeon, and I'll discover exactly what the Hendersons have been doing."

She believed him. His eyes and voice held a note of determination that she didn't doubt.

After he gave her mother a small dose and she calmed down, he took Arabella into the hall. "I'll be back. I'm going to speak to the warden and her husband and retrieve my physician to examine your mother."

Justin returned several hours later with Dr. Bancroft and a nurse who was going to stay with her mother. Dr. Bancroft examined her mother and confirmed what Justin had thought. Anger pulsed through Arabella to think her mother might have actually returned to her right mind if she'd not been addicted to opium.

When the doctor left, she turned to Justin. "You may go, but I'm going to stay with my mother tonight. I dare Mrs. Henderson to try to deny me the right."

He grinned. "You are formidable indeed when pushed far enough, I see. Alas, I find I'm slightly disappointed that it will not come to a standoff between you and Mrs. Henderson, as I would wager all my money on you prevailing, and I'm quite sure it would be entertaining."

She laughed, despite the terrible circumstances of the day. "Where is Mrs. Henderson?"

"In a cell. She and her husband attempted to deny that they had any knowledge of what their son was doing, but I don't believe them. And ledgers in her office of an overabundance of opium orders and a secret tally column of cash make me think I am correct. So I had them locked up."

"Can you do that?" she asked, praying he could.

"Of course, haven't I already told you—"

"That you can do anything? Yes, yes you have. Do you know you give very evasive answers to almost all questions?"

"Do I?" He cocked his eyebrows. "What was the question?"

She stomped her foot, half-irritated and half-amused. "You know very well what the question was, but frankly, you don't have to answer. I find I'm shamefully pleased all the Hendersons are being punished."

"And I find I like that you are shamefully pleased," he said in a low, distinctly seductive voice.

A flutter started in her belly as their gazes locked, but whatever moment that might have been was broken when the nurse came back into the room with several blankets. She immediately curtsied to Justin. "Your Grace, I swear I only left the room to fetch these blankets for Miss Carthright."

"That's quite all right, Mrs. Frockenstone. When I told you that I wanted you to stay in the room, I did not intend that it be a prison. Would you mind fetching a blanket for me, as well?"

Her eyes popped wide, but she hastily bobbed her head and scurried out of the room.

Before Arabella could ask why, Justin faced her, his eyes sparking with some emotion she could not place.

"I'm staying, as well," he said, giving her a look that warned he'd not relent, regardless of her protests.

She could do little more than nod. She was so surprised that he wanted to stay with her and put off finding Ruby but also extremely glad and touched. "You don't have to, you know."

"Of course I know," he said offhandedly. "I want to be here for you."

His words, thrown so casually to her, tugged at her emotions. The nurse returned, and Justin helped Arabella make pallets in the cramped, mostly bare room. She watched him, all too aware he was indeed dangerous to the heart. Once the pallets were finished, the nurse, with

Justin's explicit directions, went to check on the other patients and gather the necessary supplies needed for Arabella's mother. There were twenty women in the home, and all the guards on duty for the night had met Justin and had been warned he'd not tolerate ill treatment of the women.

Arabella and Justin sat on the floor and ate hunks of bread and cheese that he had surprisingly packed, and then he poured her a drink and handed her a cup. She sniffed the glass, the oaky contents almost overpowering. "What's this?"

"Scotch," he replied.

She started to push it back toward him, but he stayed her hand. "You need it. After this day, it will help ease you into sleep."

"But my mother—"

"Is now under excellent care and cannot be helped by a daughter too tired to stay awake. Now, lie down and close your eyes."

She *was* awfully tired, and with a sigh, she scooted onto her back and drifted off immediately.

Ten

$\mathcal{J}$ ustin woke slumped against the wall at such an odd angle that every muscle in his body ached. He stood and glanced across the small room to where Arabella slept on the floor near the nurse and her mother's bed. She lay on her side, curled into a small ball. Her beauty took his breath and made his heart catch peculiarly. It struck him that he'd never slept the night with a woman before. It was oddly amusing that the first time would be in a home for the mentally impaired and the woman had not even been in his arms. The peculiarity of the situation fit his life.

He motioned to the nurse, who was sitting quietly, and she followed him out into the corridor. "Did Mrs. Carthright sleep soundly through the night?"

The nurse nodded. "I'll be waking her up shortly to administer a slightly smaller dose than she's been getting. Do you want me to wake her daughter?"

He shook his head. "I...I trust you can keep it to yourself that I was here with her last night."

The nurse nodded. "May I be blunt, Your Grace?"

"By all means."

"Your kindness to that woman and her mother gave me renewed hope in men."

"Er, thank you," he replied, suddenly uncomfortable with the way she was staring at him with open admiration. "You may go do whatever it is that you need to do to see to Mrs. Carthright's care today."

The nurse bobbed a curtsy, and he was left there with his thoughts, the quiet stirring of patients and tapping of guards' shoes echoing through the hall. He was hoping Arabella would sleep late this morning. When she'd finally agreed to try to lie down last night, dark circles had surrounded her eyes. He'd been dead tired himself after leaving once more to check on her father and his caretaker. But there was no time for weariness. This morning he needed to make his ownership of this home occur. Not to mention he had the small issue of the king's lost letters to attend to.

As he left the home to see Stanhope about taking on his loan, Davenport's thoughts on love swirled through his brain. It suddenly occurred to Justin that he was putting Arabella's concerns over the king's. He was struck with a flash of guilt, but it didn't linger so long that he stopped when driving by the gaming hell where Ruby Rose supposedly now worked.

His meeting with Stanhope had successfully concluded, and he'd interviewed and hired a new warden to run the home, as well as several new guards based on the recommendation of Dr. Bancroft. He'd then stopped by the club, only to learn they had never heard of Ruby Rose, nor did they have a woman there that fit her description. He didn't imagine they would forget her if they had met her. He'd been told by Madame Chauvin, who had measured Ruby Rose for the gowns, that Ruby was almost as tall as him with long, jet-black hair and golden eyes, rather like a cat's eyes, Madame Chauvin had said.

He left Crockford's and steered his horses back in the direction of the home, aware that instead of being irritated that Arabella had not given him a good lead on Ruby Rose, he was relieved. It meant he could spend more time in Arabella's company before he had to part ways with her. But his relief was disturbing. It was another wave in the previously calm waters of his life. Just as he felt his pulse nick up and he started to count, damned if he didn't see the very extremely beautiful entanglement that was upending his world marching toward him down the road.

He pulled his carriage over and stared at her in wonderment as she neared. Surely, there was no woman on this earth as self-reliant as Arabella. "Where the devil are you going?"

"To my father," she replied and started to hike herself into his carriage.

He scrambled down to help her up. When his hands encircled her waist, a bolt of need caused a physical ache that made him clench his teeth, and he was disturbingly overpleased when he felt her tremble under his hands. He glanced at the empty road and made a decision to take for one brief moment what he wanted. A kiss. Just a simple kiss. Nothing more.

He slowly edged her around to face him. "I've seen to your father this morning," he murmured close to her ear, inhaling her scent deeply.

She turned toward him, and her mouth parted. "You have?"

He nodded as he slid his hand all the way around her waist and inched the other one up around her neck. He traced the long, beckoning, creamy column, allowing his fingers to come to a rest over the delicate skin. Her pulse beat fiercely underneath. Was she nervous over his touch or the scandalous way they were behaving? Gossip didn't concern him in the least, but in regard to her, it did. He scanned the perimeter again. Still clear.

"Your father is resting. Alice is there still. Oh, and I'm now the proud owner of the *Carthright* Home for the Mentally Impaired."

Her eyes rounded. "You renamed the home after my family?"

He nodded. "You are the reason I purchased it, after all."

"Why—"

He stopped her question by pressing a finger to her lips. "I don't know why." Only he did. He'd done it for her. To help her. Foolishness. "Do you never do anything without a good reason?"

She shook her head.

Wise woman. "Kiss me, Arabella."

"You want me to kiss you?" The question was a throaty whisper. It filled him with satisfaction and a dangerous desire to placate that need. He was fast losing boundaries and reason, and he couldn't seem to grasp them and pull them back around him.

He brushed his finger over her lips. "I don't believe I've ever wanted anything more."

She pressed her lips to his, and when her tongue touched his mouth, whatever small amount of self-control he'd still had in his possession, he willingly released for this moment. They stood on the steps of his carriage crushed together and everything vanished but her.

She ravaged his mouth with need, and he returned her longing with his own wild wanting. Their tongues swirled and retreated, then met again, until simply kissing her was not enough. Not nearly enough. He pulled her closer to him until there was not a place their bodies didn't touch. Soft mewling sounds came from her, and she wiggled against him as if to get even closer. When they finally broke the kiss—he heard the wheels of an oncoming carriage—they scrambled onto the seat and stared at each other.

It took a moment for his raging blood to slow. He wanted her to come back to his home with him. He wanted to know all of her, and in ways he'd never bothered to learn a woman. He longed to explore her body, hear how she got any scars, and learn of her fears and hopes. He desired to bring her passion she had never known. He'd not ask it, though.

"I'll take you home, if you wish."

For a moment, hope spiked as uncertainty filled her eyes. "Yes," she finally replied. "I need to go home."

His disappointment that her need for him did not match his need for her, that he had not swept her away with the tide of desire to throw caution to the wind, made him feel as if he'd been plunged into the deepest part of an ocean. She was the ocean. She'd consumed him somehow, and he'd let her.

He nodded, picked up the reins, and silently drove her home.

Near the appointed hour of five and after confirming for herself that her father was doing well in Alice's care, Arabella entered the Sans Pareil Theatre to meet Jude. Her thoughts should have been concentrated on what she was going to say to him, but all she could think about was Justin. The feel of his warm lips on hers. The way his mouth hungrily slanted over hers with passion and need. The desire for her that had made his eyes burn bright. She'd known without him saying a word that he'd wanted her. It did not scare her as she knew it should, as was proper. She wanted him, too. Very much. With an ache that almost drove her to distraction.

But it was not simply lust. In the short time she'd known him, he'd been there for her repeatedly. He may be a hardened duke on the outside, but on the inside, where it mattered, he was tender *and* he was hurting. She did want his body, but the more she thought about it, she realized with a great amount of fear and a small amount of hope that she had grown to care for him. He had somehow made her count on him, which was something she had thought never to be able to do again with another. She hoped that he cared for her, as well.

She fought to force back the grin she felt pulling at her lips as she made her way inside the theatre. The stage was full of actors and actresses practicing, just as Jude had said it would be. She glanced around the room, but there was no one in the audience. Frowning, she looked up and searched first the left and then the right theatre boxes. She was about to give up when the curtain in the last box closest to the stage parted slightly, and Jude leaned forward against the railing. He motioned her up and the curtain fell back into place. She quickly made her way to the second floor and went straight to the box.

Jude turned as she entered. "What's wrong, little bird?" he asked staring at her. "Tell me of yesterday. I got your note that your mother and father were both ill."

She didn't want to reveal all the details of her parents' sicknesses to Jude. "They are doing much better. But I had a long night, and I'm very tired," she said, taking the seat beside him.

"I'm tired, as well," Jude said with an exaggerated yawn. "My father kept me up half the night questioning my every decision."

Arabella frowned. "I thought you said you didn't know your father."

"No." He waggled a finger in front of her face. "I said I was raised by a witch. A complete truth, though she does not cast spells. What I didn't say was that my father had refused to acknowledge to me, until last night, that I am his son."

"I'm happy for you, Jude."

Jude took up her hand and squeezed it so hard that she had to choke back a cry. After a moment, he loosened his hold. "You should be. It's good for us both."

She didn't see how it mattered for her.

Jude cocked his head. "Of course, I knew it. Everything I've done was with that knowledge burning in my chest. Do you know what this means?" His question carried an intensity that scared her.

"No."

"It means that the outcome of the game we play is even more important to me now, Arabella."

"What game?" she demanded, tugging her hand away and settling it in her lap. She resisted the urge to rub her aching fingers.

"The game of life, my dear. You are one of the pieces I'm forced to move, though truly I don't want to. Yet, I can see no other way."

Jude's eyes had taken on a hard glint, and his lips pulled back into a menacing smile. She wanted to flee and never see him again.

"The Duke of Dinnisfree is no smuggler, Jude. He's a good man, and I refuse to help you spy on him any longer."

Jude jerked her forward, causing the armrest of the seat to dig into her hip bone. "Let me go," she demanded, fear pulsing with every beat of her heart.

"I wish I could," he said, the words feeling false as they rolled off his tongue. "Now you must listen to me. I want to help you, and I'm likely the only person who does. Everyone else wants to use you, regardless of how it hurts you." He released the cruel grip on her arms and clamped his bandaged hand under her chin until she hissed. "I need you to search Dinnisfree's home."

"No," she spat, even as Jude's grip became harsher.

"Arabella," he said on a long, weary sigh, "your stubbornness reminds me of myself, which is no surprise, but stubborn people die too young because they often only see their own ways. Do you want to die?"

Arabella's breath whooshed out of her lungs. "No."

"Then you will do as I say."

She fought to shake her head against his grip. "I won't. I cannot."

Jude tsked at her. "My father thinks I'll bumble this and *you* are trying to prove him right! He did not want me to meet you today. I had to threaten him."

"You're frightening me, Jude."

"I am sorry about that," he said congenially, "but I suppose in this case it's good to be frightened." He gave her chin a squeeze and released her.

"You're not really a Bow Street Runner, are you?" she accused. He'd not said a word about his assignment or his superior thinking he'd bungle the job. Simply his father...

He stared at her for a long moment, then grinned. "Brava, Bella."

The use of the nickname her father called her startled her. "How did you know—"

"It matters not. We have come to the point when we can shed a layer of lies. It's both refreshing and exhilarating. You make me proud!" He pinched her cheek hard now. She smacked his hand away. "Little bird, how courageous you are. You've met all my expectations much quicker than I could have hoped, so let us change our course."

"What course?" she demanded over the blood rushing in her ears.

"Well, we were rowing down the river of dishonesty to see if you could reach the gate of trust, and now you have. We can be honest with each other, no?"

She nodded, knowing it was a lie.

"You are a thief."

"*What?*" She immediately recalled the box, and her heart sank.

"I see I now have your undivided attention." He smiled. "My dear, not only are you a thief but you've stolen from the king."

It felt as if someone had poured a bucket of ice water on her head. Gooseflesh covered her arms and legs as images of the last few days flew across her mind.

"The jewelry box," she said through numb lips. "It was a gift, wasn't it?"

He nodded. "You're very bright. Now, little bird, I promise you that if I tell Elizabeth that I saw you stuff her jewelry box in your bag and leave with it, she *will* let the king know. He is not a forgiving man, from what I've been told."

"You set me up," she said through clenched teeth.

"Yes. I had to. I'm sorry, but I couldn't very well chance Elizabeth discovering *me* with the box."

"But you *have* the box!" she cried.

"I do. But *you* got it out of Elizabeth's home for me. Now, what I need, what I'm looking for, is something the box contained."

"You have the necklace, too! Don't you? You never intended to return it!"

"Mr. Winston has the necklace," he said with a wink. "Do you know the necklace is the most interesting part of this? The fact that the necklace remained in the secret compartment is what makes me certain that whoever took the letters we seek understands their value completely and intends to offer them to the highest bidder. It's a dangerous, dangerous game playing Whigs against Tories in a bid to control the throne."

"The throne?" Arabella's hands flew to her throat as she swallowed her fear. "I don't understand. What letters? How can letters affect the throne?"

"The letters had to have been removed at Elizabeth's house *after* I saw her put them in the box but *before* you took it, and that means whoever it was has fooled me. I hate that," Jude finished as if she were not even there, as if he were simply thinking aloud. "We need those letters. They will deliver to us what is rightfully ours. My plan was so perfect. I instructed Elizabeth to hide the letters there, after all." He frowned. "It can still be made right with your help, which is exactly, of course, how it should be. You must help me with Dinnisfree. He is the wild card in my hand. Very unpredictable, that man."

"You think the Duke of Dinnisfree is also looking for your letters?" Her voice was dull to her own ears.

"Not *my* letters, little bird. But I do feel they belong to us in a way. And as for the duke, I *know* he is searching for them. What I don't know is if he has found them. Which is where you come in. Or perhaps I should say, where you remain in the game, as really, you've been playing even before he joined us, you simply didn't know it."

Arabella's mind whirred with the odd information Jude had relayed. Justin had lied to her, but it didn't matter because she'd lied to him, too. She didn't know why he was looking for those letters, but that didn't matter, either. She'd not betray him after all he'd done for her. And Jude, he was crazy! How had she not seen it sooner?

Jude's eyes suddenly narrowed as if he could read her thoughts. He whipped out his hand and yanked her to him by her hair. She cried out, but his other palm clamped over her mouth. In the background, above the whishing of her struggle to get enough air through her nose, she could hear the actors and actresses, though muffled from the drawn curtain, still practicing onstage below. Jude stared down at her.

"Your doubt and defiance are clear on your face, little bird. Let me paint a picture for you so that you truly understand what is at stake. Dinnisfree is no mere duke. He's a spy for the king, and a very good one at that. Likely the best, though I did recently uncover his identity, which means he slipped. A very bad thing for a spy to do."

Arabella's heart slammed against her ribs. She couldn't

control the spasmodic trembling the revelation caused. Jude grinned. "I'm glad to see that changes your perception of him."

Arabella prayed that her true emotions didn't show on her face. Jude's revelation didn't alter how she felt about Justin. She wasn't sure if Jude was lying or not, but regardless, Justin was a good man.

Jude slowly peeled his hand away and released her head. She sat up and rubbed her stinging scalp.

"This is what you are going to do for me," Jude said in a matter-of-fact tone. "You will find a reason to go to Dinnisfree's home and you will seduce him. When he falls asleep, search his home."

"Search his home yourself," she spat and then reared her hand back to slap Jude.

He caught her wrist and gripped it. "It must be you."

She glared at Jude. "Never."

"Little bird, how sad I feel for you. There is much I must teach you that your false parents obviously did not. Never say never."

"I *never* told you I was adopted," she said in the most biting tone she could muster.

"And yet I know. I'll leave you for now to ponder how. But there is something valuable I want to share with you." He jerked her to him until they were so close that his hot breath fanned her face. "I have a man guarding your house, and it will take only a word from me for him to break in and kill the man you wrongly call Father. Your house is quite easy to breach."

Her gaze flew to his wrapped hand. He was holding it at an odd angle. The realization slammed into her. *He* was the one who broke the window in her father's study! He must have cut his hand in the process. "You thought *I* had the letters!"

"Very briefly," he replied. "I was immensely relieved to

learn you didn't." He patted her cheek. "I did not want to think you really *were* a thief. That is only a part you played."

She clenched her hands until her nails stung the skin of her palms, and she forced herself to relax. She'd simply tell Justin all and ask him for help.

"No, no, little bird," Jude murmured, somehow reading her mind yet again. "I'll know if you rat me out to Dinnisfree. I'm watching his house, too, and if he comes near your home to try to rescue your father, I'll have to end your father's life for your betrayal. Don't make me a murderer, Arabella. Simply play the game in the role you must and all will be perfect in the end."

Her breath solidified in her throat as her eyes blurred. How could she betray Justin? Even if he didn't have the letters and she found nothing, she would have to live with the awful knowledge of what she'd done. But what choice did she have? Jude would kill her father, unless Justin could help her. Yes, she was sure he would. "I'll do as you say, but I think I deserve to know who you really are." She trembled, praying she'd lied convincingly.

"I'm a brother," he said evenly, but his eyes burned wild. "I'm a bastard. The product of a forbidden love between a powerful man and a pitifully neglected woman. I'm a lover. I'm a survivor. I've been abused, beaten, used, and I clawed my way out of hell to sit here with you. I'm the avenger of wrongs. I'm a son who will risk all for the love of his parents. That is who I am."

She nodded. It was enough. He'd told her just enough. She'd learn who he was, one way or the other, and then she'd have the upper hand. She was sick and tired of being the victim.

Arabella left the theatre and went straight to Madame

Chauvin's. She was well aware that Jude followed her all the way. He didn't bother much to stay hidden. By the time she reached the dress shop, her nerves were a pulsating ball in her stomach. She muttered under her breath as she turned the corner and spotted Jude again.

She shot him a glare. "There is no need to follow me here! I am stopping in to see if there is any extra work that I might have."

Jude cocked his head. "Are you worried Dinnisfree will no longer want you as his mistress after you betray him?" he said in a mocking tone.

She ground her teeth. "I don't wish to be entangled with any of you when this is over!"

It was partly true. She didn't ever want to see Jude again. Her feelings regarding Justin were much more muddled. She had not known him very long, yet she cared for him. A good deal. He had been kind to her and her family. He had shown faith in her when she had told him her brother was innocent, and she felt she could count on him. And the way her made her feel... Her belly tightened as she recalled his lips on her body.

She strode into Madame Chauvin's and quickly motioned for the smiling woman to follow her into the back dressing room while pressing a finger over her mouth to show she wanted silence. If Jude did come in, she'd know. There was a bell that rang when the shop door was opened. Madame Chauvin frowned at her but nodded.

"What's this about?" the woman demanded as she closed the dressing room door.

Thank goodness the shop had been empty. Arabella had not even considered the possibility of customers. This spying thing was difficult, indeed.

Arabella moved close to the woman. "I cannot explain, but we must whisper."

"Why in the world must we whisper?"

Arabella clenched her teeth. Hadn't she just said she could not explain? "Er, because my throat is sore."

Madame Chauvin snorted. "You are a terrible liar, but all right, my dear. What is it you need?"

"Information." Madame Chauvin often seemed to know secrets others did not.

"Ah, then you have come to the right place. About whom are you seeking information?"

That was the question indeed. "I'm not sure. Why don't we start with the king and queen..." Since the letters involved the king, she suspected the queen had a part to play. And Jude's comment about the Whigs and the Tories made her wonder if the letters had something to do with the divorce the king was trying to obtain.

Madame Chauvin clucked her tongue. "You'll have to be more specific. I know a great deal of gossip about the king and queen."

Arabella thought for a moment about what she did know. The king was having an affair with Lady Conyngham, and he had recently requested the Pains and Penalty Bill be introduced into Parliament. He wanted to divorce Queen Caroline on the grounds that she was adulterous when he himself was an adulterer, the reprobate hypocrite!

Arabella bit her lip as she thought. Jude had said he was a son:

I'm a bastard. The product of a forbidden love between a powerful man and a pitifully neglected woman. I'm the avenger of wrongs. I'm a son who will risk all for the love of his parents.

"The king neglects the queen," she said out loud, her breath coming in a shallow gasp.

Madame Chauvin nodded. "Common knowledge. The king has neglected our queen since they first married. He never loved her."

Arabella rubbed her temples. The queen was a woman

just like her. And like any woman, the queen must want love. It didn't feel good not to be wanted.

Arabella knew it all too well. And because of it, she had closed herself off, locked her heart away, and told herself she hadn't wanted love, but she knew now that wasn't true. Justin had shown her that in small measure with his touch and the desire it elicited, with his being there for her. She wanted a man to grow old with and love, someone who inspired passion and admiration. The queen was married, but she was trapped in a loveless marriage, so she must have still wanted love. And if she were desperate enough, lonely enough...

"Have you ever heard whispers of the queen having an affair?"

Madame Chauvin's eyes popped wide, and then her mouth pressed into a thin, hard line.

"I am not judging her, Madame Chauvin," Arabella hastened to add.

The woman seemed to relax a bit, and when her mouth opened, Arabella's pulse skyrocketed with hope. Madame Chauvin inhaled a long breath. "Yes. Many years ago there were whispers that she and George Canning had an affair."

"The president of the Board of Trade?"

Madame Chauvin nodded and pulled her mouth into a knowing smile. "Have you read the papers today?"

Arabella shook her head.

Madame Chauvin held up a hand. "One moment." She marched out of the dressing room, her skirts swishing, and was back within seconds flourishing a paper in the air. "It says here that it's rumored that Canning has threatened to resign because of the proceeding against the queen. People whisper about them still, but I will tell you what I know as fact. I was commissioned many years ago to make a set of gowns to conceal a pregnancy. The queen left the country the day after the gowns were picked up by a woman I later came to learn was one of the queen's ladies. The queen returned a year later, and my dearly departed husband built a crib for a male child who he swore had the queen's eyes and Canning's lips."

"Might I see the paper?" Arabella said, her voice cracking. Madame Chauvin handed it to her. Arabella glanced immediately at the drawing of the queen and—

Her stomach clenched as she stared at the sketch of the man. She knew him! And not because she'd ever seen a picture of Mr. Canning. She had come face-to-face with him.

She studied the picture again to be sure. His name was printed above the sketch: *George Canning*. Her skin tingled. Canning was Mr. Winston. Except Mr. Winston didn't really exist. The president of the Board of Trade had been at Jude's house posing as someone else, and now she knew why. It had been to secure the letters Jude had thought she'd had. What did those letters say?

Arabella's heart thumped as she stared at the sketch of the queen. She'd seen those same chestnut-colored eyes when she looked at Jude, and Mr. Canning's mouth, the thin upper lip and bow-shaped bottom one, was Jude's mouth. Canning and the queen were Jude's parents. She was sure of it. And she'd use the knowledge to get out of this mess.

Eleven

$\mathcal{J}$ ustin realigned the gleaming daggers on the table and set the targets upright once more. He wiped the sweat off his brow. *Damnable sweat.* It kept rolling down his bare arms to dampen his palms. He grabbed the rag he'd discarded earlier from where he'd tossed it on his bed and used it to soak up the perspiration on his arms, stomach, and upper shoulders.

Dagger-throwing practice usually helped to clear his mind, but he'd been at it for several hours and his thoughts were still muddled. He wanted Arabella, and it wasn't simply physical. It would be so much easier to deal with if it were, because he'd known by the soft mewling sounds she'd made in her throat and the way she'd wiggled against him that she'd wanted him out there on that carriage just as much as he'd desired her.

Yet she'd turned away from that desire and asked him to take her home, and he'd done it. Without protest *and* despite the fact that to do so had made his body ache, not to mention made his chest hurt where his once-unflappable heart had constricted.

She didn't even know what he truly was and she'd sensed to keep her distance from him. It was a wise choice on her part. A good one. A perfectly sane one. However, he'd wanted her to make the opposite choice.

The revelation still shocked him. Never had he brought a woman into his home, into his head, and into his heart, and he'd been on the precipice of doing all three. He hadn't intended to throw the door of his soul wide open, but he'd been willing to crack the door. If she'd said the word, he would have brought her here and spent all night worshiping her body and learning how she'd become this woman he could not help but admire, to want to trust.

With a growl, he picked up a dagger, closed his eyes, and threw it. The steel whooshed through the air and sunk into the wooden target with a dull *thud*. He slit his eyes open and stared at the target. He'd missed the bull's-eye by half an inch. That was the difference between life and death. He'd not missed a bull's-eye since his father had beaten his arse bloody at the age of eleven with a switch for missing one. It had been his last miss. Until now. Arabella had stolen his concentration along with his composure. It was unacceptable.

He whipped another dagger through the air with a curse. The blade hit hard and the hilt moved back and forth, filling the silence with a hum.

There. Bull's-eye.

He took a deep breath and searched through his swirling emotions for the calm he prized.

He was a spy, for Christ's sake, dedicated to king and country and nothing else. He should be glad she had walked away from what burned between them, even if it did make the very air crackle when she was near. He should damn well rejoice. Because if she hadn't left, if she'd come back here, he couldn't say what he might have revealed. He could not promise that he would not have told her something personal and that would be an enormous error in the world of detachment in which he lived. That would mean he wanted her to care. That would mean he cared for her.

His gut clenched, and he scrubbed a hand across his face. Did he care for her? Truly?

When she was near it was hard to think straight and *unemotionally*, but being unemotional had always saved him. Hadn't it?

"Damn, damn, damn." He flung eight more daggers in a row, the clunking of the metal sliding into wood like a muted chorus of deadly bullets. No pleasure came. No triumph. No calm. A tempest swirled in his head and, devil take it, the woman in his heart had opened the secret chest where he kept the pain his parents had caused. Now, somehow, he had to shut it again.

He stalked to the sidebar, poured four fingers of Scotch, and threw back the contents. The liquor slid down his throat and into his belly, burning almost as fiercely as the confusion in his mind.

He picked up the decanter, poured two more fingers, and took a long sip before setting the glass down. He was a spy. Spies trusted no one. His father had taught him that with words and deeds. He'd treated him as a comrade and never a son. Hell, his mother had taught him not to trust when she'd walked away from him without a backward glance. And damn it all, hadn't he learned through the years how incredibly scheming people were? He trusted no one implicitly—only Davenport came close. What a damned foolish thing it would have been to start something with a woman he barely knew!

A knock came at his door. "Your Grace," Mumford, his butler, intoned in his typically dull voice. "You have a visitor."

Justin looked around for his shirt, couldn't immediately find it, and decided he didn't give a good goddamn if he was bare-chested or not. He was expecting Davenport, as his friend had sent him a note earlier telling him he had something most interesting to impart. It wasn't as if Davenport had never seen him in such a state before. They'd been bloodying each other in the boxing arena at

Gritton's for years. He wouldn't be surprised if his friend could recollect every scar on Justin's chest and back on command.

"Coming," Justin growled. He strode to the door and threw it open. There, standing as if it were the most normal thing in the world for her to be there, inside his home, was Arabella. A sickening, unreasonable amount of happiness filled him, followed by irritation at Mumford.

"Mumford," he clipped.

The butler turned his gaze away from Arabella to Justin. The man's once-blue eyes were clouded with a white film that had set in some years ago when he'd still served as Justin's father's butler. "Your Grace?" he said in a cracked, weathered voice as he squinted at Justin.

Whatever annoyance Justin had felt slipped away.

"Do try to remember that I've told you to make all guests wait in the library." In actuality, it would be only one guest, Davenport. He was the only person Justin had allowed in his home in ten years.

Mumford nodded, his head looking like it might roll off his stooped, thin shoulders. "I recalled, Your Grace, but—"

Arabella placed a hand—by God, it looked protective—on Mumford's arm. Surely, she didn't think she needed to protect his ancient butler from him? Then again, Arabella had been protecting people for so long it was probably a natural reaction. Justin jerked with a realization. In that way, they were *exactly* alike.

Arabella gave him a chastising look that made him want to smile. "I insisted he bring me straight back to you, propriety be damned," she blurted, her cheeks turning scarlet with her attempted boldness.

"I've always been one to damn propriety," he said lazily. "So please, do enter my domain and we will banish it to the dark cell it deserves." Her eyes widened considerably, but much to his satisfaction, she released her hold on Mumford's arm and stepped through the entrance of his bedchamber.

"Miss Carthright!" Mumford gasped at the impropriety of Arabella entering his bedchamber, Justin supposed.

Justin blinked in surprise. His butler, stoic to the point that Justin had wondered before if the man had stopped breathing, had just displayed an astounding amount of emotion. Amazing. He stared at the bewitching woman before him. It seemed she had the ability to ignite passion in not just him.

She patted Mumford on the arm. "I'll be fine, Hugh."

Justin frowned as he looked between Arabella and Mumford. He allowed his gaze to bore into his butler. "In all the years I've known you, you never told me your Christian name was Hugh."

The butler scowled. "You never asked, Your Grace," he said in a surly tone. "Nor did your father, for that matter. Miss Carthright asked me immediately. Seems she needed to know it to decide whether I was trustworthy."

"Of course she did," he said, trying not to laugh. It became increasingly difficult when Mumford smiled. Justin hadn't seen his butler smile in years. The old, deeply creased face looked strange with happiness shining from it. Justin drew his attention back to Arabella who offered Mumford—he'd be damned if he could think of Mumford as Hugh—a sweet smile that made his chest squeeze.

Arabella set her hand on her hips and narrowed her eyes at Justin. "Hugh is an excellent name. It means *heart, mind, spirit*. Any man with a name like that cannot be bad."

Mumford beamed like a schoolboy with an infatuation, and devil take it, Justin realized he was grinning, as well. He scrubbed a hand across his face and motioned to Mumford. "You may go."

Mumford gave him a beady-eyed look. "You're in need of a shirt, Your Grace."

This was certainly a day for firsts. A woman not only in his house but also in his bedchamber. A smiling butler. Then a chastising butler. "I am the employer and *you* the employee," he growled good-naturedly.

"Yes, Your Grace. I recall. I see your shirt at the foot of your bed. Shall I retrieve it for you?"

Justin glanced behind him, spotted his garment, and turned back to his suddenly bold butler. "You may go, Mumford."

"Shall I bring tea?"

"You know I don't damn well drink tea."

"I do," Arabella piped up. "Mumford, you may bring me some tea. Thank you."

"A pleasure, Miss Carthright."

Once Mumford left, Justin strolled over to his shirt and shrugged into it. He faced Arabella once more. "Not that your visit doesn't please me"—because it did, too damn much—"but what the devil are you doing here?" As she opened her mouth to answer him, Justin was hit with a thought. He held up a staying hand as his pulse ticked up a notch. "I never told you where I lived."

"No," she whispered, as if someone might hear them, "you didn't."

His survival instincts leaped to life. With a sweeping glance, he took in her expression, position of her hands, any bulges for weapons, sensible shoes for running or slippers of an innocent. Slippers. Delicate and pink. He relaxed a fraction. He swept his gaze around his room, but all was as it should be. Though, he knew something was wrong.

"Yet, here you are," he replied in a slow tone. One meant to calm her. He could see that her breathing had quickened. Her eyes darted about, and she clutched at her sides. She'd been holding herself together until, what? She got to him?

"Tell me," he said softly.

She nodded, reached out, and closed his bedchamber door. When she faced him again, she was nibbling at her lip. "I would hate for Hugh to overhear and inadvertently become entangled in this mess. Though"—she tilted her head—"I suppose if he's been your butler since you were nine—"

"Eight," Justin corrected, struggling to hide the shock coursing through him that she'd learned so much about Mumford in the short time she'd talked to him. It was because she truly cared about people. "He's old and forgets things," he said as he closed the distance between them.

"Yes, of course." She swallowed audibly. Nervously. As someone in trouble would.

"Do continue." He'd found long ago it was better to know the worst as quickly as possible.

"I suppose," she said, her words halting, "that he knows who *you* are."

"Yes," he said carefully, counting the beats of her pulsing neck. Hers doubled his, though his had most definitely increased. "I'm the Duke of Dinnisfree. Mumford is well aware."

"Not your title, but the man you *truly* are."

She could not know. There was not a chance he'd slipped. Was there? "And who am I?"

Dismay painted her face. "I was hoping you'd tell me and show the same trust in me that I'm about to give you. It would be better that way."

Justin counted to five in French in his head. He didn't feel one iota calmer. "I'm afraid, Arabella, you'll be waiting an eternity if you're waiting on me to reveal secrets. I'm an open book, so I've no secrets to reveal."

"You're a liar," she said matter-of-factly. "But then again, so am I. The difference between us is that I was forced into my lies by necessity of survival." She gasped suddenly as she stared at him. "I only just realized perhaps you were, too! I mean, with your mother leaving you and your father such a cold man. You must have told yourself that you didn't need anyone."

"Arabella." He made his voice purposely forceful and menacing.

"Oh. Yes… I'm sorry. I'm terribly nervous, but time is of the essence. I know you're a spy for the king."

He tensed instantly, his thoughts widening, then focusing in on a single one. He was relieved that she knew. *Relieved.* And speechless. He didn't know how to talk with the truth out in the open. It was foreign to him.

She nodded. "It's good you're not denying it," she said, misinterpreting his silence for confirmation. "We really don't have time to argue back and forth if we are going to come up with a plan."

He may be relieved that she knew, but that didn't mean his reaction was wise. He struggled to sort his thoughts and put them in the damnable order they required. He had a duty to protect the king, and that could not be forgotten. He was still a spy for the man, after all. "What makes you think I'm a spy, Arabella?"

"Oh." Her shoulders drooped. "You *are* going to deny it. All right, then. I do understand. The thing is that I know because Jude told me."

"Your cousin?"

Her brow furrowed. "What? Oh…no. Jude is not my cousin. I don't have any cousins. I had to tell you that. Jude is, well…" She bit her lip. "I honestly am not sure if I even know his real name. He said it was J.I. Devine, but when I asked him to tell me what the J.I. stood for he said Judas Iscariot. You know, the man who—"

"I know," he growled. His patience—had he any more?—snapped. He grabbed Arabella by the arm and dragged her toward one of the large, matching leather chairs in his adjoining reading room. "Sit," he said, gently pressing her down as he took the seat opposite of her. "Start from what you perceive is the very beginning of your tale, but skip *all* unnecessary details."

She scowled but took a deep breath. "It all started with Lady Conyngham refusing to buy the dresses she commissioned, and then ensuring Madame Chauvin had to let me go."

She knew Elizabeth? His gut clenched at the thought and the implications that came with it.

Arabella paused and frowned. "I suppose it actually started the day the king and queen married, but of course, I was not drawn into it until years later."

"Arabella, the facts as they occurred in chronological order, please."

She nodded, took a deep breath, and spilled her tale. His mind turned over each thing she said and examined it as she spoke. Jude—true name unknown—was the probable bastard of Queen Caroline and Canning, as Arabella had already hypothesized. That went along with what Justin already knew, though he'd not had so much as an alias for the child's name.

The way Justin understood it, this Jude had set Arabella up to ensure Justin did not find the king's letters, which Jude obviously knew about. Jude was working for someone. Who? The Whigs, or Canning, or the queen? Ruby Rose and Fitzherald were part of Jude's plot, but they were simply being used as distractions. An expertly planned false lead.

Arabella had pilfered the box; therefore she had stolen from the king, even if she had not known it. She claimed to have never seen the letters, though she had seen the queen's necklace—again, that she had not known was the queen's—which the king had stupidly given to Elizabeth. Canning, posing as a collector, had taken the necklace, and Arabella assumed he was still in possession of it. Likely correct.

Justin took a deep breath. It was a lot to take in, but the first thing he needed to determine if she was even telling him the truth. His gut said yes, but the greater question was, could he trust himself when it came to her?

"And then," she wailed, snapping Justin's focus back to her completely, "Jude threatened to kill my father if I did not do as he said." She looked him straight in the eyes. "I'm supposed to seduce you. That's why I'm here."

"Well, by all means, then," he teased, even as desire gripped him in its iron hold.

Her mouth parted, and she stared at him for a long moment. She inhaled slowly, her chest rising tantalizingly. "I'm also supposed to search your home for the letters."

He cocked an eyebrow. Anger pumped through his veins that she, an innocent, had been drawn into such corruption.

"Justin, I don't intend to seduce you."

"How utterly disappointing," he murmured. He had to take a deep inhalation to try to return his heartbeat to a normal rhythm. If she'd attempted to seduce him at this moment, he would have let her with no hesitation at all. He would have compromised his mission to touch her, kiss her, and hold her in his arms.

Hellfire. He swallowed the lump of longing lodged in his throat. "I assume by your coming here and telling me all this that you are entrusting me to help you."

She nodded. "I have not relied on anyone in years, but I know I can count on you. I'm certain of it. I am betting my father's life on it. I'll stay here long enough that Jude believes I have done what he demanded. I'm to meet him at midnight tonight near the corner by my house and give him the letters or any information I've discovered."

Her bright eyes implored him, but there was no damn need for her to plead. She had his trust, and he suspected a great deal more than that, as much as he did not want to admit it. The overwhelming need to protect her fairly choked him.

"Arabella"—he cleared his throat when it cracked—"you can count on me. I will deal with this man Jude. And Canning." *And the king.* Prinny could never know she had stolen from him. "I'm not admitting I'm a spy to you, of course," he added, knowing it was futile.

"Oh, do be quiet!" She jumped up from her seat and kneeled before him. She grasped his hands in hers. "I wish you'd trust me as I'm trusting you. And," she said, her lashes lowering to blanket her eyes, "I wish ever so much that you'd kiss me."

Had she really just uttered that plea? She could hardly believe her boldness or the longing to feel his lips on hers that coursed through her. He'd accepted her words as truth, and he was going to help her. She knew she could count on him in her heart, but his proving it yet again banished any lingering doubts about what she wanted. He would not fail her or leave her floundering.

Her breath caught as she raised her eyes to him. He was so proud and honorable all alone behind the wall of indifference he'd built. She understood his aloofness because she'd been much the same. She'd convinced herself that she didn't have time for love, but now, dear God, *now* love had made time for her. She didn't simply care for Justin. She loved him. He had her heart, and she wanted to obtain his. For his love, she'd risk it all.

"You want me to kiss you?" he asked gruffly.

She nodded.

Desire flickered to a bursting flame in his eyes. "You're sure you are not trying to seduce me?" His words were bantering, but his voice was gruff.

Her pulse beat a thumping rhythm in her throat. She swallowed. "I'm sure I am. Will you let me?"

"Let you?" An incredulous look swept his face. "I will do more than let you, sweet Arabella," he promised.

He bent his head to hers and claimed her mouth in a kiss of possession that branded her as his, whether he wanted her to be or not. He traced her lips with his tongue, nipping and kissing, each contact of his skin to hers drugging her and lulling her toward euphoria. She scooted between his thighs to get closer to him, and the intoxicating smell of liquor mingled with his masculine sweat over-whelmed her. She broke the kiss because she had the desperate need to press her lips to the corded muscles that tensed under her hands. When her lips met his chest, he groaned and grabbed her shoulders, pushing her away from him. A quiver surged through her veins at the look of raw need he gave her.

"If you keep kissing me like that," he growled, "I won't be able to control myself."

"Good," she replied. "It will do you good to lose the control you so prize."

His fingers curled tightly around her arms. "Arabella, I'm speaking of more than seductive kisses."

She shook with fear, hope, and need. Forcing herself to be bolder still, she raised her hands to his shirttails and slipped them under the garment. She hissed when her fingers made contact with his hot, taut skin. Slowly, she slid her hands over the hard, chiseled planes of his abdomen.

A groan escaped him as he clutched her hands and stilled her. "You are sure?"

The sensuality in his voice caused a deep ache to grow in her throat, making it almost impossible to respond. "Very."

He pulled her to her feet and seemingly weightlessly into his arms. She tilted her head and he stared at her with a sort of wonder that surprised her. "You are the only woman I've ever allowed in my home."

A surge of happiness coursed through her. Perhaps he'd let her into his heart, too. "I'm glad of that," she said, knowing it meant a great deal that he'd not simply booted her out the door. He had let down his guard a bit, whether he realized it or not.

An uncertainty slid over his face as he gazed at her. "I don't know what I can promise you, but I know you make me feel things that I've never experienced. Softness. Yearning. Weakness." The last he said with a scowl.

"I don't desire any promises," she said, meaning it. She desired a chance at real love. Consuming love. Passionate love. Surely that sort of love required a great risk. Following all the rules with a man like Justin would simply never work.

He nodded and silently closed the distance between the chairs and the bed. When they reached the mattress, he laid her down gently and then straightened, standing before her as he peeled off his shirt to reveal a body sculpted by what must have been hours of grueling exercise. The daggers protruding from the multitude of wooden targets in the room had not gone unnoticed.

He crawled over her, his weight making the bed creak. Staring down at her with his arms on either side of hers, he said, "You make me want to—"

"Your Grace!" Mumford boomed from the other side of the door, making Justin frown fiercely. Arabella stifled a nervous giggle at the man's poor timing. "Miss Carthright's tea is ready."

"She doesn't want the bloody tea. Go away and stay gone. I'll call you if I need you!"

"Thank you, Hugh!" Arabella called out on a gale of escaped laughter.

Justin grinned down at her, and the genuine happiness

and ease she saw in his face made her heart lurch. He
reached down and brushed a strand of her hair away from
her cheek. "God, you make me feel happy."

She frowned up at him. "You say that as if it's a bad
thing."

He ran his hand down her face, featherlight, as if she
were glass that he might break. "I'm unsure. Had you asked
me three days ago, before you came into my life, I'd have
said it was an impossible circumstance, one of which I
wanted no part."

She grasped his hand in hers, brought them to her lips,
and kissed his fingertips. "And now?"

"I want you. Therefore, I must desire how you make
me feel. But with such feelings comes vulnerability. I *cannot*
afford to be vulnerable."

"Perhaps," she murmured, finding boldness again as she
stroked a hand down his taut stomach, "what you cannot
afford, what will make you less than human, is to *never* be
vulnerable. Be human with me for this small moment in
time. I tried to need no one, too, and I've decided it's no
way to live."

"I think you may be right," he said, lowering his head
and brushing his lips against hers. She thought he might
claim her mouth in another of his wondrous kisses, but he
moved lower, deftly sliding one hand behind her back,
lifting her slightly, and loosening her gown as his other hand
trailed over one breast and then the other.

Her breasts grew heavy with aching need as he teased
her. "Curse this gown!" she blurted and pushed against his
chest until he rolled to her side with a chuckle. She
scampered off the bed and yanked out of her gown and
unmentionables until they were naught but a crumpled pile
on the floor. The cool air hit her hot flesh like a blast of
wind and made her suddenly very aware that she stood
naked before a man for the first time, and he was *not* her

husband. She braced for the shame to singe her, yet it didn't come. She loved this particular man. Her mouth parted with the knowledge that poured through her veins, made her heart pump faster, and swirled the thoughts in her head.

He smiled wickedly. "I never thought I'd say this, but I do believe I adore an impatient woman."

She cocked her eyebrows. "*Any* impatient woman?"

He was off the bed and standing in front of her before she could comprehend that he was moving. "Only you." He brushed a hand along her neck, gooseflesh rising in the wake of his touch. He offered her a grin of clear amusement. "But now I will show you how being patient will bring you great pleasure."

"All right," she whispered, heat pooling in her belly.

"For instance, if I were not a patient man I would not do this…" Justin cupped her breasts and then flicked his tongue teasingly over the tips of each hard bud.

She could not contain her exclamation of delight. His gaze flew upward and locked with hers, and he offered a smile that promised more sinful lessons.

"If I were the impatient sort, I'd only think on the fact that I long to plunge myself deep within you, and I'd forget what a sweetly excruciating ache doing this can bring."

His strong arms wrapped around her waist, and his hands splayed across her back and pushed her toward him once more until he took her right breast into his mouth. His hot lips suckled her breast, and then he teased her bud. She was certain she would collapse from desire. Her legs and arms shook with such force that she had to cling to him.

He straightened slowly to tower over her. When he looked down at her, her heart fluttered wildly at the tenderness in his gaze. "A hurried man would not take the time to simply drink in the beauty of the strongest, most compassionate woman he'd ever met."

Her skin prickled with pleasure at his words. "Thank

you," she said.

"No," he replied in a velvet voice, "thank you for trusting me." He traced a path down her waist with one hand while his other unbuttoned his breeches. When they fell to the floor to reveal that he wore nothing underneath, she marveled at the strange beauty of his body that sprang forward, long and hard.

She started to move her hand to reach for him, but he shook his head. "Not yet," he choked out. "I desperately want your touch, but even I'm not patient enough to slow myself once you do that. Let me bring you pleasure first, and then we will find it together."

She opened her mouth to offer her agreement, but when his fingers softly plunged into the hair between her thighs and expertly found the nub pulsing there, she could not speak. All she could do was gasp as he rubbed across the nub with slow, gentle circles. Her thoughts spun away from her as his circles became faster, harder, and pinpointed the exact spot that made her scream. She could not hold it back. He captured her mouth with a kiss as his fingers moved deftly until the blood raged through her veins, and her belly cramped as, deep inside, her body clenched and then unclenched on wave after delicious wave of pleasure.

"I cannot stand any more," she said through her pants and the thundering of her heart.

He swooped her into his arms and laid her down. The bed moaned with his weight, as he loomed above her. She struggled to bring her heartbeat back under control. It was hopeless. He gently nudged her legs apart with his knee, and when he was hovering between her thighs, his hands slid under her, grasped her buttocks in a firm grip, and lifted her hips high in the air.

"Now," he said through clenched teeth that indicated how the wait was costing him physically, "we shall see the fruits of patience together."

Her heart leaped as he thrust deep within her. There was a momentary pinch, followed by the feeling that he filled her unbearably. Yet swiftly upon those feelings, his heat enveloped her. She grasped onto his back as he moved in slow, careful strokes.

"Are you all right?" he asked in a gentle voice, his gaze holding hers.

All right could not possibly describe it. She wanted to explain, but she was afraid she'd blubber on about how incredible he felt. She nodded. "Perfect."

He leaned down as he glided in and out and brushed his lips to hers. "You've entranced me," he whispered, his hot breath fanning her face.

"Likewise," she replied, unable to say more when the turbulence of passion captured her once again.

He must have sensed her growing need because his long strokes became faster and harder until her body vibrated like liquid fire.

"Arabella," he rasped.

She focused on his face. It was lined with tension and desire. Perspiration covered his brow, his straining arms, and his chest.

"No more patience," she demanded.

She could see the relief dance across his face as he gathered her toward him and plunged even deeper within her, carrying her with him over some edge of bliss she never cared to return from. They cried out together, her body tensing at the same moment as his. He pulled out quickly with a shudder, and collapsed onto the bed beside her. Their mingled panting filled the silent room, and now, bereft of the heat he had offered when he covered her with his body, she shivered. Putting his large hand around her waist, he drew her to him, then glided his hand under her back. She turned into his chest and nestled her head into the space between his shoulder and chin. It was a perfect fit.

He traced his fingers softly through her hair. "I've never done this."

"Oh, please," she managed. "I *know* you have."

He chuckled, and she could hear the merry rumble deep within his chest. "No," he replied. "I've never held a woman in my arms after bedding her."

She held her breath, praying he would continue.

He glided his hand over her head as he spoke. "I never wanted to. But with you…" His hand stilled and he hooked a finger under her chin until their gazes met. "With you I find I want to very much. And not just this once. I want…" His brow furrowed. "I want…"

"What do you want?" She couldn't contain the question.

"*You.* And it scares me. I can only be so open. Do you think you can accept that?"

Tears burned her eyes as she pressed her lips to his. "Yes." She could accept that, because if he was willing to be vulnerable with her at all, she was sure the rest would come.

He cupped her face and gave her a long, sweet kiss. When he drew away, he said, "I don't want to move, but we must. We need to make a plan, and I still need to complete my mission, if nothing else."

She wasn't sure what *if nothing else* meant, but now was not the time to ask, for she was certain the answer was not simple. And she had to go home. Jude was watching and waiting, and her father needed her. She followed Justin's lead and scooted off the bed and hurriedly dressed. They moved in silence, and it struck her with both happiness and fear how natural it felt to be with him.

He came behind her as she struggled with the buttons of her gown. "Let me," he offered in a gentle voice.

She nodded, lifted her hair, and waited. After he finished, he pressed a kiss to her neck. "Let us go."

She whirled toward him. "Us?"

He nodded, a dark expression crossing his face. "Did you think I'd let you go alone?"

Her stomach clenched. "But you must! Jude has someone watching my house, and they'll kill my father if you come back with me."

"Arabella," he said in a tone she recognized as soothing, "*trust me.* I can handle Jude and anyone else who means to harm you. You are safe with me."

Safe. Yes, she believed it with all her heart, which was why she had come here in the first place. That and the little fact that she had fallen in love with him. She wanted to tell him, but she feared it would send him running in the opposite direction.

"What is your plan?" she asked instead.

He motioned for her to follow him as he strode toward the door. "Well," he started as he opened the door, but she didn't hear whatever else he was going to say because she screamed. A tall blond man with narrowed green eyes and a two-inch white scar down his right cheek stood there with a pistol aimed at them.

He gave a swift mock bow. "A pleasure."

Twelve

J ustin scowled at Davenport for scaring Arabella so much. "Does no one bloody knock anymore?" he demanded as he grabbed Arabella's hand. "This is my friend, the Marquess of Davenport," he said to Arabella as he shoved past Davenport.

"I did bloody well knock," Davenport thundered. "No one answered your door."

Damned stubborn Mumford. Justin had told him to make himself scarce until he called for him, and the damnable man had done exactly that.

"Naturally," Davenport said, his footsteps close behind, "I became worried since you *did* respond to my note that you'd be here."

"As you can see," Justin growled, stopping at the bottom of the long stairwell to give Arabella a moment to catch her breath, "I'm here, and I'm not in danger from Miss Carthright."

Davenport's eyes narrowed further, and his mouth pressed into a thin line. "So you say."

Justin frowned. What the hell was wrong with Davenport? He knew who Arabella was because Justin had told him. "She's as trustworthy as *your* wife," Justin growled.

Arabella's fingers tightened around his hand as she faced Davenport. "I swear your secrets are safe with me."

Davenport's mouth fell open. Then his face turned red as he glared at Justin. "Did you tell her—"

"No," Justin clipped before his friend foolishly revealed

his own past, which Justin knew he did not want known.

Davenport's jaw visibly clenched. "Might I speak with you alone, Dinnisfree?"

"No," Justin said, making to start toward the door, but Davenport grabbed him by the arm. Justin jerked around, swinging Arabella with him. He glanced at his friend's hand, then up at Davenport, who ought to know better than to grab him. "Let me go. You can tell me what you know on the way to Miss Carthright's."

Davenport shook his head. "I need to speak to you *alone.*"

Justin sighed. He understood Davenport's reluctance to talk around Arabella, but it irked him. "We will be alone."

"You will?" Arabella asked in surprise.

"Yes." He encircled her in his arms and pressed a kiss to her forehead, well aware that his friend was gawking at him once again. "We'll follow on foot well behind you, so whoever is watching your home does not see us."

"Yes, that makes perfect sense," she replied. "But what is your plan after you follow me home?"

"Once you are safely inside, Davenport here will ferret out who is watching you." He glanced at his friend, who gave a reluctant, rather skeptical-looking inclination of his head.

"I'll do whatever must be done to protect you, *Dinnisfree,*" Davenport replied. "You know that."

Justin didn't miss the stress on his name, nor the fact that his friend had left out that he'd protect Arabella. He'd have to assuage Davenport's mistrust when they were alone.

"After Davenport has captured the man, I'll wait for Jude to show his face, and then I'll apprehend him. From there," he said grimly, "one way or another the man will tell me everything he knows."

She nodded. "What will you do with Jude after you capture him?"

That was an excellent question. If he was not truly Canning's son, he would ensure Jude took a long, one-way trip to a remote country with no hope of ever returning. It was a different, more delicate matter if Canning was indeed his father, as Arabella thought, and even more delicate if Canning was involved in a plot to obtain the king's letters. Those damnable letters! He had to find those blasted things.

Putting Arabella first was blatantly compromising his mission, but he could not make himself turn away as he should. Still, it did not mean the mission did not have to be completed. He turned Arabella to face him. "You need to go first. If someone is shadowing you, they'll likely follow. Davenport and I will depart out the back, but don't worry. I will be behind you protecting you. You just won't see me."

"Of course you will," she said matter-of-factly. "I have no doubt."

His chest squeezed with her words. In the three short days since meeting Arabella, he'd done the two things he'd always sworn he'd never do: compromise his mission and give his heart to a woman. He allowed the truth to sink in and then shoved it out of the way when it did. He'd deal with the ramifications later and assess how to handle the situation. Right now, he needed the necessary cold calculation to rise up and consume him. He kissed her on the mouth and watched as she opened the door and stepped out into the twilight.

"Let's go," he said without turning to Davenport. Justin took off toward the back of the townhome, slipped out the gate, and then rounded to the opposite side of the street. He darted into the shadows, aware that Davenport was behind him from the man's heat and nothing else. His friend was still very good at being quiet. Justin's breath didn't release until they were on the sidewalk and he spotted Arabella ahead.

"Any motion?" he asked in very low tones as he scanned the perimeter.

"Nothing. Whoever is trailing her is very good or *not* trailing her because she is *lying to you.*"

If Justin had a moment to spare, he would have stopped and punched Davenport in the face, but he could not take his attention from Arabella. Instead, he clenched his fists. "She's not. She's innocent." And before Davenport could argue, Justin told him everything Arabella had revealed as quickly as he could.

"That's an excellent story," Davenport responded in a whisper when Justin fell silent, "but now you must listen to me. Let me tell you what I have discovered."

Justin nodded as he walked and watched. There was no point arguing. Davenport would not be quiet until he'd said what he wanted.

"I followed Canning as we agreed and he went to the Garden District to see the man you said is threatening Miss Carthright. I overheard a woman, a fiery redhead—"

"I believe you are talking about Miss Mary Morgan."

Davenport nodded. "Miss Morgan knocked on the door after Canning went in, and demanded in a loud voice that Jude let her in. He told her *no* in very clear terms. She started screaming that Jude was in cahoots with Miss Carthright and that he had forgotten about her."

"No," Justin denied, though a spurt of anger surged through him. "Miss Morgan is mistaken."

"You cannot be sure," Davenport growled.

Justin paused for the space of one inhalation. "I *can* be," he replied, refusing to say more. He would not discuss the fact that he'd bedded Arabella and she had most definitely been an innocent. He picked up his pace once again.

"You bedded her," Davenport said in a voice of utter astonishment.

Justin refused to acknowledge his friend's words.

"Jesus Christ, Dinnisfree. What happened to never getting involved with people who can blur your mind? Compromise the mission? People you don't know."

"I know her," he ground out.

"I don't think you do. I think she may be the cleverest opponent you've ever come up against and you don't even realize it."

Justin clenched his jaw, then counted to ten in French, Japanese, and Italian. Still, he wanted to pummel Davenport in the face. "Just spit out what it is you have learned. The facts only."

"All right," Davenport growled on a huff. "Miss Mary Morgan, the irate redheaded demirep, was quite chatty in her anger. I pretended to be an interested client who knew the man she is in love with, J.I. Devine, also known as Jude, also known as Phineas Darlington to those who truly know him, according to her."

As they turned the corner and Arabella's house came into sight, Justin frowned. Darlington? Why did that name ring a bell?

"Because you do know it," Davenport drawled, answering the question Justin had not uttered aloud. The man had always had that uncanny ability.

"How do I know it?" Justin asked, crouching behind a tree. He brushed a branch out of his face and inhaled the smell of dirt and pine.

Davenport kneeled beside him. "You know it because I mentioned the name to you a few years ago. I recall the conversation because it was the only time I've ever withheld information from you."

Justin snapped his gaze to Davenport. "Remind me."

"We had just finished a mission, and when I told you I was going on another one, you assumed it was for the king, but it wasn't. I never corrected you because I'd promised to tell no one. When I returned, you asked me if I had found my quarry, and I told you I had located the hidden Phineas Darlington. I don't know why I mentioned his name. Guilt, I suppose. You made a remark that it was an odd name and the subject was dropped."

"You've now broken your promise," Justin snapped, angry that the one person he'd thought had always been truthful with him had not.

"I suppose so. Let me finish."

Justin nodded.

"The queen, having no one to turn to, approached me after she and I had an innocent conversation at a ball one night and I'd expressed sympathies about her plight with the king."

Justin stared into the black night. "You did what? Before you'd ever retired from service?"

"Prinny had made me very angry, and I'd imbibed too much that night. Very foolish, but it has turned out to be the best mistake I ever made."

Justin scowled. "I'll judge for myself, thanks."

"As would I, Dinnisfree. The queen came to see me a few days later and asked me to help her. She wanted to find out the location of two children, a boy and a girl, *twins* born at the same time but who did not look alike. She said it was for one of her ladies-in-waiting who'd had the children out of wedlock, given them up without knowing where they had been placed, and was now racked with horrible guilt and wanted to know simply if the children were faring well. I suspected by the guilt swimming in the queen's eyes and lacing her tone that the children were *hers*. And when I started digging, the trail led me to Canning. He had been the one to take the children from Paris, where they were born, and bring them back here. One child was raised by a madam in a brothel house. I'm sure you can guess which one."

Justin's boot snapped a twig under his foot as his mind snapped the facts into place. He didn't want to speak the words. Everything Davenport said was leading to something terrible. He knew it in his gut. "Madame Sullyard."

"Yes. The other child, the girl, I could never locate. What I learned back then was that Canning had given the girl *and* boy to Madame Sullyard, and he'd instructed her to only keep the boy. She was to find a new home for the girl. One he didn't ever want to know." Davenport cursed under his breath. "I never imagined—"

"Finish," Justin said woodenly.

"My theory is that Canning didn't want the children or anyone else to ever find out that the twins were born to the queen. I think he thought to protect the queen from her own guilt, as well as what that blame might one day cause her to do, such as seek out her children."

"What happened to the girl babe?" Justin asked, knowing damn well if Davenport did not now know, they'd not be having this conversation.

Davenport gripped Justin by the arm. "I swear, had I known before—"

Justin jerked his arm away. "Just continue."

"Madame Sullyard told me years earlier that she gave the baby to a man who was traveling through and said he could sell the child for a great amount of money that he'd split with her. I stupidly accepted it as fact because it seemed something the woman would do. I even told Canning that is what happened. But yesterday, as Miss Morgan was screaming about Jude, J.I., Darlington, whoever, not loving her anymore, she said something that made me realize my mistake. She said he was sick in the head and sinful because he loved a woman who looked like his sister. She didn't know, of course, of his twin who had died."

It was as if Davenport's words physically knocked over a domino in Justin's head. Suspicions tilted one by one onto one another until a pile of doubts formed a crystallized question. "You said you discovered hours ago exactly what happened to the baby girl?"

"Yes. Let's say I persuaded Madame Sullyard with an exorbitant amount of money to try to recall the name of the man to whom she gave the babe so long ago. It seems she, in fact, gave the child to a woman, not a man. A seamstress she had grown to know, who at first had sewn gowns for an Italian actress who lived across from Madame Sullyard, had offered to sew gowns for Madame Sullyard when no other seamstress would. The woman had one child, a boy, but could have no more. The woman's name is—"

Justin squeezed his eyes shut. "Mrs. Carthright."

"That's right," Davenport confirmed. "Her full name is Mrs. Ophelia Carthright, and her daughter is Arabella. The only other person Madame Sullyard has ever told was Darlington, who she complained has renounced her. As far as I can tell, Madame Sullyard has no clue that she raised one of the queen's bastards and gave the other away."

"Jude, J.I., Phineas." Justin forced his eyes open and dug his hands deep into the dirt on either side of him. He needed to grip onto the earth because he felt he was floating in a nightmare. "Do you think she knows who she is?" he asked without looking at Davenport.

"I think there is a great chance she does. On the one hand, she could be an accomplice to get those letters to protect the queen and everything she's told you is a lie or a partial truth. On the other hand, she could be clueless and being used by Canning and his son, as she claims."

"We shall see," Justin replied, slapping down every feeling save the calm that tried to emerge.

He settled his gaze back on the house. Was Arabella a liar or an innocent? His head told him *liar*, but his heart said *innocent*. He wanted to smack his skull against a tree to quiet the roar of doubt. His control slipped, and raw emotion flooded him. He felt like a crazed person. This...this feeling of being ripped apart from the inside out was exactly what he'd experienced when his mother had left. How had he gotten here again? How the hell did he return to the numbness he'd dwelled in for so long?

"Dinnisfree," Davenport hissed. "We have movement on the left and the right. I'm going left."

Justin nodded and took off toward the right.

Thirteen

$\mathcal{A}$rabella sat in the chair beside her father and stared out the window into the dark night, watching for any sign of movement. The house was silent except for Alice's rattling snore. Arabella had not had the heart to wake her father's caretaker and tell her she could go home. Even in sleep, Alice's exhaustion had been obvious. There were dark smudges under her eyes, and the woman had not so much as twitched when Arabella had come into the room. So she'd covered her with a blanket and left her in the chair where she slumbered. It was likely best she was here. If Arabella had to go anywhere with Justin, she would be free to do so without worrying about her father.

"Arabella."

Arabella jerked toward her father and smiled in relief. "Papa!" she cried out and leaned over to give him a hug. "Oh, Papa! Nothing has ever sounded so good as to hear my name on your lips once again."

He chuckled and patted her on the head as he used to do when she was a child. "Bella."

The moniker was thick and halting, but she'd take it. The physician had said his speech would improve with practice, and Arabella intended to make him practice a great deal once he felt a bit better.

She sat up and grasped her father's hands, tremendously glad he was finally completely alert. She needed to speak to him. She needed her father's council more than ever. Ever since she was a child, whenever she'd had a problem, she would seek out her father's advice. Daniel had been her mother's favorite. It had been no secret, and Arabella understood why. Daniel was her true son, and though her mother had told her many times and in many ways how glad she was that Arabella had been given to them, it was Daniel her mother had always had a special smile for.

Arabella shook the useless thoughts away and squeezed her father's hands. "Let me get you some water and broth. I'm sure you must be famished."

He nodded, even as his brow creased. "N-n-need to t-tell you something."

"Yes, yes," she said, standing and moving toward the water pitcher. "First things first, though. I need to tell you some things, as well."

"Bella," her father rasped behind her.

She whirled around with a full glass of water and scowled at him. "Papa. Your voice sounds like sandpaper on wood. Let me give you some cooling water and healing broth, and *then* we shall talk."

He shook his head. "N-n-no." His face was mottled red, and he slapped the covers with his palm. Arabella flinched. Her father never showed anger.

She rushed toward him and sat on the bed beside him. "What's wrong?"

"L-leeshan—" He growled when he could not get the word out correctly.

Arabella bit her lip. "Would you like some paper?" Ordinarily she would have made him talk to practice, but he seemed so distraught and impatient.

He nodded, and she quickly retrieved some parchment and a quill pen and handed it to him, along with a book to lean on to make the writing easier.

He hunched over the paper and scribbled furiously.

Get my blue coat out of the wardrobe and bring it to me.

She started to ask why, but he waved an impatient hand at her, so she rose, went to the wardrobe, and retrieved the coat he'd worn the night he'd had his brain attack. Whyever he wanted the coat at this moment, she couldn't imagine. "Here you are," she said, handing it to him.

He fairly snatched it out of her hands, fumbled around in an inside pocket, and pulled out what appeared to be a bundle of—Arabella's breath caught in her chest. Dear God, those were *letters*. Or they certainly appeared to be. It could not, *could not* be mere coincidence. "Papa?"

He glanced up at her, and his eyes widened. Her shock must have been written on her face. He clutched the letters to him as he scribbled.

You're a pawn. Dangerous political game. I need to protect you and your mother.

He knew something. Her mind could not form more than that thought. As he continued to scribble, she read:

Brougham came to see me the day you were at Lady Conyngham's. He had spies in the lady's house, the butler. He was supposed to secure the lady's box, but you stole it before he could. Why?

"Oh, Papa!" Tears filled her eyes. "I was desperate. She refused to purchase any of the gowns I had made her, and she promised to have me dismissed from Madame Chauvin's. We needed money."

He sighed wearily and started writing again.

Thought that might be why. Assumed you stole it thinking you could sell the box, not knowing what it contained.

"How are you involved in this?"

I threatened to shoot him if he stayed and tried to get the box from you. Didn't want you to know. Didn't want you involved. He vowed to have your mother taken to Bedlam where he would ensure she was never released unless I retrieved the letters immediately and brought them to him. He has the power to do it, too. Claimed he wanted only to help the queen, but I know him. He is a liar. I took the letters to Howick to reveal to him what Brougham was trying to do, but Brougham was already at Howick's when I arrived the night of the card game. Demanded the letters. I lied and told him I had not brought them, and he became enraged. I had the attack when we started to argue.

He thrust the letters at her. "Take *theeeese*," he ground out.

Her pulse thumped in dread as she clutched the letters. "What would you have me do with them?"

"Go to Howick. Protect your m-m-mother. And help the queen."

A hard knot formed in the pit of her stomach. If she did as he asked, she'd be betraying Justin. Yet if she gave the letters to Justin, did he have the power to stop Brougham from locking her mother in Bedlam forever? He did own the home now, but did that mean he could stop Brougham from taking her mother? He was the king's man. To help her would be to betray his vow. She brought her fist to her mouth to stifle her cry.

"B-Bella?" her father choked out.

"Papa. Oh, Papa. I've something I must tell you!" And there wasn't much time to do so. She quickly explained about Justin, who he was, what he had done for Mother, Daniel, and her father by sending his physician. "If I take these letters to Howick, I will betray Justin, but if I don't…"

Her father gripped her hand. "Trust *inshtincts.*"

The word was slurred, but she understood what he'd said. Trust her instincts.

She nodded and stood. "I'll be back, Papa. Justin is outside, and I know he won't let us down."

Justin raced back toward Arabella's street, cursing as he ran. To have allowed himself to be drawn away from her home was an amateur mistake. For a moment, he reconsidered not having pummeled the young lad he'd finally caught up to, who'd been paid by a stranger to creep around Arabella's house. He redirected his anger toward images of throttling Arabella's twin brother, Darlington. He had no doubt the man was the stranger who'd paid the boy. He fought the fear that was gnawing at him, causing him physical pain. Did Arabella truly have something to do with all this? As he ran, he searched the darkness for Davenport but saw no sign of him.

Arabella clutched her father's pistol in her trembling hand as she picked her way through the darkness.

"Justin," she hissed, trying to keep her voice low. "Justin!"

She circled the front of the house, whispering his name to no avail. Where was he?

"Justin!" she called again, louder this time. Had he abandoned her? No. He wouldn't. She could rely on him, couldn't she? "Justin!"

"Here!"

She cried out in relief and raced toward his voice. Out of the darkness, he reached for her and pulled her violently to him. Her father's pistol dropped to the ground between them.

"Justin?" The moonless night made it impossible to see his face.

A hand came around her neck and gripped hard. "No, sister dear. It's Jude. I've come to bring you home."

Pure terror drove her to react. She thrust her palm upward, and it connected with his face with a *thunk*. A lip? Maybe a nose? She crouched to search for the pistol, her heart hammering as she patted frantically at the fog-dampened grass. The air swished above her as Jude came down beside her with a grunt. Her fingers brushed the slick, cold barrel of the pistol, and with a cry of relief, she gripped it. A tug of resistance came immediately.

"Let go," Jude growled.

She grasped the barrel tighter. Jude was mad. His words proved it. He'd called her his sister, which was deranged!

She jerked upward on the pistol with a scream that momentarily pierced her ears, only to be drowned out by a deafening shot.

The force of the bullet entering her shoulder threw her backward against a tree. Her head hit the wood with a crack, and the black night filled with bright specks of light as hot, searing pain engulfed her right arm. She tried to suck in, air but coughed as pistol smoke filled her nose. Jude jerked her to her feet, and a wave of pain washed over her as the shining flecks dulled and all went black.

Fourteen

$\mathcal{J}$ustin's chest constricted when Arabella's piercing scream filled the night. Before he could recover his composure, the sound of a pistol exploding sent him racing forward into the darkness. Branches snagged his shirt and grazed across his face, leaving stinging marks as he ran. Curse the damnable clouds, fog, and pitch-black night.

A horse's loud whinny gave him just enough notice to lurch out of the way. He jumped to the right as the wind, moving with the horse's speed, whispered across his cheek, and he stared in shock into the dark night, into which the creature must have disappeared.

"Arabella?" he thundered.

Deafening silence answered him. He didn't waste a second wondering what had happened. He knew two things with sickening certainty: she'd been taken against her will, and he'd promised to protect her and failed. His heart squeezed within his chest. Damn the mission and damn the king. Arabella came first.

He tore through the dark toward her father's home and didn't stop to knock. He slammed through the door and stopped cold. Her father sat in a wheelchair with a pale-faced woman standing behind him, clutching his shoulder. The man had a pistol aimed at him.

Justin lowered his own pistol and held up his hand to show he meant the man no harm. "Please, is there anything I need to know? I mean to go after your daughter and save her."

The man's shoulders slumped as his pistol lowered. "Bedroom," he croaked. "Pa-apers," he struggled to get out.

Justin stormed toward the room Arabella's father had pointed at and glanced around quickly. On the bed lay a pile of papers. He snatched them up and read them one by one as he walked back out into the hall.

Carthright motioned him close. Justin walked over and bent down when he realized the man was going to speak. Arabella's father grasped Justin's shoulder. "She t-trusts you. Picked you."

Justin nodded as his pulse ticked a furious beat. Emotions roiled inside him, but he beat them back with an iron will. He had no time to feel anything. Allowing himself to soften might very well cost Arabella her life, if it had not already. His gut clenched at the possibility. "I'll bring her back to you," he promised, praying it was one he could fulfill.

As he was walking out the front door, Davenport appeared with Miss Morgan in tow. Fresh claw marks ran down the right side of Davenport's face. He slapped a palm over the bellowing woman's mouth and regarded Justin with an irritated gaze. He jerked his head toward the woman. "Miss Morgan tried to kill me, but luckily I prevailed."

"Does she have a horse?" Justin demanded, ignoring the woman glaring at him.

Davenport furrowed his brow. "What the devil sort of response is that?" He glanced warily over Justin's shoulder toward the foyer of Arabella's home. "Where is—"

"Taken," Justin snapped. "And I tell you she knows nothing," he thundered.

Davenport wisely nodded in agreement, then twitched his head toward Miss Morgan again. "She has a curricle parked up the street."

"Excellent." Justin brushed by Davenport.

"Where are you going?" his friend called after him.

"To Darlington's house. My gut says he's headed there."

Davenport, dragging Miss Morgan behind him, fell into step with Justin. "I'm coming with you."

Justin refused to feel gratitude. He refused to feel at all. Feeling *hurt*. He wanted numbness. He wanted logic. He wanted to return Arabella to her father and mother alive. They needed her. He did not need her. He *could not* need her. It had been foolish to even let the notion enter his head.

⚜

"Bella."

Arabella swatted a hand at her ear. Why was her father bothering her? She was so tired.

"Bella, this won't hurt. I've made sure of that. I'm *so* sorry. I didn't mean to shoot you."

Her eyes popped open at that. Jude's face was so close to her that she yelped and flinched. She cried out again while reaching for her arm, except it seemed she was moving in very slow motion.

Jude's hand flashed out and stopped her movement in midair. "You mustn't touch the wound, lest you infect it, sister dear."

"I'm not your sister," she spat. Or tried to. Her tongue felt too thick for her mouth.

He gave her a pitying look that filled her with dull fear. Arabella tried to shrink back, but he still gripped her hand.

"You are my sister." His tone was insistent. Menacing.

He quirked his mouth in a manner so similar to something she would do that doubt pierced her heart. She squeezed her eyes shut for a split second. She didn't believe this. It was madness. She opened her eyes and shook her head. "No," she insisted again, shoving the uncertainty away.

A hard smile settled on his face. "The witch will tell you. She knows the truth, as do I. Though the slut didn't even know what she knew." His grip tightened a fraction more, making her wrist throb. "I had to put it together for her." He released her and knotted his hand in his hair.

Arabella gulped in a breath. She had to make him see reason. "Jude—"

He slapped his palm over her mouth. "Stop it! Stop denying me. You're making me very angry, Arabella."

She bit the inside of her cheek on the desire to cry and nodded instead.

His sweaty palm slid away and she gulped in a breath. "The witch took you as a babe from Canning and believed you were the by-blow of a lady-in-waiting to the queen. I had to tell her when Canning came to see me. I knew I was too good to be the witch's true son, and my gut told me my sister was not dead. You were not dead."

"Jude, this is madness!"

She never saw the slap coming. His hand connected with her face and sent her head sideways. Her skin instantly burned and tiny sparks of pain vibrated across her cheek and down her neck. He jerked her head to face him. "You are my blood."

"I'm not," she spat. At that moment, she didn't give a damn if he slapped her again. She was furious. "My mother found me in the street and rescued me."

Jude raised a sharp knife and wiped it on a rag until it gleamed. He glared down at her. "Lies. She told you lies. The witch gave you to the woman you call Mother." He pointed the knife at her, the tip almost grazing her nose. "Do you understand?"

Fear and a hefty dose of self-preservation doused her anger. The notion that what he said might be true made her stomach roil and her fuzzy thoughts tilt in her head. "Who are your parents?" The words took effort to form. She frowned at how she was feeling. Was it blood loss? She tilted her head to the right to glance at her arm and grimaced at the blood covering it.

Jude's finger came under her chin, and he drew her gaze back to his. "*Our* parents are George Canning and the queen. Now, I'll tell you all later. I've not spent the last two years of my life discovering who you are and plotting to bring you back to me only to have you die."

Could what he said be true? The question echoed in her mind, but she could not truly wrap her thoughts around it. It was as if her ability to think clearly had been broken.

"We are meant to be a family," Jude said. "I've sent word to Father to come immediately and bring Mother with him. So what I'm going to do now is make sure you stay alive."

He started toward her with the knife. She tried to roll away, but her body would not cooperate. Jude simply put out a hand and stilled her. "Don't be stupid. I won't hurt you. I love you, and I want to help you. Hold still."

He wanted to help her as long as she agreed with everything he said. Yet, at this moment, she needed his help. She did not feel right. All she could do now was play along. She nodded, her head heavy and her heart beating in her throat. "Where am I?" she asked, the painted ceiling above blurry.

"At our house," he replied, as if it were the most reasonable thing in the world to say.

"In the Garden District?" she asked, feeling hopeful but trying to recall why.

"Of course." Jude leaned over her arm and brought a rag up to wipe it.

She clenched her teeth against the expected pain, but she could not even feel his touch on her arm. Fear gripped her. Was she dying, then? Would she lose her arm?

Jude tossed the rag behind him. "We'll move, certainly, now that you are joining me, and after Father and Mother acknowledge to both of us that we are their children. The son and daughter of a powerful man and the Queen of England certainly can't live across from a brothel."

Her mind tried to sort through what Jude was saying, but she felt funny, dizzy, her head swimming. "I feel strange," she said, her words sounding slurred to her own ears.

When he nodded, it was as if there were two of him. "I gave you a hefty dose of laudanum so you'd not feel the pain when I cut out the bullet."

"Ohhhh," she said, thinking she should feel scared, but her body was floating. She laughed as her eyes fluttered shut.

"Untie me, Phineas!"

Arabella understood every word being screamed near her. The command had been repeated several times, and though she tried to ignore it, she could not anymore. She wanted to drift in the warm darkness, but someone was ruining her peace. She struggled to open her eyes for several moments, and when she did, she was looking at a painting of fairies done in pale blues, yellows, and lavenders. She squinted, trying to recall what had happened, and slowly turned her head to the right. Tied to a chair, facing her, was Mr. Canning—the president of the Board of Trade and, she was positive, Jude's father. Her heart lurched. Was he her father, too?

No. She gritted her teeth. She had a father.

"I have a father," she croaked.

Canning gawked at her, and Jude stepped into her line of vision to block Canning momentarily. "You do," Jude said, "and he is sitting there tied up because he refuses to acknowledge you, and he came without Mother. She may be the queen, but she is our mother," he roared. "We deserve her attention!"

"Jesus Christ, Phineas."

"Jesus Christ, Phineas," Jude mimicked. He held out a hand to Arabella, his demeanor changing in a flash. "Can you sit up?"

She nodded, her thoughts finally becoming clearer. She had to get out of here. Jude was beyond reason. She took Jude's hand with her good one. Her other arm throbbed dully. The pain, she suspected, was still lessened by the laudanum. At this moment, she was grateful for that. The room spun a little as she sat up, and once it quit moving she started to stand.

Jude placed a staying hand on her shoulder. "Stay seated," he commanded, waving a bloodied knife in the air.

With *her* dried blood on it, she realized.

He sat beside her on the edge of the table and threw his arm over her shoulder. "I shall let you decide what you want to do, Arabella," Jude said, gazing at her.

Fear curled in her belly. "About what?"

He frowned. "Our father, of course. I've done everything he asked and more. And all I demand in return is that he acknowledge you, my sister, as he acknowledged me. Though, he still needs to claim me as his son to the world. It's only fair."

Canning groaned and lowered his head. "Phineas," he murmured, his words muffled from the angle. "I should have never made contact with you. I was weak. I wanted to know you."

Dear God! Arabella shivered. Was Canning going along with Jude, too, or was he admitting there was truth to Jude's story?

"Don't say that, damn you," Jude cried and jumped up. "I'm glad you did, but you must accept Arabella, too. You and Mother abandoned her, too. I won't abandon her as you did."

Canning raised his head, his face a mask of twisted pain. "No. I see that. But you used her. Even when I told you not to do so. Even when I demanded you stop your plan."

"She had to prove she was cunning and loyal to me," Jude snarled, "so I could know she'd chosen me as I did her. You wanted the letters. Well, here they are."

Panic prickled across Arabella's skin. She'd forgotten about the letters. She had to get them back somehow.

"You've made a mess," Canning whispered. "I've made a mess."

Arabella shook as she stood, her legs weak from the blood loss. She judged the distance to the door. Ten paces. Jude was at least twenty paces away. She wasn't sure she could even make it, and she certainly couldn't flee without the letters, nor could she abandon Canning to Jude's mercy. She didn't think there'd be much of that.

No, she couldn't leave him, even if the man had left her, she thought sourly. She shoved her anger away. She *had* parents, and she was blessed that they had been given to her.

Jude reached behind his back and withdrew a pistol. Arabella cursed. It was her father's. He raised it and pointed it at Canning. "Either admit Arabella is your daughter so she can know the truth, or I'll shoot you. I'd rather go back to having no father than a coward for one."

Arabella's gaze was drawn immediately to the man. His gaze locked with hers. "I am your father." His words were laced with misery, regret, sorrow.

Arabella gasped as she moved toward him, unable to stop herself. Was he truly her father? Or was he simply trying to appease Jude? She stopped beside him. His eyes seemed to be pleading. "I cannot claim you, don't you see? There is more at stake than my desires. There always was, except for the moment I let my desire get away from me, when Caroline and I conceived the two of you. She is the queen. To lose her throne would be devastating."

"But to lose her children was not. We were expendable to keep her throne," Arabella said. Sadness filled her for this man and the queen, followed by an overwhelming sense of gratitude that she'd been loved so much by her parents. "My mother lost her eldest son, and it almost killed her. She would have given up a thousand thrones to have him back."

"This is wonderful!" Jude exclaimed. "We're all talking and working things out as a family should. We will go together to meet our mother face-to-face since she couldn't be bothered to come here, and we'll give her the king's naughty letters."

Arabella exchanged a long look of mutual understanding with Canning. They had to stop Jude from trying to see the queen, and Arabella had to somehow get those letters. She kneeled by Canning, but the motion made her woozy. She set her palms to the ground to steady herself and cringed at the pain that danced up her throbbing right arm. "The room is hot," she muttered, swiping thick perspiration off her brow.

"You're flushed," Canning replied. "Jude, you must let me fetch a physician for Arabella. Fever is setting in."

Arabella suspected Canning was right. She was hot, but as she struggled to untie the rope around his wrists, she suddenly felt cold and nauseated. She got the last knot undone and went to stand, but the room tilted and her knees buckled. Canning caught her with a grunt and steadied her. Jude rushed toward them with an expression of panic.

"Arabella!" he cried, his gaze focused on her.

Now was her chance. Possibly her only one. She gave Canning a sidelong look that she hoped he understood. When Jude put his arms around her to hug her, she grasped the letters and Canning lunged at the pistol, but Jude easily shoved the older man away. Canning scrambled near her, panting.

Jude faced them, his face a portrait of wild fury. He

swung the pistol toward Canning. "Betrayed again," he bellowed.

Arabella tensed, sure he was going to shoot Canning when Jude altered his aim in a flash and pointed the weapon at her chest. "I loved you," he cried out in anguish. "Everything I've done was for you. All I wanted in return is for you to love me as your brother! You're supposed to love me now that I've finally revealed all to you! You were supposed to be thrilled and want to care for me. Stay with me! Always." He hit his head with his free hand. "You're such a disappointment."

The click of the pistol firing exploded in Arabella's ears, followed by a bellow from Canning and the deafening boom of the shot. One moment she was standing and the next she was flying sideways through the air. She slammed into a small table, clutched it in desperation, and went down hard on her back. Her head hit the ground, spiking pain through her skull to join the agony of her burning arm. Above her, the table tilted and then fell and smacked her on the head. Warm blood ran in a path down her forehead and pooled in her ear. She screamed, or she thought it was her screaming, but a deep roar filled the air.

Panic hit Justin like fists. Darlington was going to shoot Arabella. Rage swept the panic away in a tide and calculation sent his hand to his dagger. His fingers closed around the hilt, and with a breath for steadiness, he threw the weapon at the same moment the pistol shot exploded in the room. He let out a bellow of anguish and fear, and for one terrible moment, he was sure he was too late.

Except suddenly Arabella was flying sideways instead of backward as she would have if she'd been hit. Darlington swung around, his face twisted with fury. A crimson stain spread rapidly down the man's arm. As Darlington reached up to pull the dagger out of his shoulder, Canning—to Justin's shock—let out a bellow that filled the room and smacked his son over the head with a large candelabra. Darlington's legs buckled under him, and he fell to the floor, unconscious.

The pounding of footsteps behind Justin alerted him to someone's approach. He glanced over his shoulder to see Davenport, tight-lipped and red-faced, clutching Miss Morgan with one hand and his pistol with the other.

Justin swiveled back around and raced across the room to where Arabella lay with a table on top of her. Blood covered her forehead, the side of her face. It soaked her hair and left a crimson stain on the tile beneath her head.

"No!" he roared, ripping the table away from her still body and falling to his knees beside her. "Don't die," he demanded, afraid to touch her lest he hurt her more, yet afraid she'd die and he'd never get to hold her in his arms again. Flinging caution to the wind, he gathered her to him and cradled her head.

"Arabella," he whispered, his fear of losing her over-whelming him. Trembling violently, he brushed his lips against hers. "Don't leave me. I need you. *I do.* I don't want to, but I cannot seem to crush the need. Please, please stay with me."

Tears blurred his vision as he stared down into her pale, unresponsive face. Behind him, feet shuffled, and then Davenport clasped him on the shoulder. "Is she—"

"I think so," Justin said brokenly, crushing her to him. He'd lost her and he'd never even really had her. "Arabella," he moaned.

"Did you check for a pulse?" Davenport asked.

His hands shook as he pressed his fingers to her neck, groping for a pulse, willing one to come. A faint beat throbbed against his skin, and he let out a shuddering sigh of relief.

Fifteen

$\mathcal{A}$rabella awoke with a gasp and a scream. And to blackness. Fear choked her. She tried to bolt upright, but a strong, firm hand pressed her back against pillows so soft that she knew instantly she was not in her bed.

"Shh, Arabella. You're safe," came a deep, soothing voice she recognized at once as Justin's. She turned her head—by God, that bloody hurt—toward the body she sensed beside her.

"Justin?"

A sharp inhalation filled the air, followed by a scrape and a sudden flaring of light. She winced immediately and squeezed her eyes shut.

"My God, I'm sorry," he croaked, his voice sounding raw.

"No," she managed through teeth clenched against the pain. "Don't be sorry."

His hand cupped her face. "That was unthinking of me. The physician did say light would likely bother you for several days, but I was so eager to see your eyes open once more."

"Leave the candle lit. I want to see you, too."

"As you wish," he replied, and then a rustling sound filled the silence, followed by the scraping of wood against the floor. "I'm moving the candle so it's not directly in your face. There now. Open your eyes again."

She did so tentatively. He'd placed the candle on a bedside table that seemed somehow familiar to her and moved the furniture away from her head. It was near his leg, and his face was illuminated by the flame. Her breath caught as she stared at him. Reddish-brown stubble covered his jaw, his green eyes had dark shadows underneath them, and his eyes were bloodshot. "You look terrible."

He grinned. "You don't look so terrific yourself what with your head wrapped in a bandage and your hair all matted. I washed the blood out, but—"

"You did what?" She didn't bother to try to disguise her surprise.

He shrugged, displaying his discomposure. "I didn't trust your lady's maid to protect your head as it needed to be. So I did it myself."

"I don't have a lady's maid," she murmured, her mind reeling with the knowledge that Justin had been so worried for her that he'd washed her hair himself. A duke. A spy. A hardened man who didn't display emotions had shown her how much she meant to him without telling her. Warmth spread throughout her body.

He cupped the side of her face with his palm. "I hired you a lady's maid because you need one."

She pressed her hand over his much larger one. "I appreciate that, but it's not necessary."

"It is," he said fiercely. "*To me.* I want you better as soon as possible, and a lady's maid will ensure you are not trying to care for your mother and father while you are healing."

"My parents!" she gasped, overcome with the realization that she had no idea what had happened after she hit her head or even where she was. "Where am I?" she demanded. "Where's my father? Jude? The letters?" She struggled to sit up, but he gently stopped her. She scowled. "Justin, I have to—"

He set a finger to her lips. "Canning and Davenport took Jude to the Carthright Home to get help. He will be under lock and key until he is sane, if ever. You are at my townhome because your house was too small for me to stay there along with a lady's maid, your father, your mother, and the nurse for your mother."

She batted his hand away. "My mother?"

He nodded. "Your father told me, or rather he told me some and wrote the rest, about Howick and Brougham and the threats against your mother. I put the fear of my hands into Brougham."

"Your hands?"

"Yes. I explained how quickly a man can die when I use them as weapons. Especially men who forget their places. He quite forgot he was the queen's lawyer, and he should not be making threats to innocent people such as you or your father, who know nothing about any letters, again."

"I see," she whispered. Her gratefulness made speaking hard. Justin had ensured her father would not be bothered again and he'd ensured her mother's safety, as well. "What of the letters?"

"What letters?" He cocked an eyebrow.

"Justin," she chided. "I know you are trying to protect me, but I must know."

"I promised to keep Brougham's treasonous behavior a secret from the king in exchange for his and Howick's words that they would use the letter I gave them to ensure the king did not obtain his divorce."

Relief made her almost dizzy, but then another concern gripped her belly. "What if they lied to you?"

"I read the letter I gave them. It's enough to keep the king from getting what he wants but not to topple him from his throne. Besides," he said with an air of nonchalance, "I made it very clear that I could not speak for whether you would keep the secret of who your parents were. But I thought perhaps if they kept their promises, you might agree that keeping your true identity a secret would be for the best." He stared into her eyes with an unwavering gaze. "But if you don't wish to do that, I will back you. I will be there for you no matter what."

She bit down on her lip to keep from blubbering her love for him. "My parents are George and Ophelia Carthright. They are the only parents I have ever known. They are the only parents I ever want to know."

He nodded. "I thought you'd say that."

The pride in his voice made her smile, but when she thought about what his actions to help the queen could mean for him, fear gripped her. "What of you? I mean with the king? Will he—"

"He'll never know. I am going to see him tomorrow, and I will explain that his letters were burned so he need not fear anything."

"But your vow."

His lips pressed together in a thin line. "Yes, my vow. I can no longer keep the vow to put the king above all else. Thus, I'll be retiring."

Guilt and nervousness pricked her. Did he blame her? Was he angry that she had inadvertently put him in this situation? She swallowed hard, afraid to ask. "What will you do?" she asked instead.

"Oh, I imagine I'll be quite busy." He leaned in close, a devilish look coming into his eyes. "I'm getting married, you see."

It took a moment for what he said to sink into her muddled brain, but when it did, she could do nothing but stare at him.

"Say something," he urged in that velvety tone of his. He took her hand and squeezed gently.

"Why?" she asked, settling on the most important question clamoring in her head. "Why do you want to marry me?"

He placed a hand on her belly while holding her gaze.

"You could be carrying my child."

Disappointment filled her, but she battled it back. She knew he did not speak of his emotions, but that didn't mean he did not love her. She needed to be sure, though. "I may not be. And I have decided I want to marry for love. Nothing less."

He gave her a narrowed, glinting glance. "You love me." His voice was carefully colored in neutral shades, but suddenly his vulnerability displayed vividly in his shining green eyes.

"I do," she said, trying desperately to keep her own voice from shaking, an almost impossible task given telling him how she truly felt required letting go of every barrier she'd ever erected and standing naked and vulnerable before him. "I do love you. Desperately. Crazily. Madly. For as long as I've known you. But how do *you* feel about *me?*"

He glanced away, turned back toward her, and then abruptly stood.

Her heart jerked as he strode to the window and stared silently out into the darkness. She wanted to call to him and tell him never mind to her stupid question, he could grow to love her, she loved him that much, but it would not be true. She needed to know he loved her.

He jerked a hand though his hair and then came close to her again, looking down at her with an intensity that wrapped around her and made her shiver. "I cannot put the king first because now there is you. You are first. You have my hands to hold you, bathe you, nurture you, kill for you if need be to protect you. I do not want to live without you." He sat on the bed and gripped her hands in his. "Will that do?"

"That will do," she whispered as tears of happiness rolled down her cheeks. He'd not uttered the words, but she knew they were in his heart. One day he would say them when he felt safe making himself vulnerable to her. He would tell her he loved her.

Sixteen

*J*ustin awoke long before anyone else in the household, and as he had done every day for a week—except the day he had gone to see the king and resign as a spy—he crept down the hall to the bedchamber where Arabella was recuperating, and he cracked the door to ensure his bedridden patient was still well. From the doorway, he trained his gaze on her chest, hidden under the white coverlet, and he waited for the rise and fall that would let him know she was breathing evenly. When it came, most of the tension drained out of him, but not all of it.

He was intensely cognizant of how important she had become to him. It was as if he could not breathe properly until he was sure *she* was breathing properly. He had to gain some control over himself and his rampant emotions. He needed her in his life, could not imagine it without her, but he refused to rip out his heart and hand it to her. His damnable heart had to stay in his chest where it was safe.

How hard could it be to manage that? He didn't want to be like his father. Never that. He would never be a cold and uncaring husband. He would lavish attention and affection on Arabella so that she would know in her heart how he felt. But to say the words... He shuddered. That would be to willingly give her control of his heart.

She wanted that. He knew she did. He could see the desire for him to tell her he loved her in her eyes. All week, he'd contemplated how to make her happy now *and* when they were married, and he'd settled on ungodly amounts of attention, which was quite easy to give her. Every single moment with her felt like a gift, but he could not rid himself of the notion that the gift would be taken away if he fully gave in to the way her presence made the beat of his heart shift.

He watched her breathe for several more minutes before he eased the door shut and went back to his own room to change and fetch her breakfast. The house was now teeming with servants he'd hired for her. It made him uncomfortable to have so many people underfoot and tangled in his personal life, but he wanted everything to be perfect for her. He knew the maids thought it very odd that he brought her a breakfast tray every morning himself, but he didn't give a damn what they thought. After collecting the tray and the paper, which he'd been reading to her every morning, he made his way back to her bedchamber and knocked.

"Come in," she called.

The sound of her sweet voice tightened his chest. He opened the door, and he grinned at the sight of her, sitting in the enormous bed, propped against a mound of pillows, bright-eyed but totally disheveled. This woman was going to be his wife. It both filled him with joy and terrified him at once.

"You look ravishing," he said as he closed the distance between them, set down the tray, and leaned in to kiss her on the forehead. He inhaled her flowery scent and, for once, welcomed the onslaught of emotions she made him feel.

Her eyebrows drew together and her hand came to her hair as he sat on the edge of the bed. She pursed her lips, but there was a playfulness in her gesture. "I can feel my tangled hair and know I don't look ravishing. I look frightening, I'm sure, but I love how you lie to me." She grinned.

"It's not a lie," he replied, thinking how his soon-to-be

wife used the word *love* quite a lot. "Has your maid not been in to see you and dress your hair?"

Arabella nodded. "She has, but she's rather rough with the brush and I have a sensitive scalp."

Now he frowned. That was *not* perfect. "I'll dismiss her at once and—"

"Don't you dare!" Arabella gasped. "She is young, but she will learn. I simply didn't feel up to instructing her this morning. Besides, it's awfully odd to have someone else, a stranger, brushing my hair when I'm used to doing it myself." She glanced at her bandaged arm. "It's too bad for you that the arm I use to fix my hair is the one that was injured." She cocked her head, her eyes twinkling mischievously. "I suppose you will have to put up with my looking unkempt."

An absurd idea struck him, but one that quickly transformed from absurd to tantalizing. "I'll brush your hair for you."

"You?"

He nodded and slid his gaze to the top of her creamy breasts. He longed to touch her in any form or fashion, even if it meant simply holding her head to brush her hair. "I promise," he said, purposely making his voice deeper, "I will be *very* gentle."

She rewarded him with a pretty blush, and her tongue darted out to wet her lips. "My brush," she replied huskily, "is over on the dressing table."

He nodded and retrieved the silver brush, his blood simmering slowly at the idea of the intimate gesture he was going to perform. How odd that such a normally mundane task could kindle his desire for her. She scooted forward on the bed, and he settled behind her, unaccountably aware of her heat and the thin dressing gown she wore. He slid his hand behind her hair, fighting the urge to delve his hands under her gown and cup her breasts. As his fingers closed around the delicate column of her neck, he groaned at the need that hardened him, and she hissed through her teeth.

He stilled and leaned so near her that his chest brushed her back. "What is it, darling?" The endearment felt completely right. "Am I hurting you?"

Her hand found his thigh and settled there as she turned her face toward his, their lips a hairbreadth apart. "I ache because I want you. And I want you *because* I love you."

There was that word *love* again, but he rather liked how it flowed from her mouth. He pressed his lips gently to hers, and they both sighed into each other's mouths. He kissed her slowly, carefully restraining the need ravaging him. She was still recovering.

After a moment, he broke the kiss and brushed his fingers across her swollen lips. "If I don't stop now, I'm afraid I won't be able to, and then I might hurt you in your present state. So be a good girl and help me."

She giggled but nodded and faced forward. He picked up the brush he had set beside him and eased it gently through her hair. "Is this good?"

"Oh yes," she said, her weight seeming to settle in the hand that gripped her neck. He was awed and humbled by the trust she freely gave to him. They sat in silence for a bit, as he slowly rid her hair of tangles. When he was finished, they settled together side by side on her bed, and he read to her about the queen, her mother. The trial was going well for her. She had the favor of the people of London, and it seemed that the king's ploy to get a divorce would likely fail. When Justin had read every detail there was, they sat for a moment, hands intertwined and gazing at each other.

Arabella finally spoke. "I hope for her sake the king does not get his divorce."

Justin nodded. "You are kind and have a forgiving heart. Many people in your situation would hope just the opposite."

Arabella quirked her mouth. "I suppose. I don't hate her, though. Yet, I cannot say I feel love for her. I have a mother, who in my heart is my true mother, and I love her. And my father. And you."

She stared expectantly at him, and he shifted, uncomfortable. She wanted the words, but he could not say them. He could not hand over every last bit of control. "Arabella—"

She suddenly grinned as if she knew how uneasy she was making him, the minx.

"Teach me French," she pleaded. "I have always wanted to learn to speak French. It sounds so very romantic."

"All right," he agreed, relieved that she'd willingly changed the subject. "Why don't we start with—"

"The words *I love you*," she inserted with an unmistakably impish smile. "That way I can tell you how *I* feel in two languages."

The muscle in his jaw ticked, but he nodded his head. He'd not deny her that. He didn't want to deny her anything, damn it, and he knew deep within he already was. He took her hand in his and stared into her eyes. "*Je t'aime* is how one says *I love you* in French." He started to pull his trembling hand away, but she gripped it tightly.

"*Je t'aime*, darling. Now and forever."

He nodded. "Yes, I know, and I have never felt luckier in my life." He lowered his head to hers and claimed her mouth with a kiss that he prayed conveyed what was in his heart.

The weeks of recovery flew by at Justin's house. It seemed to Arabella that the harder he tried to fight saying *I love you*, the more things he did to show her how he felt. She was determined to break down that small barrier he was trying to keep between them.

They were married a month and a half after the day she'd broken his nose in Madame Sullyard's brothel. The ceremony was quick but touching, with her father and her mother as her witnesses. Her mother smiled at her, and Arabella's heart clenched that her mother was finally coming back to herself. Justin's witnesses were dear Hugh Mumford and the Marquess and Marchioness of Davenport. Arabella liked Lord Davenport's wife immediately, and afterward, at the wedding breakfast, she'd invited Audrey— as she insisted on being called—to the dinner party she had spontaneously decided to throw. Justin had agreed to it with an obvious amount of discomfort, and Arabella knew it was because having people around who cared for him and demanded he do so in return threatened a bit more of the control he prized.

"I'd love to come to the duke's home," Audrey gushed as she eyed Justin with a smirk. "He's never invited me, though I have hinted many times," she said in a playful but chiding tone.

Arabella stole a glance at Justin, who was scowling at Audrey. The woman simply winked at him before turning her full attention to Arabella. "I shall stay today and help you make a guest list."

"No," Justin replied in such a harsh tone that Arabella frowned at him.

"Whyever not?" she asked.

He leaned toward her and pressed his lips to her ear. "This is our wedding day, my dear. I have definite plans on how I want to spend it."

Heat singed her cheeks and filled her belly. He'd resisted all the flirtations and silent invitations she'd sent him in the last week, as she'd been feeling better. She'd not been hurt by his caution. She knew him a bit better now and had assumed he feared he could harm her if he bedded her.

"You think me well enough?" she teased under her breath, though conversation had carried on without them between her mother and Lady Audrey.

He frowned. "Of course. I've known you were recovered for the past week."

It was her turn to frown. "Then why did you not bed me?" she whispered fiercely, not caring a bit that she sounded wanton. With him, she *was* wanton. And now he was her husband.

He gave her a look that smoldered with promise. "Because I did not want to compromise you any more than I already have."

"What?" She gasped. Too loud apparently because heads swiveled in their direction.

"Excuse us," Justin clipped. He shoved his chair back and then pulled hers out with her in it.

She blushed as she looked around the table of her family and, she supposed, new friends. "I'm terribly sorry," she said. "We'll be right back."

"No, we won't," Justin announced in matter-of-fact tone. "Thank you for sharing in our celebration, but we are retiring to my chambers for the day."

Her father frowned, her mother smiled, and Lord Davenport gave what appeared to be a nod of approval while Audrey winked at Justin. "That's what I like, a husband eager to please his wife."

Arabella quickly scooted her chair back the rest of the way before Justin commented further. "Enjoy the breakfast and, er, the day," she said as she twisted around and took her husband's proffered arm. As they left the dining room, she elbowed him. "You really *are* bad."

"I know," he said on a chuckle, "but you must forgive me."

"Why must I?" she demanded at the foot of the stairs.

He swept her off her feet and into his arms and gave her

a long, toe-curling kiss that stole her breath and her wits. "I'm desperate to be alone with you, and desperate men act without thought."

She giggled as she nuzzled against his chest. "You are forgiven."

"Wonderful," he replied as he carried her up the stairs. "I'd hate for you to be angry when you see your surprise."

She lifted her head and gazed at his face. "What surprise?"

"This," he responded as he strode into his bedchamber and shut the door behind him with the heel of his boot.

As he set her on her feet, she gazed around the room in wonder. The once-bare room now contained matching settees, one covered in the palest feminine yellow and the other covered in dark-blue velvet. On the far wall of the bedchamber were two towering wardrobes.

Justin pulled her to him until her back was pressed firmly to his chest. He wrapped his arms around her waist and kissed her neck. "The wardrobe on the right is yours and the one on the left is mine."

She blinked back the tears blurring her vision and twisted around to face her husband. "We will share your bedchamber?" She had worried he might insist on separate chambers.

"Of course," he responded, kissing her chin, her nose, and her eyelids. "I want to go to sleep with you in my arms and wake up to your beautiful face every day." He paused for a beat. "Do you mind? I know many married people keep separate chambers, but I thought you would like this as much as I would."

"I like it very much indeed," she said past the large lump in her throat. "I love it, just as I love you." She pressed her mouth to his and felt the moment his control slipped from his grasp. His body hardened all the way down the length of him and he nearly tore the material of both of their clothes while taking off everything as fast as he could. The need she sensed in him thrilled her, and her own need grew from an ache to a living, breathing thing that stole her own control.

He swept kisses down her neck, over her bare chest, down her belly, and back up to her mouth. He took possession of her mouth as if he were possessing her soul. She gave it willingly and with abandon. He suckled one breast and then the other, expertly giving her pleasure and eliciting her moans of delight. She ran her hands up and down his arms, memorizing how he was formed. When he gripped her under her buttocks and commanded she wrap her legs around him, she did so without hesitation.

His gaze locked with hers as he moved them against the wall and then thrust deep within her. It was so exquisite that a cry ripped from her lips, and he immediately froze. "Have I hurt you?"

"No." She kissed his mouth. "But you'll kill me if you don't continue." And he did, at a frenzied pace of raw need that she reveled in. When they had both reached their climax, she collapsed against his chest, and he carried her to the bed, laid her down, and settled beside her. They lay in the middle of his large bed, now covered with a beautiful blue-and-yellow bedcover and mounds of delicate pillows that she knew he had purchased so she would feel this was her bedchamber as much as his. She turned onto her side and stared at his profile, so strong and beautiful. He'd still not said the words *I love you* to her other than in the French lesson, but he said them with everything he did every single day.

An odd trepidation filled her. Surely this could not last. She wanted him to tell her it would. "I'm so happy," she whispered, placing her hand against his arm.

He turned on his side to face her and frowned. "Why do you say that as if it's a bad thing?"

"I'm worried it won't last."

He pulled her into the crook of his arm and stroked her head. "It will last. I will make it last."

"You cannot keep all bad things at bay," she said, his words striking fear in her. She didn't want him to try to do that. It was futile and would make him crazed.

"Of course I can," he replied cheekily. "I'm the Duke of Dinnisfree. I can do anything I wish. And at this moment, I wish to take you again, *if* you desire to be taken."

"There is nothing I want more," she replied. This time their lovemaking was slow and sweet, and when she found her release for the second time that day in her husband's arms, she collapsed onto the bed and fell promptly asleep.

Arabella woke hours later and realized with a start that the room was in shadows and she was under the bedcovers being cradled by Justin. He had one hand wrapped around her waist, and the other rested protectively over her belly. She had yet to tell him she was with child. She had been waiting for today, but he knew. Of course he did. He missed nothing. She smiled in pure happiness as she listened to the easy rhythm of his breath, and eventually, she drifted back to sleep with the thought that if any man could stop bad things from happening it would certainly be her formidable husband.

Their days soon found a pattern of long strolls in the garden, followed by French lessons, poetry readings, and hours of Justin relentlessly practicing throwing daggers, doing target practice with his pistol, and performing sweat-drenching exercise while she watched in utter fascination. Some days they would visit her parents, who were living at their home together again, and once a week, Justin would accompany her to visit Jude, as Arabella would forever think of him. He raved like a lunatic each time, and she learned from his ravings that his life at Madame Sullyard's brothel had been horrific. Madame Sullyard had allowed men to do despicable things to him for money when he'd only been a child, helpless to defend himself. But when he grew stronger, he had killed a man who dared to touch him and threatened to kill Madame Sullyard if she ever tried to use him again. The revelations were heartbreaking for Arabella, but Justin always listened to her after each visit and helped her work through her sadness for Jude.

Things were wonderful between them, and they seemed to be growing closer. Justin told her of his father's harsh treatment and relayed many stories of missions he had gone on, but he never discussed how he felt about them, which bothered her. Every time she tried to get him to talk of his feelings, he would change the subject or simply cut her off.

As the weeks passed into months and she increased her efforts to get him to open up, he started to grow distant. Until eventually, he spent more time practicing weapons and exercising and less time with her. Their lovemaking went from several times a day, to a few times a week, to once a month by the time she reached eight months of pregnancy. She was so distraught one day that she burst in on one of his dagger-throwing practices, which he no longer invited her to, with the sole purpose of confronting him.

He stopped immediately upon seeing her and grinned, though a wary look came into his eyes. "Hello, my dear. You look ravishing, as always."

She glared at him. The words sounded wooden, as if he'd said them just to please her. "If I look so ravishing then why do you not touch me anymore?" Her chest heaved with her question and her cheeks burned, but she was glad she'd asked it.

Justin, who always went bare-chested when practicing daggers, shrugged into his shirt as her hungry eyes drank in his beauty. He regarded her for a long moment. "I've simply been preoccupied," he finally answered, but his words did not sound truthful. He was pulling away from her, and she didn't know why. She was desperate to reach him before he retreated completely behind his cold barrier once again.

She rushed toward him and raised her hand to cup his face, but he flinched and she stilled in horror. "Do you no longer like my touch?"

He reached out as if to touch her and then pulled back. A pained expression crossed his face. "God, yes," he said, his voice ragged. "Too much. I crave it night and day. Do you understand?" he pleaded.

She didn't understand at all, and she was done being accommodating. The problem, she decided angrily, was that Justin had been going through life without really living it. He had managed to strip emotions away and replace them with cold order. She prayed that what he was facing now was the struggle to maintain the coldness he had made a part of him. And she prayed what she was about to do would shove him toward her and not away. "I need you to tell me you love me. I need you to say the words or...or—"

"Or what?" he demanded, his voice razor edged.

Or what, indeed... She didn't want to say she'd leave because she knew she wouldn't. Not yet anyway. Maybe never, she loved him that much. She had to say something. She inhaled sharply. "Or I will remove all my belongings from your bedchamber and deny you entrance to my bed. If you cannot say you love me and *mean* it, then you can no longer have me." Dear Heavenly Father above. What if he simply agreed? She'd die. Yet she'd die if the wall he was trying to keep between them stayed. Oh the death would be slow and emotional, but all the same it would be the death of her soul.

His eyes widened in a completely uncharacteristic display of emotion. He opened and shut his mouth several times as if he were going to speak. Her hopes rose and fell each time she thought he might say the words, and then a mutinous look crossed his face and his nostrils flared. "You agreed that what I could give you was enough. Do you remember?"

She heated with guilt. "Yes," she whispered. "I remember, and I'm sorry. Truly I am, because I know how hard this is for you, but it is not enough. I want all of your heart, and instead of softening toward me as I hoped, you seem to be growing more distant. As if the closeness we have gained scares you. I want you to relinquish control of your heart to me. Trust me as I have trusted you."

He flinched and drew back a step. "I have business in Town," he said, raking a hand through his hair. "I'll be home late, but I pray you are still in our bedchamber. You belong there with me."

Angry tears burned her eyes as he turned and disappeared out of the room.

After he left, she paced the house for hours before finally deciding she needed the advice of a woman who had been married longer than she had. She needed a friend, and the only person she knew that came remotely close to filling that requirement was Audrey. Arabella asked Hugh to get the coachman to ready the carriage, and she went to visit Audrey.

She was shown in immediately to the marchioness, who was in her drawing room. Audrey rose upon Arabella's entrance and met her with outstretched hands. Her green eyes crinkled at the edges with her large smile. "I'm so glad you called! I'm bored to death with trying to embroider, and Sin has gone into Town with your husband to box, but of course, you know that."

Boxing? Arabella frowned as she sat in an overstuffed chair. "I know nothing," she said grouchily. "I don't even know who Sin is."

Audrey grinned and waved her hand. "Sin is a moniker

only a very few people call my husband. You must forgive the slip."

"There's nothing to forgive," she replied, feeling sorry for herself. "I wish I had a moniker for Justin. I wish I knew him so well as that!" She sighed and rubbed her aching back.

Audrey frowned. "Sit here instead. It's the most comfortable and will support your back."

Arabella nodded gratefully and moved chairs.

Audrey took the seat opposite her and then raised a bell and rang for tea. A servant immediately appeared, forcing Arabella to hold her tongue. Audrey gave her an understanding look but launched into a diatribe against the king, who had fallen from grace—and rightfully so—as far as the man could possibly fall with the good people of England. As the maid poured the tea and served the scones, Audrey and Arabella spoke of the queen and how she had fared very well in the trial and how beloved she was.

Arabella's thoughts drifted a bit as Audrey spoke about fashion next. Her mind was on the queen; and truly, no matter how hard Arabella tried, she could never think of her as anything other than the queen. She was not her mother, despite their shared blood. The sound of the door shutting drew Arabella's thoughts back to Audrey. She realized with chagrin that the marchioness was studying her.

Slowly, Audrey tilted her head. "I recognize that look on your face."

Arabella frowned. "You do?"

The woman nodded and curled a very freckled nose. "I had hoped you were here to finally plan your dinner party."

Arabella pressed a hand to her cheek. "I need to do that, but I've been so consumed with—"

"Your husband," the woman said with a knowing look. "It's perfectly normal. Has he been equally as consumed with you?"

Arabella plucked at a nonexistent string on her gown. "He was. Until the last few months. It seems the more advanced my pregnancy becomes and the more I say I love him, the more he pulls away. He does not—" She swallowed her embarrassment. "He does not touch me anymore. I had thought I could get him to admit his love for me, but now I simply do not know. The situation is intolerable."

Audrey came out of her seat and sat on the arm of Arabella's chair. She leaned down and hugged her. Arabella gave a loud sniff. "He's never told me he loves me. Perhaps he never did." She groaned, doubt flooding her mind. "Perhaps I only believed what I wanted to."

"Nonsense," Audrey chided and handed Arabella a handkerchief to wipe her tearstained face. "You would not have married him if you didn't know he loved you, and besides that, Sin says the man is a lovesick pup trying desperately to deny his feelings."

"He is?" A bubble of hope welled in her chest. If someone else believed it, too, then she was not being delusional.

"He is," Audrey replied and squeezed her shoulder. "And I'll tell you this, when I was pregnant with our daughter, Sin handled me like glass he would surely break. And he did not handle me enough to my liking, so I had to take matters into my own hands. I had to seduce him."

Arabella stared up at her friend. "Do you think that's what I should do? Seduce him?" She had to admit the idea held enormous appeal, though she had said she would deny him her body if he would not say the words. She quickly told Audrey of the desperate threat she had given Justin today.

Audrey stood and tapped a finger to her chin. "This is not awful. This is rather good, I think. His will to deny his feelings must be crumbling, which scares him and is making him fight harder. Seduction is perfect. Except, once you have his desire at a boil, demand the words. He will say them, and after he says them once the fear will be gone. Problem solved!" she exclaimed with a grin. "Now, I must go to the nursery to see the baby as she wakes from her nap. Do you want to come?"

Arabella nodded and spent the rest of the day with Audrey and her daughter. By the time Arabella arrived home for dinner, she ordered a light repast be sent to her and Justin's bedchamber. After she'd eaten, she stripped naked and took a long luxurious bath infused with rose water. After toweling off and dressing for bed, she waited eagerly for her husband to return.

The crowd at White's had thinned to five people, none of whom Justin gave a damn about talking to, including Davenport, but as he'd gone to Davenport and asked him to come with him into Town, he could not very well demand his friend leave him alone. Justin had thought to attempt to ask Davenport's advice on his problem with Arabella, but he could not seem to find the right words.

Davenport smirked over the rim of his Scotch glass, then set it down. "Are we going to simply stare at each other for the remainder of the night or are you going to finally get to the heart of why you asked me to come to Town with you today?" He gave an exaggerated yawn. "It's getting late, and my wife will be eagerly awaiting my return, as I'm sure yours is."

Justin tensed. "Perhaps not. She threatened to move out of our bedchamber today and deny me access to her new chambers."

"Finally, we have come to the problem," Davenport said. "Why did she do that?"

How could he explain? It was hard to even think about it. Justin growled, tipped his tumbler up, and drank every last drop of whiskey. He set the glass down with a thud. He didn't talk of his feelings to anyone. He didn't want these feelings. They were too strong, too consuming, too terrifying. "I thought I could control how I felt about her. How much I let her in."

Davenport picked up the decanter they had ordered to be left on the table. After filling both glasses, he slid Justin's back to him. "We all think that at some point. It's foolish. You will never be happy attempting to deny how you feel for her, and you will make her miserable. You may even cause her to hate you or leave more than your bedchamber. She may eventually leave *you*."

The idea of a life without her appalled him. "I thought I could have her as my wife and keep control of how I felt about her, but I can't. Every day I spend with her, every time I touch her, she closes the distance between us a little more. I thought I could hold part of myself back, but I'm making her miserable, just as my father made my mother miserable."

Davenport nodded. "You have two choices. Keep on as you are and you will become your father. Your marriage will be unhappy, and likely, she will eventually leave you. Or give her what she wants." Davenport stood, moved to Justin's side, and clapped him on the shoulder. "It's what you want, too, you know. If you really think about it." Davenport released his hold and shrugged on his coat. "Shall I secure you a ride or are you coming?"

Justin looked up at his friend, but he saw Arabella in his mind. Her smile. Her twinkling eyes. Her proud face. Her belly swollen with the child they had made out of love. His gut clenched. *Love.* He loved her. They were to have a child together, and he damn sure never wanted that child to go through what he had endured with his cold father and the loss of his mother. He had been a coward and a fool. Well, no longer. He shoved his chair back. "Wait, I'm coming. I have some groveling to do."

Davenport chuckled. "I can assure you, it won't be your last time, my friend."

Seventeen

$\mathcal{A}$rabella was beyond furious when she woke near midnight and realized Justin was still not home. But then she was struck with a terrifying thought. What if she had pushed too hard, and he was not coming back? She knew of lords who lived separately from their wives.

Her heart grew heavy. She feared the battle was lost if he was not returning home, and they were to no longer live together. Just as she started to pace the room, she heard carriage wheels in front of the townhome. She flew to the window and saw his carriage and the coachman, but she did not see him. Her stomach knotted, but then she heard the downstairs door open, and Justin's voice as he spoke to the footman was loud and clear. Relief flooded her. Of course he had come home! The need to see him and not just hear him coursed through her. She dashed out of her room to go to him and embrace him. First she'd tell him she loved him, and then she wasn't certain what she would say. They were at an impasse, but surely he would relent.

She raced toward the stairs, and when she reached the top, she saw him coming toward her, taking the stairs two at a time.

"Arabella, I'm sorry!" he called from the first curve in the stairwell.

"I love you, Justin!" In a rush, she started down the stairs, but the toe of her slipper stuck on something sharp. When she jerked her trapped foot, the weight of her pregnancy threw her forward and no amount of flailing her arms would send her back toward safety. A scream filled her head, heart, and lungs. She saw his eyes widening, his mouth opening in a cry of horror, his hands reaching, grasping, missing. The stairwell was expansive, and her body flew past him just a hairbreadth too far to the left for him to get a firm hold.

He'd never known true panic before, but he knew that it welled within him now. It choked him as he raced down the stairs after Arabella's falling body. She hit the floor with a hard smack that shattered his soul. He stumbled in his haste, gripped the railing, and kept going. Mumford was already there, hovering over her. Then the man was standing, moving faster and with more animation than Justin had ever seen, shouting for the footman and then barking orders to fetch Dr. Bancroft.

Justin fell to his knees beside her. Pain twisted her face. He moved to touch her, but jerked back as she let out a bloodcurdling scream that shattered every ounce of composure he'd cultivated in his life.

"The pain!" she screamed, gripping her belly.

Justin's heart constricted as he took in the dark stain spreading between her legs and covering the floor. "Shh. You'll be fine," he murmured, willing it to be so. He turned toward her, and she stared back with wild, glazed eyes.

"Get him out!" she yelled.

He froze with a hand hovering near her face, thinking for one moment she was talking about him, but she meant the babe, he realized, as she clawed at her stomach. She thought she was having a boy.

He placed a hand on her damp forehead and leaned near her ear. "I'm going to pick you up and take you to the bed."

She didn't answer. Didn't acknowledge him. She twisted her head back and forth, panting, gasping, crying that the
babe had to be delivered now. He scooped her into his arms
as she flailed. *Jesus Christ.* Was she going to die? Would the
babe die?

As he climbed the steps with a hammering heart, his
own legs trembling, he struggled to gain control and find
some small bit of the cold composure that was like breath to
him. It was as if he were blind and searching for something
thrown into a never-ending pit. His chest physically ached
and tears burned his eyes.

When he reached the bed, all he could do was look at it.
He could not put Arabella down. She wailed incoherently in
his arms, and he knew with perfect terrifying clarity that it
was too late for him. He loved her beyond reason. He could
put continents between them, and the distance would not
be enough to make him indifferent to her. He'd never again
be the man he once was, but he understood in this moment
that he was glad for it.

She'd been correct to say going through life numb was
not living. He wanted to inhale life with her. "Arabella," he
whispered raggedly and pressed a kiss to her forehead.

Her eyes fluttered open briefly, but she squeezed them
shut on a grimace. Behind him, he heard the rapid approach
of footsteps, and then Dr. Bancroft was there with his nurse,
instructing Justin to set her down gently and get out.

Justin laid her on the bed and went around to the other
side to kneel by her. He could not leave her. This was his
fault.

"Your Grace," Dr. Bancroft snapped as he leaned over
Arabella and ran his hand over her stomach. "Please go."

"No," Justin replied. "I'll move if you need me to, but
I'm not leaving her."

The nurse's eyes went wide, but Dr. Bancroft shook his

head at her. "As you wish," the physician said. "But I must warn you that there will likely be a great deal of blood with the birth."

"I'm not squeamish," Justin snapped as he watched the nurse prepare Arabella. "Will she—" God, he could hardly form the question because the possible answer terrified him. He gritted his teeth. "Will she live? Will the babe live? Be all right?"

Dr. Bancroft's sympathy-filled eyes made Justin's stomach clench into a hard, pulsing knot. "You don't know," Justin whispered, feeling as if his heart had been ripped from his chest.

"I don't, but I'll do all in my power to help them both." The physician leaned over Arabella and whispered in her ear. "You must push to save the babe. Do you understand?"

Justin was sure she'd not respond, as incoherent as she'd been, but her eyes flew wide and locked on Dr. Bancroft's face. "Yes," she said in a voice so full of determination that it filled Justin with hope.

He squeezed Arabella's hand, and she slowly turned her head toward him. "Arabella, I'm sorry. I was stupid. So stupid. Can you forgive me?"

She opened her mouth and let out a scream that pierced his heart with a shaft of terror.

Hours later, Arabella's screams had died to whimpers and then silence. She lay listless on the bed, her gown soaked with sweat and blood, despite the nurse's best effort to clean her up. Justin's own shirt was drenched with the sweat of fear. He ran a hand through his wife's matted hair while Dr. Bancroft tried once again to get her to push. "One last time, my dear. I can see the crown of the head now."

Justin's breath froze in his lungs when Arabella didn't respond at all.

Dr. Bancroft rose with a curse and motioned for Justin to rise. They met at the foot of the bed. "She is spent, and I fear has nothing left to give. I can try to pull the babe out, but it is much safer for her to push the child out. Can you think of anything you could say to her that might reach her?"

Justin started to shake his head, and then he froze. He rushed back to Arabella's side and pressed his lips to her ear. "I love you, Arabella. I love you, do you hear me? Darling, I love you. *Je t'aime*. And I love you in Russian, my darling. я люблю тебя. And Greek. *Σε αγαπώ*. Darling, I will say it in every language spoken if you will just push one more time."

He held his breath, waiting, hoping, and when a smile flitted at her lips and her eyes opened and locked with his, his heart filled with such joy that he cried out. She mouthed, *I love you, too*, and then pushed as he held her hand and whispered over and over, "I love you."

⁓⚬⚬⚬⚬⚬⁓

Arabella watched with a smile from her bed as Audrey walked back and forth and sung softly to Jonathan, the Marquess of Steele, the most perfect child ever born. Audrey paused and turned to her. "He has his father's eyes."

Arabella nodded. "But he has my nose. See how straight it is?"

Justin entered the room at that moment, carrying a small black box in his hands. He strolled over to Arabella, leaned over her, and kissed her. He went to Audrey, shoved the box in his coat pocket, and held out his hands. "My son, if you please."

She smiled and handed Justin the sleeping baby. Arabella's heart tugged as Justin cradled Jonathan snug against his chest and cooed to their son with unrepentant pleasure.

Audrey chuckled. "This is something I never thought I'd see."

Justin looked up and grinned, then turned his eyes to

Arabella. Her breath caught in her lungs, and she wondered for the thousandth time if she would ever derive less pleasure from seeing Justin's love for her in his eyes. She was certain she would not.

He moved silently toward her and sat by her side, the bed dipping with his weight. But he turned toward Audrey. "You should get used to seeing me thus, because I intend to have as many children as my wife will give me."

"Right now, that would be one," Arabella murmured good-naturedly. "But it's only been three days. Give me a few weeks to recover totally, and I'm sure the number will go up."

"Well then, darling," Audrey said, "I better go now and let you rest so you can give your husband a nursery filled with joyous bundles."

After they said their good-byes to Audrey, Justin laid a still-sleeping Jonathan beside Arabella and then reached into his pocket, withdrew the box, and handed it to her.

"What is this?" she asked, staring at the box.

"Open it, my love." She smiled at the term of endearment he'd taken to using. Hearing *love* from his lips would never grow old, either.

She opened the box and gasped with delight at the thin gold chain with a perfect, rather large, gold heart attached to it. Carefully, she picked up the chain, the heart dangling in the air between her and Justin.

"Turn it over," he directed.

She did, and as she read the inscription silently, Justin read it aloud. *"My heart for my love."*

She blinked back tears of happiness as she handed him the chain. "Will you put it on me?"

He nodded, did so, and then kissed her. When he drew back, she pressed her fingers to the golden heart. "Your heart and your love are always safe with me," she said.

"As yours are with me, my love. As yours are with me."

World of Johnstone Teaser

When a Laird Loves a Lady
(Highlander Vows: Entangled Hearts Book 1)

A need to belong drives her. A longing to forget compels him. Fate may send them into each other's arms, but only love can mend their hearts.

An Outlander

Raised by a tyrannical father, Marion de Lacy yearns for the comfort of belonging to a loving family. So when her father announces her betrothal to an evil knight in exchange for his help to overthrow the king, she concocts a desperate scheme to avoid the marriage: feigning her own death and then fleeing England. But when her plan goes terribly awry and she's captured by the knight, not even her careful preparations could ready her for the Scottish barbarian who rescues her and then informs her that he's to marry her by edict of her king. Certain her father will defy the king's orders and wed her to the knight if she refuses the Highlander's hand, Marion agrees to marry the strangely compelling but obstinate laird of the MacLeod clan.

A Highlander

After the death of his beloved wife, Iain MacLeod has no desire to marry ever again. Yet when he finds himself obliged to do so to secure the freedom of his childhood friend and king, he reluctantly travels across England to collect his unwanted bride, expecting to find a cold Englishwoman. Instead, he discovers a fiery, bold beauty who is fiercely loyal, protective of those she loves, and defies him at every turn, challenging his certainty that his heart is dead.

Ensnared

Following a hasty marriage and perilous journey to Scotland, Marion harbors no illusions that her new husband loves her. Still, her heart cannot resist the noble, brave warrior, and she cannot suppress the hope that she has finally found where she belongs. However, the harder she tries to fit in with the clan and gain Iain's love, the farther away her dreams drift. Iain is more than willing to give his respect to his courageous wife—her kisses and caresses even ignite his blood and demand his passion—but he refuses to give up his heart. That is, until enemies near and far threaten to take Marion from him. Now the demons that haunt him can only be conquered by surrendering body and soul to Marion, if only it's not too late...

Dukes, Duchesses & Dashing Noblemen
(A Once Upon A Rogue Regency Novels, Books 1-3)

Be swept away by two dukes and a rake-in-training in the three complete novels of the Once Upon A Rogue series!

"My Fair Duchess"

After years of playing the rogue to hide a dark family secret, the Duke of Aversley feels tainted beyond redemption and cynical beyond repair. Never does he imagine hope will come in the form of a quirky, quick-witted lady determined to win the heart of another aristocrat.

Thanks to a painfully awkward past, Lady Amelia De Vere long ago relinquished the notion she was a flower that had yet to blossom. But when her family faces financial ruin and the man she has always loved is on the verge of marrying another, she'll try anything to transform herself to capture her childhood love and save her family—including agreeing to participate in a bet between her brother and the notorious, dangerously handsome Duke Of Aversley.

Bound by the bet, Amelia and Aversley discover unexpected understanding and passion beyond their wildest dreams, if only they can let go of their pride, put trust in each other and chance losing their hearts.

"My Seductive Innocent"

Miss Sophia Vane, a wallflower of sorts, makes an unlikely match when she weds Nathaniel Ellison, the rich and wary Duke of Scarsdale. What starts with an unexpected friendship soon blooms into a fiery passion. But a betrayal plunges Sophia into the thorny world of London Society and entangles her in a labyrinth of manipulation and jealousy that will test the strength of her marriage. Behind her husband's sudden icy facade, Sophia believes dwells the caring, passionate man she loves. To break through the barriers and reclaim their happiness, they must do more than simply cast away their pride. They must fight for their very lives.

"My Enchanting Hoyden"

A bargain born of desperation ignites into passion as one lord's quest to save his family leads to the discovery that he can never settle for less than love.

Forsaken, abandoned, and duped, Miss Jemma Adair has no other recourse but to request her grandfather's help to avoid living on the streets. His asking price? She must marry a neighboring lord's odious son. Thankfully, there is a way out of her dilemma—ensuring the rake never asks for her hand. But what is Jemma to do when her ally is an all-too handsome silver-tongued lord with a penchant for poetry that makes her question giving her heart to another man?

Philip De Vere, Lord Harthorne, wishes to marry for love, but inherited debt and family obligations force him to seek a wealthy wife. Yet experience has taught him that ladies of the *ton* prefer rogues to gentlemen with a poet's soul. But when an unrepentant hoyden claims to know a thing or two about how to make a man a rake, Philip finds he cannot resist Jemma's offer or her.

Also Available

About the Author

Julie Johnstone is a **USA TODAY** best-selling author of Regency Romance, Victorian Romance and Scottish Medieval Romance. She also has written a new urban fantasy/paranormal romance book. She's been a voracious reader of books since she was a young girl. Her mother would tell you that as a child Julie had a rich fantasy life made up of many different make believe friends. As an adult, Julie is one of the lucky few who can say she is living the dream by working with her passion of creating worlds from her imagination. When Julie is not writing she is chasing her two precocious children around, cooking, reading or exercising. Julie loves to hear from her readers. You can find Julie at these places:

Julie Johnstone on email:
juliejohnstoneauthor@gmail.com

Julie Johnstone on the web:
www.juliejohnstoneauthor.com

Julie Johnstone on Facebook:
facebook.com/authorjuliejohnstone

Julie Johnstone on Twitter:
@juliejohnstone

Julie Johnstone on Goodreads:
goodreads.com/JulieJohnstone

Julie Johnstone's newsletter:
juliejohnstoneauthor.com/extras/subscribe

You May Also Like

Secrets to A Gentleman's Heart

WITH UNCLE CHARLES AWAY, THE RAKES ARE OUT TO PLAY

When Regina Darlington's globe-trotting guardian doesn't return from his latest adventure before the start of the Season, she finds herself the object of a scandalous challenge. It seems every scoundrel in London is trying to seduce her right under the nose of her nearly blind and beloved great-aunt. Fortunately, her eccentric uncle taught her an ancient warrior art for just these circumstances, and she is adequately equipped to defend her virtue. Protecting her heart is another matter. When a down-and-out thief accidentally knocks himself unconscious at Wedmore House, Regina takes pity on him and becomes his nursemaid. But her patient is no ordinary thief, and Regina is woefully unprepared to defend herself against the charms of the handsome stranger.

New Orleans gadabout Xavier Vistoire made a powerful enemy during his stay in London two years ago, and he has been paying for it ever since. Imprisoned at a remote farmhouse with nothing but a burly simpleton for companionship, Xavier jumps at the chance to earn his freedom. All he must do is break into an earl's house and steal a map, which should be easy when the only male servant has resigned and the ladies of the house are attending a ball. But complications arise when he surprises a goddess during her bath and her little dog causes him to fall down the stairs. He wakes to find he has a beautiful new jailer, and nothing about his situation is easy except falling head over heels for Miss Darlington.

CPSIA information can be obtained
at www.ICGtesting.com
Printed in the USA
BVHW031931030520
579117BV00001B/62